The LONELY FAJITA

ABIGAIL MANN

OneMoreChapter

One More Chapter an imprint of
HarperCollins*Publishers* Ltd
1 London Bridge Street
London SE1 9GF

www.harpercollins.co.uk

This paperback edition 2021

A catalogue copy of this book is available from the British Library.

ISBN: 978-0-00-840818-3

Set in Birka by
Palimpsest Book Production Limited, Falkirk, Stirlingshire

Printed and bound in the UK

Chapter One

I've come to accept that I am honestly and truly terrible at my job. Like, seriously bad. Until recently, I thought I'd naturally 'come into my own', like one of those women who gesticulate wildly in front of a flip chart with red nails and swishy hair fresh from the blow bar. I've had jobs where I've been decidedly average, like the bakery gig I had at university (I overstuffed the baguettes), or the two bar shifts I managed at the campus club (I self-diagnosed sleep deprivation and had to quit), but never wholly incompetent. Ironically, I'm not even earning a wage at this internship and it's where I feel most out of my depth.

I look down at the notes I made on the tube this morning and feel a lurch in my stomach like I've driven over a humpback bridge. How it's possible to interpret these blunt scribbles into a meaningful report about the past week's social media engagement is entirely beyond me. But last week I sat through a three-hour-long webinar on Big Data without slipping into a coma, so I can surely get through this. When it comes to anything digital, my only saving grace is that my boss Mitchell knows less about social metrics than I do, which is really saying something.

Adam, who has worn flip-flops and a salmon-pink polo shirt throughout winter, is coming to what I think is the end of his presentation. He's slightly sweaty and puffy-looking under the glare of the projector lamp. I shift on my yoga ball, which squeaks like a fart and makes my heartbeat quicken. Suki is the only one who breaks into a smile from across the desks, which have been wheeled in front of Mitchell's glass cube of an office. This is the 'conference zone' and it's a sign that we have to switch into 'serious mode'. The rest of the time we're in 'self-governed workplace allocation', which basically means 'sort yourselves out and don't fucking bother me'.

'I made progress, yeah. They were just about tugging me off for another meeting next week, so I'll get on that, Mitch.' Whilst Adam talks, he pulses his hips. Eurgh. If I did that, it would definitely be considered indecent.

Last night, Adam took two Indonesian investors to a Hoxton-based craft-beer brewery followed by crazy golf and penalty shots, which, according to him, isn't the reason I was swapped into today's early-morning conference call with our developers in San Francisco.

My phone, which I've placed over a shopping list I'd been writing, buzzes loudly and scurries a centimetre or two across my notebook. This doesn't bother the rest of Lovr's seven employees, who are all scrolling through digitised notes, but it does make Mitchell glance from my phone to my paper, which he looks at with a slight twitch. A few months before I got here Mitchell gave an impassioned presentation on the necessity of going paperless, influenced in no way by Louis, the successful Stanford dropout and CEO next door, who had done the exact same thing earlier in the week. So thoroughly applied is this new ethos that Rachael, who works on the front desk, meets the postman every morning on the pavement outside and types up anything worthy enough to ping over in an email.

As it buzzes once more because I didn't pick it up the first time, I slide the phone onto my lap and unlock it. In the darkened room, my face is upwardly lit with the light from my screen and I catch my concertina of chins staring back at me as I accidentally switch the front camera on. I jab at the screen to open my messages and glance up at Suki, who watches Adam with her chin propped up on a fist. Without catching my eye, she gives a slight Mona Lisa smile.

Her message reads,

Do you think Adam purposely wore shorts that show his ball sack to best advantage or is this a happy accident?

I try to suppress the laugh I'm holding in my ribcage and instead trace the outline of my lower lip with my finger in an attempt to look appropriately thoughtful. Rhea – our infuriatingly competent PR manager – starts nodding, so I nod too.

Adam clicks through to his last slide, which shows a stock photo of two suited executives grinning like maniacs whilst shaking hands. He lifts one foot onto a chair that he's swivelled round to face him in what he likely thinks is a 'power pose', but instead causes everyone's gaze to drop three feet to his eye-level bulge. I bite my lip and try going back to my grocery list. I don't really feel like adding to it now. Of all the long hours spent in this room, this has surely been the longest.

'People do business with people, guys,' Adam says with an expression of mock pride, 'especially if those people are three Jägerbombs down and have scored a hole in one!'

Another buzz. Suki has sent a string of green 'sick' emojis. I slowly shake my head and purse my lips, focusing on the corner of the ceiling.

Mitchell, notoriously unpredictable in his reaction to these briefings, is silent for a moment. Looking down at his highly polished brogues, he chuckles and waggles his finger at Adam as though he's a cheeky grandson who has taken an extra chocolate biscuit. 'Good man, good man. You're seeing Gabrielle and Raj from Pound tomorrow?'

'Yes, boss,' Adam says, thankfully now sitting on the edge of his seat. He crosses his ankle onto his thigh, flip-flop bouncing against the sole of his foot. 'Drinks in the Sky Garden then press night with the British Olympic boxing team – my mate over at Red Bull sorted us some passes.' Adam pouts and smugly leans back against the springs of his chair. God, I hate him.

Suki, in what I now recognise is her version of an eye roll, blinks rapidly and pulls her face into a vacant smile. A meet and greet with boxers? How Adam's overeager public-school lisping, and a clear sense of the obligations owed to him by others, works in any way other than to expose his brazen arrogance is beyond me. Mind you, Mitchell believes and talks bullshit in equal proportions. It's like they speak the same language.

Do you think he'll wear closed shoes for that?

I message Suki, tapping on my phone under the table. Within seconds, it buzzes back a reply.

High tops and his Yeezy shirt – he'll want to make a good impression, obvs.

I smirk, looking down at my nails still half covered in a shellac manicure I'd paid for with a Harvey Nichols gift card, courtesy of Mum. The midnight-blue polish is now scuffed and waxy, but I can't afford to have it taken off, so I'm letting it grow out. Another couple of weeks should do it.

Just when I think Rhea might announce coffee, and thus the end of the meeting, Mitchell turns to me with his chin held in the air. 'You're up, darlin'.'

Like always, I choose to ignore his slightly sexist introduction. Instead I think back to last Thursday, remembering how utterly miserable it was. In an attempt at 'market research', I'd set up a little 'dating booth' in Waterloo station (a table for two, an M&S picnic selection, and a ten-minute timer), and although my presumption that singles would be lured by a mini lamb kofta was right, my hope that they would feel an obligation to stay and chat was wishful thinking. One guy didn't even bother sitting down. At one stage, I was actually lunging for commuters as they walked past – which I'm sure is harassment of some kind – and a group of secondary-school kids swiped handfuls of pretzels whilst my back was turned.

'Yes, thanks, Mitchell.' I am going to be sick. Today is the day I am going to vomit on someone.

I bounce myself up and off my ball and side-step once, just behind Jonathon, purely so I don't have to see his face as I talk.

'Do you need the projector, Elissa?' he says with a half-smile, using this moment to comb his hair along the ruler-straight line of his parting.

'No thanks, Jonathon, I've got it all here.' I flop my notebook a little too enthusiastically in my hand. Deep breath. 'So, the pop-up Lovr stall in Waterloo had a really strong reception from the public.' *Not a lie. Not technically a lie.* 'And we had constant footfall next to the booth, which is great for brand exposure.' *Of course there was footfall; it's literally the busiest train station in London.* 'We had fourteen couples take part in spontaneous dates whilst we were there.' *A bicycle courier stayed on for five dates, asked me to watch his bike, and chomped on antipasti for the best part of an hour.* 'And seventeen of them downloaded Lovr to start chatting with the person they'd had a date with.' *Okay, this one's a flat-out lie. They'd signed up because I said they'd get a push notification when we'd be there with free food again. Half of them had deleted the app in the hours that followed when they were prompted to fill out a profile.*

'Seventeen?' Mitchell says, looking at me over the rim of his glasses, which I'm pretty sure aren't prescription.

'Er, yes. Yes. Seventeen.' I glance down at my notes, half expecting a number to magically appear that would sound more impressive. I have circled two figures, neither of which are seventeen, and one has a heavily pencilled question mark next to it. Thank you, Past Elissa. Very useful.

'Because if it was seventeen, not every couple signed up. So where's that extra person come from?' Mitchell asks. Jonathon slips into a wry smile and presses his fingertips together in a pyramid. *Shit.*

'Um, well—'

'An interrupted download could account for the mismatched figures. This has happened over at MeowCall in the past when users are hooked into public WiFi networks. What I did notice –' Suki swipes quickly on her iPad, her mouth pursed to one side and her cheekbones sharp in the uplighting from the screen, '– is that conversion rates from first and second connection users had a sharp increase in the hours that followed Elissa's pop-up.' She looks around

7

the room expectantly. 'Which is a sign that those who came across the booth told friends and acquaintances about the app, and they in turn downloaded. That kind of traffic is a far more valuable metric of engagement, because it's word of mouth.' God bless you, Suki. I have no idea what she's talking about, or if it's even true, but by Christ I could lean over and kiss her beautiful bald head.

I adjust my stance and put a hand on my hip, closing my notebook with a twang of elastic. Mitchell is nodding, which doesn't mean I'm entirely in the clear, as his facial expression rarely matches his mood. But then he traces a circle on his tablet and the office solar shades oscillate to let daylight in. I mouth 'thank you' to Suki, who sticks her tongue out in way of reply.

Jonathon gets up with such alacrity that his yoga ball bounces out of its chair frame as he strides towards the kitchen. 'Drink tonight?' Suki says as she slots her iPad into the pocket of her lime-green dungarees. The tech team have been moved up to the second floor as a better access point for the six start-ups that share The Butcher Works, a co-working space with a very expensive postcode. As a result, Suki and I don't see each other every day any more. I'm glad I got to know her when we shared a desk, because she's way too cool for me and I would never have approached her if I hadn't seen her playing Neopets when I know she was meant to be editing code.

'I can't. Tom's heading off on a Vegas stag do tomorrow and I should really get home to see him.'

Suki pulls a face at me and makes a gameshow 'whamp-whamp' noise.

I do love Suki. She's one of the best people I've ever met and is so perceptive. When Mitchell or Jonathon have said something really tactless, or I've accidentally deleted all my scheduled tweets, Suki is there, pinging me an inappropriate emoji or giving me an excuse to go upstairs to the break-out space for a bit of venting. She's mentioned going out before, or has loosely asked if I'll join her at a Saturday-morning HIIT gym in Hoxton, but the actual invite rarely follows. We became chummy really quickly, but I've only seen her once or twice outside of work and she often cancels plans at the last minute. She's always popping up on my feeds doing something fun, usually on a Saturday night when I'm halfway through a tub of Nutella. If she knew how little I had going on in my life outside of this building, I worry she'd drift even more.

'Hang on, isn't it your birthday soon?'

'Yeah ... wait, what's the date?' I say.

Suki perches on the front of Adam's desk, leans backwards with enviable core control, and wiggles the desktop mouse. 'The sixteenth.'

The sixteenth? Well, that's crept up.

'Christ, it's tomorrow,' I admit. 'Twenty-six. Had to think about that for a second.'

'How could you forget?' says Suki, slinging an arm across my shoulders.

'I'm not sure. I've already had my birthday present from

Tom, so I've not been looking forward to anything. Like an "event event", you know?'

'Right, that's it then. It's decided.' Suki thumps me triumphantly on the chest like we're about to run onto a football pitch. 'We're going to Snatch on Saturday.'

'That's your favourite club, not mine.'

'You say that now, but when you're grinding along to 90s hip-hop without any dudes trying to grab your arse, it'll be your favourite as well,' says Suki. She bites her tongue between her teeth and clicks her fingers, rolling her body as she walks backwards towards the office kitchen.

'That does sound good.'

'So, it'll be me, you, Jazz—'

'What happened to Fiona?'

'Ah, we broke up. Long story. Your friend, what's her name? The teacher?'

'Maggie?'

'Yeah, Maggie. Get her along. And your other friends, whoever!' Suki lowers her voice. 'Shall we invite Mitchell?' she says, wiggling her eyebrows.

'God, no!' I laugh, racking my brain to think of these 'other friends' I supposedly have. Suki shoves a filter in the coffee machine and tips in an alarming mound of ground coffee beans.

'Mine first for a cheeky drink and then I'm popping your Snatch cherry,' she says.

I'm trying to think of reasons why I couldn't, or shouldn't, go. Other than the obvious: the fact that I'm already in my overdraft and won't be able to afford more than a lime soda. Then again, the thought of cooking a two-person packet of tortellini, promising I'll save half for lunch the next day, then eating it and going into a carb coma whilst watching the Keira Knightley version of *Pride and Prejudice*, is too much to bear. Fuck it. I'll take Suki's offer of poorly mixed cocktails and a lesbian club.

Chapter Two

My stomach grumbles and gripes as I walk up the steps of Stockwell station. I'm itching to stop at the deli on the way back to the flat for one of those sausage rolls that turn the paper bag see-through, but I really, *really* can't. I've already spent my daily budget on a double-shot coffee, a pastry that stopped me being hungry for about ten seconds, and the miso soup that stood in for a proper lunch. Unless it is liquid-based and devoid of all nutrition, I swear it is impossible to buy lunch in London for under a tenner. It's madness. Once, I was tempted to pick up a token for a 'pay it forward' coffee, but those are for actual homeless people.

I had an idea to cook a fancy dinner for Tom from scratch, and I even looked up a recipe on the internet during the slow hour between three and four, but I left the print-out at work and, to be honest, I lost the will somewhere between Old Street and Oval.

I nod at the man who runs the corner shop underneath our place and go to unlock the door, the metal scratching and grating from a cheap, poorly cut key. Although undignified, there's a real knack to it. You have to tease it in, flirt with the lock, if you will, and then quickly jerk the key round whilst furiously rattling the handle. I must be lucky today; the door opens on the fourth attempt and I've only sworn once.

When I get inside, the smell of burnt cumin hangs in the hallway and I can hear Yaz tapping a utensil along to the beat of a Primal Scream track from behind the closed kitchen door. Down the corridor, our bedroom door is ajar. I chuck my scarf in the direction of the coat rack, miss, and kick it to the skirting board instead. Tom's hiking rucksack is propped up against the bed, a row of folded outfits lined up on the duvet, complete with socks and a rolled-up pair of underpants for each day he'll be away.

'Still refusing to use a suitcase?' I say, opening the wardrobe to pull on a jumper. The office carpet that runs through the flat feels cold, almost damp, underfoot.

'What?' he says, scratching behind his ear in irritation.

'Your rucksack? For a stag trip?'

'Yeah, well, I'm going with the lads, aren't I?' he replies, as though this explains it.

'Ah, of course. What was I thinking?'

He doesn't pick up on my sarcasm and instead sits on the bed with a travel-sized bottle pinched between his knees. 'Can you pass me the shower gel?' he says, holding out a hand. I turn and pick up a tube of sea-salt and black-pepper body wash that I've long since been banned from

13

using because it's 'manly and expensive'. When he takes it from me, his hand slides up my forearm and he pecks me so briefly that I hover stupidly, mouth open, preparing for a deeper kiss that never arrives.

'Hello then,' I say, squatting down to look under the bed for my slipper socks.

'Hey. Sorry, I'm just trying to get everything sorted so I don't wake you up later. You all right?'

'Yeah, fine. I was thinking stir-fry for dinner. And cheese-cake.' Tom frowns and lifts things up one by one from the bed, looking for something.

'I ate already. With Ben, after work. I told you about it yesterday, remember?'

He didn't.

'Oh, right. I thought it might have been nice to eat together, seeing as you're going away,' I say, trying not to sound hurt that he's ditched me and my offer of slightly dry ribboned carrot and sweaty noodles. 'And ... it's my birthday tomorrow, so, yeah.'

'It would have been nice, sure, but I had a load of stuff to sort out at work and I needed to talk over some logistics with Ben.' Ah, logistics. That delightful turn of phrase that could, quite literally, mean anything. 'We had last weekend, didn't we?'

'Hmm,' I reply, thinking back to my 'birthday meal', which wasn't the all-you-can-eat sushi restaurant I'd been hinting at for weeks, but curry night at the local pub – a real treat, especially when the boxing came on. If I wanted

14

to see two blokes fighting for an audience, I'd get the night bus more often.

I run my hands along his shoulders, pushing his knees apart to place myself squarely between them, his head level with the waistband of my jeans. He looks up and I hold his gaze with doe eyes, silently willing him to hold me by the hips, to pull me down onto his perfectly folded t-shirt collection, but instead he frowns and is, if anything, embarrassed.

He taps my leg with one hand.

'Can you move? I need to get my shoes.'

I don't answer immediately. Tom raises one eyebrow and I have an overwhelming urge to kick his bag across the room. I don't, though. Of course I don't. I smile away the tightness in my throat and squeeze his shoulder as I scooch past him to sit on the desk chair – a relic from a previous tenant.

When we first got together, we barely left his bedroom, except to get coffee and walk in the park for an hour before the sun went down. But when Tom got a job I couldn't explain to my parents on the phone, the broken chairs we'd picked up during lazy mornings at flea markets were put back outside on the pavement, the intention to fix and paint them abandoned as weekends became a negotiation between the office, golf awaydays, and time spent with me.

'Did you put this in here?' says Tom, pulling out a disposable camera from a side pocket of his bag. *Oh, I'd forgotten about that.* I cross my legs, struggle to pull my ankle into my lap, and silently chastise myself for not keeping up with yoga tutorials on YouTube, as had been my resolution this year.

'Yeah! Thought it would be cool for you guys, like in *The Hangover*? You could have it developed on the way back and piece together the bits between tequila shots. Pose with Mike Tyson, that sort of thing.'

He sucks on his lips and turns the camera over in his hands. 'Hmm. Not sure how it would go down with the boys.'

'What do you mean?' I say, irritated now. 'There isn't anything to "go down"; it's just a fucking camera, Tom.'

He looks up at the ceiling, his face partway between a smirk and a smile. As he goes to reply, a neat knock at the open door turns our attention towards Shamaya, the most recent addition to the house and – most unnervingly – the landlord's daughter.

'Any chance I can interrupt? We're having a house meeting, so could you come through, Tom? Elissa, you too?'

Not again, I think. If this is another lecture about putting clingfilm on leftovers, I'm going to weep.

* * *

When we head through to the living room (well, it's more of a living room-cum-kitchen-cum-dining room) Yaz gives us a nod from the beanbag and ladles a spoonful of chilli into his mouth. I perch on the back of the sofa and Tom sits on an upturned stack of empty plastic boxes, left over from Shamaya's move last month. The four of us cast glances at each other, no one keen to speak first.

'I don't want to make it sound like I'm being, like, the "house boss", says Shamaya, using her fingers to make quote marks in the air, 'but I thought it might be a good idea to talk about a couple of issues that have come up.' Oh, no. This doesn't sound like one of *those* meetings. Usually, she brings in evidence of our deviances and lays them out on the kitchen counter like a domestic member of the KGB. She's only been here three weeks and so far we've covered morning bathroom arrangements, pungent food items that are now banned from the fridge (basically all the good cheese), and a detailed chore chart that I have completely neglected to obey.

Shamaya leans against the kitchen cupboards and weaves her hair into a braid that drapes over her left shoulder. 'This has got nothing to do with Dad being the landlord, though. I'd say this in any house I was living in.' Now *that* I don't doubt. She ties her plait off with a twang of black elastic and folds her arms across her chest. 'Now, I know we all came up with a set of house rules – well, not rules really. What were they? Guidelines? Well, I've noticed that we're not *all* taking them seriously.'

'Are you talking about my gym stuff in the airing cupboard?' says Yaz, scraping at his plate. 'Because it's not sweat. They're damp because I washed them.'

'No, you're good, Yaz,' says Shamaya, tapping her forearm

with a row of manicured fingers. 'It's more this. All this washing up.' I notice it now. On the counter, a number of cereal bowls have been stacked up, along with smeared plates and a few mugs, sticky with hot chocolate and marshmallows. My stomach does an awkward little jump. *Shit.*

From the corner of my eye, I catch Tom looking over at me.

'Er, I think some of those might be mine,' I say.

'They're all yours.'

'Right. Okay. Sorry about that, I'll just ...' I walk over to the sink and reach for the Fairy Liquid, but Shamaya interjects.

'It's not just that. And I'm not saying it's you necessarily, but I've noticed that someone's been using my hair oil in the bathroom.'

'Definitely not me,' says Yaz, pointing to his buzz cut.

'Can't claim that one. Sorry, Liss,' says Tom. Bloody traitor.

Shamaya raises her eyebrows at me and I root around inside, searching for any semblance of guilt, but ... no, I don't regret it one bit. That oil has been a wondrous gift from the heavens. The *curl* definition. It defies logic. I've been flicking my head about at work so regularly that I'm sure I've got mild whiplash.

'It might have got knocked over?' I offer lamely.

'Hmm. I don't think so, do you?' says Shamaya. *Ouch.* 'Look, I've been helping Dad out with some of the property maintenance, and to be honest, this place was only ever meant for three tenants. Technically, it's me, Yaz, and Tom on the lease. Oh, and the utility bills,' says Shamaya, trying and failing to seem like she's only now remembered a clearly rehearsed piece of evidence. 'So, I don't know what you guys want to do, but according to the multiple-occupancy license, two adults sharing a room need a minimum bedroom space of 10.22 square metres, which we can't provide for you here. It would be different if it was just Tom, but when you moved in ...' she trails off, angling her head towards Tom, who sits on his hands and refuses to look up.

Is she ... is she suggesting I move out? because of a few crusty dishes and some fucking argan oil?

'Look, this hasn't been a problem before. We're fine! I'm sorry about the dishes – seriously – but me and Tom have an arrangement about the bills and stuff. Don't we?'

The sound of crunching polystyrene balls comes from the corner, as Yaz does his best to sink deeper into the beanbag.

'Don't we, Tom?' I repeat.

He looks up as though I've yelled his name from across a park. 'Well, yeah. I mean, we said I'd pay for both of us until you got a job and then we'd move somewhere nicer. No offence, Shamaya,' he says, turning to her briefly. She shrugs. 'And, well ... you've got one now—'

'– that pays me enough to get the tube to work and buy a Freddo at the end of the week. I've hardly got enough to start banking in the Caymans,' I say. Tom always complains

19

about the fact we live somewhere grotty when he could afford a place without lino on the floor. He likes lingering at estate-agent windows – a pursuit I've never seen as anything other than self-flagellation. Although it increasingly seems like fantasy, Tom knows I want to share the rent equally.

'The thing is, Elissa, it's not a case of wanting you out, but Dad would have to apply for a new license from the council, which he's not keen on,' says Shamaya.

'That sounds sort of ... fair enough,' says Tom, shrugging.

'Yeah, I mean, if we have to find somewhere else, that's that,' I say. I look over at Tom. He's cleaning muck out from underneath his nails.

'Look, I know this is awkward.' Shamaya exaggerates a grimace. 'But there are probably loads of flats happy to take a couple. Elephant and Castle is on the up.'

'We could, yeah,' says Tom, slowly. 'But if we break the lease early, we'll have to find someone to take our room.'

'What difference does that make?' I say.

'I'm just gonna—' murmurs Yaz, easing himself up from the floor to slip between us, silently leaving through the kitchen door.

'Well, it's a lot of faff, isn't it?' says Tom.

'Yeah, but we'd have to do that in a few months anyway,' I say. The strip lighting of the kitchen feels razor sharp and I notice the beginnings of a headache pinching at my temples. I have an overwhelming desire to sleep, and to

20

keep on sleeping until everything is simple and soft and uncomplicated. Shamaya clears her throat.

'It's inconvenient, that's all. I've got a lot of work stuff coming up,' Tom says.

I have a vision of tense room viewings sandwiched between arguments about affordability and yet another conversation, instigated by Tom, about asking my boss for a wage. If he'd met Mitchell, he'd know you can't just *ask* him something like that.

'I'm just the messenger,' says Shamaya, wide-eyed and slack-lipped with concern, 'but if you wanted to get your own hair products, you know, until you figure out the room thing, that'd be great.'

£17.50 for a 100ml bottle of perfumed oil? She must be having a laugh.

Tom gets up from his plastic-box perch and clicks his fingers absent-mindedly. I'm chewing on the skin around my little finger and don't notice him near me until he's slipped his hand into mine, pulling me over to stand beside him. His grasp is a little too tight around my fingers and I can feel his rough, bitten nails digging into my palm.

'We'll have to sort something out,' says Tom, breathing through his nose. I twist my hand free, feeling heavy and hollow with the realisation that my housemates clearly find me an utter drag to live with.

It's true that I haven't really made an effort with Shamaya, but to be honest, passive-aggressive Post-it notes about 'bin etiquette' aren't the best foundation from which to build a friendship.

'Come on, we don't need to decide on anything right now,' says Tom, his voice soft, eyes insistent. He gives me a little tug and motions towards the door. As we turn to leave, Shamaya puts down her bowl with a loud clunk.

'Oh, one more thing. Could you also remember to separate stuff for the recycling? I found an After Eight box stuffed in with the milk cartons yesterday.'

'Elissa?' Tom prompts, half out the door. He nods towards the neatly labelled recycling tubs and yawns. I swallow with immense effort and kiss my teeth.

'Recycling. Sure. Not a problem.'

When I try and smile, I bite my cheek and wince at the pain.

22

Chapter Three

Last night whilst Tom brushed his teeth, I climbed into bed and tucked myself as close to the wall as possible, my back to the door. I don't know what I thought it would achieve. A prompt to pull me closer, perhaps, even though I'm still angry that he hasn't once mentioned Shamaya's smear campaign against me. Aside from grazing the back of my head with a kiss, he's apparently unconcerned. I spent an hour blinking at the flaking plaster on the wall before I gave up and turned over, hooking my arm across his chest. He shuffled back to nestle into the curve of my body, at which point I must have drifted off. When Shamaya woke me up at 5.30 a.m. with her military stomp to the shower, he'd gone.

The pipe from the basin runs along the wall above our bed and, in my half-conscious state, it sounds exactly like a trickle of wee. I would say there are worse ways to wake up, but after the rampant foxes that shag on the green opposite the flat and sound uncannily like a woman being attacked, the pissy shower is a close second.

There's a small flurry of birthday messages on my Facebook page and I wonder if it was incredibly narcissistic of me to reactivate my account just before I went to bed last night, largely from a fear that otherwise this day would go entirely unrecognised. They've ranged from Maggie's 12.03 a.m. re-post of an old picture of us from school, aged ten and doing 'girl power' peace signs at the camera, to a video clip of my mum and dad on the deck of a cruise ship somewhere in the Caribbean. I can't hear exactly what they're saying because of all the wind, but there's lots of blowing kisses from Mum, and Dad is wiggling around and dancing with his elbows up near his ears to avoid spilling his pint. Other than that, a couple of people I haven't spoken to since school and a guy called Paul I slept with once at uni (bit weird) have sent birthday wishes. Oh, and my brother, who has sent me an emoji of a birthday cake. Nothing from Tom. I guess it's early.

I've missed my designated bathroom slot, as Shamaya is followed by Yaz, who has been singing in there for a full twenty minutes. Tom so irrationally hates Yaz's singing it makes me laugh. In fact, I've always found Tom's cynicism and general intolerance of other people's quirks endearing. But then again, it means he also won't let you talk during a film, or when *Pointless* is on, or during the cricket, which is sadistic because sometimes those matches go on for actual days.

Earlier, I'd jumped out of bed to put my dressing gown on the radiator and only now manage to slide out of my marshmallow duvet, straight into the gorgeously pre-warmed robe. It had been my nanny's before she died a few months ago and I'd brought it back to London with me, seeing as she'd hardly used it before she went into hospital. Tom thought that it was morbid and weird, but I find it quite comforting. The thick towelling material had swamped her when she'd worn it; her little bespectacled face peeked out of the top, the belt tied twice round the waist. With Mum and Dad declaring early retirement a few years ago, Nanny had been the only one I could call for a chat without someone thinking I needed money.

From the midst of my bedcovers I hear the muffled tinkling of my snooze alarm, now on its eighth repeat. I look at the screen whilst scraping my hair into a rough bun:

REMINDER: Friday 8.30 a.m. Smear Test @ Vassal Medical Centre

No! How is that today?! No, no, no!

I look at my phone, which now reads 8.11 a.m., and throw it back down on the bed. Mentally calculating my options, I quickly assess the two most likely. One: I could skip it, but that would mean I'm struck off the surgery's patient list and I'll have to sneak over the border into Southwark to register under a pseudonym. Or, two: I could go, somehow explain to Mitchell why I'm not coming in, and turn up unshowered with a faint red wine stain around my mouth.

Why would I have booked a smear test on my birthday?!

Happy Birthday, Elissa. Here's your present: having your fanny winched open in front of a total stranger. In addition to the horrifying fact I'd read this morning (at age twenty-six, your cells decay more quickly than they are replaced, so you essentially begin dying. What a treat!) this has to be the worst start to a birthday I've ever experienced. Worse than waking up in my second year of university with a sticky pillow, because my housemate had climbed into bed with me and promptly vomited the previous night's snakebite all over the sheets.

I'd put off asking work for a late start because I couldn't bear the thought of having a talk with Mitchell about anything even remotely associated with my vagina. I'd tried writing out different versions of the conversation in my notebook, but I'd torn out all the pages like an indecisive teenager writing a love letter.

Last time I went for one, I'd had a mini freak-out in the waiting room when I realised the doctor was a man, so I panicked and told the receptionist that I'd left an egg boiling on the stove and needed to rescue it immediately.

I leave the house with mottled skin from the splash of cold water I'd chucked at my face as I left the flat, and jab Suki's name into my phone as I quick-walk up the road. Suki picks up on the third ring.

'Suki, I'm in a—'

'Happy birthday to you! Happy birthday to—'

'Suki! Suki, I've had a 'mare of a morn—'

'– YOU. HAPPY BIRTHDAY TO ELLISSAAAAAAAA.'

A pause.

26

'Suki, I've—'

Oblivious to my plight, Suki breaks into a Maria Carey style riff and runs up and down the scales like a has-been 90s diva. 'HAPPY BIRTHDAY TO YOUUUUUUUUU!' The last note turns into a screech and I hold the phone away from my ear.

'Thanks, Suki, that was, er ... lovely,' I say, my body straining from the burst of movement I'm forcing it into. I take a breath and glance at my screen to check I'm still heading the right way. 'Suki, I've got a problem. I've booked a fucking smear test and I'm already late and I've forgotten to tell Mitchell. Is there any chance you could make up something that explains why I'm not in? Like I've ... twisted my ankle or dropped my phone on a tube track or something?'

'A smear test on your birthday? Fucking hell, Elissa, you know how to celebrate.'

'I know, I know.' I don't know if it's the sharpness of the cold air on my throat, but I've got a sudden urge to sink onto the floor and have a bloody good cry. She's laughing down the line and I force a smile even though I know she can't see me.

'I absolutely would – in a heartbeat – but I'm not in the office, babes. Louis' got some bloke over from Seattle and he's using my desk. I'm working from home. Well, I'm playing *Street Fighter* with Jazz at the minute but I will be working. Soon.'

'Okay.' I take a ragged breath and hear my voice crack

on the line. 'Okay, don't worry. I'll sort it out.' I try to feign enthusiasm, but it sounds like I'm in a hostage video with a rifle-clad soldier standing just out of shot. 'See you tomorrow then!'

'Snatch night, babe!'

'Can't wait!' My voice wobbles and I bite into the casing of my phone to stop myself from screaming. A man walking in the opposite direction recoils, flicks up the collar of his navy woollen coat, and quickens his pace. My phone now reads 8.26 a.m. and according to the map I'm ten minutes away. Lurching into a quick walk with a hop every other step, I dial Mitchell's work number and wait for him to pick up. I chew my top lip as it rings for the fourth time.

Just as I'm about to celebrate the far less intimidating prospect of explaining myself to Mitchell's voicemail, his clipped, nasal voice breaks across the hum of rush-hour traffic on Clapham Road.

'Mitchell Chandler speaking.'

'Um, hi, Mitchell, it's Elissa.'

'Who?'

'Elissa. Elissa Evans?'

'Oh right, Els, what's going on?'

My rehearsed explanation slips entirely out of my head.

'Are you running?' asks Mitchell.

'Yes, well, no, I mean, I am running but I'm not on a run. Hahahaha!' *Come on, Elissa, initiate brain!*

'Unless you're about to give me a visual description of your sports bra, I'm not interested, darling.'

'I'm phoning to ... I'm phoning because ... I'm having a ...'

'I'm having a fucking existential crisis listening to you. Would you please get to the fucking point?'

'I'm a ... I'm ... It's my vagina! I've got vagina issues! It's a vagina thing!' I scream down the phone.

What. The. Fuck. I've lost it. I hold the phone away from my ear and stare at it in disbelief, gaping as the call lengthens by the second. I want to shove my whole fist in my mouth. I'm effectively fired now, aren't I? And if I'm not fired I've got to quit. And move cities. Possibly countries.

'I'll be in later. Thanks, Mitchell! Doctors, you know, the appointments always run late, what can you do! Okaythanksbye!'

Well, that's one way of dealing with it.

By the time I arrive at the surgery, I'm puce, panting, and sticky from the run.

I strip off my coat and fan myself with a meningitis leaflet to try and appear as anything other than a sweaty monster. The waiting room is bulging with elderly people and parents with tiny, sticky-fingered children who squabble over toys and frayed cardboard books in the corner of the room. A mum, straight out of a Boden catalogue except for the slightly swollen and bloodshot eyes, yawns wearily and pushes a pram back and forth, despite the fact that her chubby baby is gurgling happily on her lap. Behind her, a noticeboard hangs heavy with community adverts: kittens for sale, a request for a French-speaking au pair, mother and baby groups, and local litter-picking walks (I will never be a good enough person to do that.) Just as I'm considering whether 'mother and baby' groups are an example of everyday sexism, my name flashes up on the obtrusively large LED screen and I'm called through to room five. Gender politics will have to wait.

Chapter Four

Okay, not the horror show I was expecting. I could have done without being shown that strange speculum thing before it went in (why does it have to be made of clear Perspex?), but in all honesty I've had far more awkward sexual encounters with Tom, so this was an upgrade if anything.

As I leave the surgery, I tuck into the wall, allowing a man in an electric wheelchair to navigate expertly round the socked feet of crawling toddlers. I hitch my bag up onto my shoulder, but when I do it catches on thumbtacks and dry Blu-tack, sending a flurry of notices to the floor.

'Oh, bollocks.'

Hurrying over with small clicky steps and a jaded expression, the receptionist helps me pin the adverts back up, some of which are stiff and crinkled with age. I pass her each notice and after a quick glance, she scrunches and drops most of them into a bin that she's dragged beneath us using the pointed tip of her shoe.

As I hand over the last one, I waver, and we end up

clutching either end of a purple-bordered flyer lettered in bold Comic Sans. From under her thumb, the phrase 'rent-free' peeks out at me, along with a picture of a young woman perched on the arm of a winged armchair. In it, an elderly lady sits, her eyes crinkled with a strained smile.

'Hang on, can I keep this one? Is that okay?'

She looks down at my hands and shrugs, speaking out of the corner of her mouth to save the pins from falling. 'Sure, saves me some space.' I look at the flyer and squint to read its sun-bleached words:

Are you seeking a unique opportunity to care for an elderly member of your community? Are you looking for low-cost accommodation, whilst greatly adding to another's quality of life? The ElderCare Companionship Scheme could be for you! A rewarding and fulfilling opportunity, our scheme is open to anyone patient, friendly, and helpful (over 25 years) willing to be a live-in companion. Contact the ElderCare team to find out more about matchmaking, locations, and availability.

It shouldn't feel aspirational, but the people on the flyer look so ... content? I thought companionship would be easy if you lived with someone, but recently I've found myself apologising to Tom for asking to spend time with him. It's like I need permission to be his girlfriend.

I fold it up and slide it into my back pocket.

I wind my scarf around my neck and walk out of the

surgery feeling oddly proud of myself, kind of like when you use a trolley to go food shopping for the first time. I'd done a grown-up thing! And I hadn't cried! Yes, the doctor may have referred to the scraping of cells as 'a bit like caving'. Yes, I may have shouted the word 'vagina' to my boss, but I have achieved something today!

I stand outside the surgery, take my phone out, and flip the camera round. I grin and point to the sign above the door, adding a spattering of 'thumbs up' emojis around my face along with the caption:

I had a smear test and it wasn't horrendous!

I send it off to Maggie. Within seconds she's pinged one back, her face grimacing in front of a plywood stage.

Well done Supergirl! I'm auditioning Year Two for the Easter musical. All trying very hard but tone deaf. Only one recorder so far! Bless them!

Oh, Maggie. She has oodles of patience and an unrelenting ability to see the best in everyone, even screechy children. At university, she had the reputation for being the 'mum' of our group, so naturally she's fallen into teaching. Whilst we all took advantage of five-for-£10 sambuca deals at the bar, she'd happily nurse a single pint of snakebite and she'd always put us to bed with a glass of water and two paracetamol laid out on the bedside table. She lives over in

Richmond and I wish I saw her more, but she's busy and I pretend to be. When she does moan, it's about middle-class mums who linger at the school gates to discuss Japanese counting methods or trampolining club. She says I can call her whenever I like, and she does really mean it, but I know I'll only have her for ten minutes before she has to get back to marking, or the vital stage of a complicated Ottolenghi recipe. I sound quite bitter. I am, I guess. She's always known what she wants to do and she's even been putting money into some sort of ISA that's designed to help you build up a house deposit, which is an alien concept to me.

Whereas Maggie went straight into teacher training after school, I spent a few years waitressing at a pizza restaurant, gained ten pounds (a calzone for dinner five times a week will do that) and did the odd bit of admin temping until I applied for an internship at Lovr. I'll admit it: I was seduced by the idea of legitimately working from a beanbag, a Cilla Black for the new age, pinging off witty tweets between coffees (made by the in-house barista, of course).

I inflated my experience; they gradually deflated my hopes of a decent wage, and nine months down the line I've barely anything to show for it.

***

As a birthday treat, I buy myself a meatball marinara sub and clutch it like a baby on the tube platform. The train arrives and I sit down, carefully pulling away the wrapper, at which point the train lurches and a fat meatball plops onto my lap. I pick it up and put it straight in my mouth. I'd be mad not to. This thing cost me £4.

I wipe my mouth with the back of my hand and scrunch the soggy wrapper into a ball, licking each finger clean before I pull out the flyer I kept from the surgery. I smooth it out on my leg to study in closer detail. The old lady pictured is buttoned up in a lilac cardigan and next to her a woman with pastel hair and a nose ring holds a plate of bourbons between them. It reminds me of the battered biscuit tin my nan kept in a cupboard of her little council house. My chest aches a little at the thought.

I read over the flyer again: *'Live-in companions wanted in London.'* This might, *might*, just be my last resort, if Tom's still weird about breaking the lease early. *Sigh*. If it's only for a few months before we can find somewhere new together, what have I got to lose?

Chapter Five

I leave the station as one of a sullen mass, jostling our way onto the streets of East London, until the crowd spreads and splinters down side streets and into glass-fronted buildings. The smell of sweet, fried dough from a churros stand mingles with the remnants of last night's gnawed chicken bones, which are scattered around Shoreditch's 'Silicon roundabout' – the grubby cousin of California's 'Silicon Valley'. They might have palm trees and curated gardens, but we have a hot yoga studio inside a shipping container and baristas who sigh when you ask for cow's milk.

I pull out my phone. Am I completely mad? Is this a decision that will frame my quarter-life crisis? I could just get a fringe, or start going to CrossFit classes and then humblebrag about how enriched my new life is all over social media. I hover over the green 'dial' button on my phone and press it before I can convince myself that prostitution is also a feasible option.

It's ringing. They'll hear my desperation on the phone, won't they? From the list of companion credentials, the only bullet point I can mentally tick off is 'friendly', but beyond that I'm not sure what I could offer a pensioner. If a burglar tries to break in, I'm hardly going to stop them from nicking anything; I'm about as intimidating as Eddie Redmayne in an arm wrestle. I'll hang up. Mum and Dad were right. I'm not cut out for London. Maybe if I moved back to Hereford for a bit and took up that job at the garden centre with Auntie Rena and—

'Hello, this is ElderCare, Alina speaking, how can I help you?'

'Um, hi there.' My stomach lurches. 'I've seen a flyer for your home-share scheme and I wondered if you might, by any chance, still have a need for a companion? You've probably got everyone you need, but if—'

'No, no, no, we're far from full! Thank you so much for calling! What's your name?' I tell her, along with how old I am and how long I've lived in London, leaving out any details about this companion gig being a very likely temporary situation.

'So, let me give you the rundown about how the scheme works.'

'Sure.' She sounds so chipper. I wonder, how many people have actually rung through about it?

'We're a charity who work within a number of residential villages for the elderly, as well as older people who want to continue living at home, but for whatever reason are struggling to retain the same level of independence they had in their younger years.'

Oh God, please don't say it's wiping bums, please don't say it's wiping bums ...

'They're not at the stage where they need a full-time carer, but what they often have in common is a sense of isolation. They might only have the TV for company, not have the confidence to leave the house, or cook proper meals for themselves, because it can be depressing eating dinner alone, right?'

It sounds like she's describing me. All the evenings I've reheated pasta with a heap of grated cheddar on top, only to eat in bed with *RuPaul's Drag Race* for company. 'Yeah, I can imagine that's horrible,' I say.

'So, we've established a mutually beneficial arrangement: our companions move into a spare room in the home of one of our gorgeous older people, rent-free, and keep an eye on them. They do small things that make a big difference, like going for a walk, cooking a meal together, getting books out of the library, making sure they don't rob any banks ...' Alina starts laughing and I join in, now within sight of the office.

'Honestly though, it isn't too much responsibility. I always say that it's like living with your grandma, without the uncalled-for observations about weight gain, or how her other grandchildren visit more than you.' She laughs again and the sound makes me smile.

This might be the longest conversation I've had with a stranger for ... weeks? Maybe she's being too nice. Like she's trying not to put me off because volunteers are thin on the ground. She needn't bother, because if Tom doesn't want to live with me right now, it's not like I've got any other options.

'Elissa?'

'Sorry, I'm here. What was that?'

'I said I'm sending over an application form with all the nitty gritty details in it. Try to be as detailed as possible in the longer answers, because if it turns out that you're eligible, we use that information to match you with one of our lovely older residents who we're sure you'll get on with, okay?'

'Okay, sounds great!' I say.

'Speak soon, Elissa!'

I hang up and stand there for a moment, looking up at The Butcher Works, a building I recognise as Georgian from countless Sunday mornings spent watching Jane Austen adaptations whilst nursing a hungover with Maggie. You wouldn't be able to tell from the inside, what with all the exposed pipes, polished concrete, and surplus of bean bags.

There could be loads of benefits to moving in with an elderly person, right? I like talking to old people. I feel a bit weepy when I see an elderly man at the bus stop, especially if he's got medals pinned to his chest, although you hardly see them nowadays. I used to love staying at my nanny's house, too. We'd have a dinner I'd never think to cook myself, something like minced beef pie with cabbage and watery gravy. Then again, knowing my luck I'll match with an old pervert who worked in advertising fifty years ago when it was normal to sexually harass your secretary.

***

Even though Mitchell bangs on about how the 'hot desk' system was designed for 'self-motivated, free-flow work cycles', everyone ends up in the same spot each day. Rhea spends the morning at the 'walking desk' (essentially a slow treadmill with a laptop stand), Jonathon is nearest the kitchen (makes a lot of tea to avoid work), Bismah is next to the radiator (always cold), Adam faces the door (to monitor the attractiveness of incomers), Rodney's tucked round the corner (sometimes I don't notice he's there until the afternoon), and I sit in the middle at an angle (so no one can see my screen and question why I watch so many videos of hamsters eating tiny versions of regular dinners).

I've managed to slip in without talking to anyone. After a lunch that lasts the best part of two hours, Jonathon walks in flanked by a guffawing gang of tech guys, one of whom sways on the spot, having reacted badly to Jonathon's day drinking. I can't hear exactly what he's saying because I'm watching a TED talk about human altruism in an effort to look busy, but it's clearly hilarious because his little group of cronies laugh and shake their heads. I pull one of my earphones out just in case I overhear something I can add to my secret list of 'Reasons Why I Hate Jonathon'.

'And then one of you dickheads spilt a White Russian all over the ping pong table. How much did you pay for that again? £15? What a mug!' Adam, who for unknown reasons was invited to Jonathon's lunchtime schmoozing – possibly to help legitimise the £500 bill – smiles and shrugs awkwardly.

'I still won, didn't I?' he says. 'What was it? Five games for me and how many for you? Four, I think?'

'All right, mate. No need to get all Billy Big Bollocks about it.' Jonathon laughs and smacks Adam on the back, and he bluntly smiles in suppressed annoyance. The others titter around him. From my desk, this display of male posturing is so potent I can almost hear David Attenborough's commentary: *'And here we have the young corporate man, defeated by the alpha male for failing to "banter" with necessary vigour.'* Jonathon waves them out the door and exhales deeply, cricking his neck from one side to the other.

'I'll pop a cafetière on, shall I? Enough for …' Jonathon points to those gathered around him and mouths numbers. 'Rhea? Coffee?' She shakes her head from her treadmill by the window. Jonathon looks around the room, catches my eye for a split second, and turns back to the others. 'Four then.' Ha! I don't even want a coffee. I've got one already; a coconut latte with butterscotch syrup that I spent £3.70 on.

Bismah comes in wearing a huge puffer jacket that she sheds like a chrysalis under a blast of heating above the door, draping it over the radiator near her desk. She puts down a Pret a Manger bag and opens her drawer, pulling out an impossibly long scarf that she winds around her neck and shoulders as she sits down. 'Cold today, isn't it? I've got two head scarves on. Have you spoken to Rachael on reception?'

'No, I haven't been in long, why?'

'Something's going on. Something big.' Bismah looks at me in earnest and lowers her voice. 'Rachael was flitting about and I overheard her on the phone trying to order a cold buffet, but not from that place we had last time with the brown food and soggy salad. Do you remember?'

'For the market research thing? Yeah, gross. Bleurgh.' I'd actually enjoyed that food. It was free and there was loads of it. I'd even snuck back up before the cleaners came in and filled a tub with dry brownies and veg pakoras.

'Mitchell's ordered from the delicatessen in Selfridges. The stuff they only get in when the investors are here. Have you seen it? They carve the carrots into lotus flowers and emboss the app logo onto macaron shells. It's too nice. I doubt there'll be leftovers we can swipe.'

'You're right. We might get to scoff some dry sandwich crusts.' I tap the table with my pencil. 'As a treat, you know?'

'Potentially. If we still have jobs by then.'

My stomach twists into a knot and before I can question Bismah about what she's just said, Mitchell opens the doors with a double-handed shove and strides towards his glass cube, stumbling over a loose laptop cable as he

42

goes. I really want to laugh but going from the look on his face I decide that this would be akin to signing my own death warrant.

'RODNEY!' Mitchell stands rigid, having recovered from his trip. Rodney's head appears, meerkat-like, from behind a whiteboard that he's wheeled in front of his computer. His eyes are magnified and watery from the thick-lensed glasses he wears.

'Why, in Chairman Mao's name, is there a FUCKING LAPTOP CABLE ON THE FLOOR?'

Adam skips across the room and picks it up. 'Er, it's mine, boss. Left it out – no big deal,' he says casually. Everyone tenses and looks from Mitchell to Adam to Rodney, like we're watching a match on centre court.

'Put it down, Adam.' Mitchell's cockney voice has turned soft and supple. You'd think he was comforting a kid who'd just grazed his knee on gritty tarmac. 'There's a good lad.' Adam looks around. No one moves. 'Come here, Rodney. That's it. Come on. What's this, Rodney?' Rodney pushes his glasses back up his nose.

'It's an AC adapter.'

'Is it? An AC adapter?' says Mitchell, pinning Rodney to his side, who visibly stiffens at such contact. Mitchell laughs and turns Rodney to face us all. 'Guys, it's an AC adapter! Bismah!' Bismah squeaks. 'Did you think this was an AC adapter?'

'Um, yes.'

'Who else thinks this is an AC adapter?' Mitchell looks

around the room, winching Rodney round under his arm. 'Come on, Bismah, get your hand up! Jonathon? Rhea? You?' He looks at me, his neck stretched and sinewy. This is a trick question. We all know this is a trick question. I look at the corner of the ceiling and raise my hand like all the other muppets in the room. 'Right! So we're all agreed, are we? This is an AC adapter.' We've all put our hands down, except for Bismah, who looks so terrified she must have mentally detached herself from her own limbs. Adam and Jonathon nod.

'WELL IT'S FUCKING NOT! IT'S A TRIP HAZARD.'

Mitchell plonks Rodney down on a beanbag, which makes a 'pfffff' sound as he lands. Watching this is like sitting through a dinner party with people you don't like, whilst the hosts bicker in the kitchen. Mitchell rolls his head in a semi-circle and stands behind Rodney, who must be meditating or something, because he's completely expressionless.

Mitchell rests his hands on Rodney's shoulders, massaging them in a way that is clearly painful. 'Relax, Rodders! All that stress!' His voice is almost a whisper. 'Forgetting to replace the laptop batteries ... leaving cables all over the floor ... what're you like, eh?' Oh God, there is nowhere to look. I've gone a bit hot and feverish. Abruptly, Mitchell releases Rodney and makes a show of helping him to his feet.

'Ten minutes. Upstairs. Conference Room.' We remain deadly still. Mitchell gives Rodney a final withering look, picks a bit of fluff from his shoulder, and continues into his office, kicking the door closed.

'Bismah.' I scoot round in my yoga ball chair. 'You can put your hand down now.'

***

I make another cup of coffee, which is unusual for me so late in the day (I get jittery and paranoid), and head upstairs. I've only visited this level of The Butcher Works once before, when I was given a tour on my induction day. Lovr's meetings never take place here. They involve nights out, beer, and a lot of blowing wind up someone's arse, which is best done outside the office.

When I get to the landing, the others are huddled in the corridor like moody teenagers loitering outside an off-licence in the hope that a passing adult might buy them alcohol. 'How come we're all out here?' I say.

'Mitchell doesn't know the code to get in,' says Rhea, nodding towards a tablet sitting on a podium beside the door. She looks more impatient than amused and I find it odd that no one sees the irony in a tech CEO locking themselves out of the 'smart security' system. We stand there in silence, except for Adam and Jonathon who are talking about last night's rugby match. After a few minutes, Mitchell appears, refusing to make eye contact with anyone. He inputs a four-digit code that he's drawn in biro on his hand.

'Voila.' He goes in first and paces the room whilst we take our seats. Not wanting to infuriate Mitchell with my notebook, I left it downstairs (hidden out of sight), but now I feel naked and underprepared. Needing to do something with my hands, I wrap them both around my mug. I wonder if I look all cosy and warm like the cover of a Danish lifestyle book?

'Do you want the shit news, or the shit news first?' Mitchell says, putting his hands on the table. *Oh, it's this kind of meeting.*

'Er, the shit news?' says Adam.

Mitchell turns a chair around and sits down with one leg crossed over his thigh. He looks out of the window and scratches his chin, pushing his orange-framed glasses up onto his head. He doesn't acknowledge that anyone has spoken. 'Bismah, you got a calculator on you, darlin'?' He's talking in soft, quiet tones – the Mitchell equivalent of a rhino scraping the floor with its foot.

Bismah dives under the desk and pulls out a scientific calculator that I vaguely remember using in maths at school, mainly to work out different sums that would all provide the answer '80085', which looks like 'BOOBS' on an old mercury display. Ahhh, those were the days.

'Type in £270,000.' Bismah taps it into the calculator. 'Good girl.'

Mitchell lists a number of costs and expenditures that Bismah inputs with a long, manicured nail, deducting from the total. Some of it seems obvious (domain subscription), but a lot doesn't (£576 drinks bill from Adam's last water-polo-themed client meeting). Finally, Mitchell finishes with a breakdown of the rent he pays for each desk in The Butcher Works.

Numbers have never been my strong point (the only thing I know is that they go down whenever I post something on our Instagram account, which is the opposite of what's supposed to happen), but even I can tell that this isn't adding up properly.

'Now take away £179,489. That's what I pay for all of you.' He motions to us. I inwardly scoff. It's not like I see much of that money.

'What does that leave us with, Biz?' Bismah blinks slowly. She hates it when people shorten her name.

'Well, er ... nothing.'

'Be more specific,' he snaps.

'Minus £117,983. And 72p.'

Mitchell nods slowly and turns to face us all. 'Well, I see university wasn't wasted on our Bismah, was it? That's the news, fellas. We're in the fucking shitter and no one brought a paddle. MediaCell – our only guaranteed source of investment for the next fiscal year – are going to pull their funding if we don't show some serious fucking improvement.' He looks at us with accusation.

'So, what to do?' I've realised by now that this is not a meeting in which we're expected to contribute. Mitchell looks like he's delivering a Shakespearean soliloquy; he's all narrow eyes and dramatic irony.

'Bake sale?' pipes up Jonathon, tittering to himself.

I can see the exact moment he realises what a terrible mistake he's made. His face sort of ... spasms and he shakes his head rapidly, biting his lips as though they've betrayed him. Despite his clear discomfort, it's brilliant to watch. I wish I could turn it into a looping GIF to watch whenever I feel a bit sad. Mitchell fixes Jonathon with a hard stare. 'Get out.'

'What?' says Jonathon, eyes darting around the room as though the 'bake sale' joke had come from a phantom body elsewhere. 'Like, out of the room?'

'Like out. Out, the opposite of in. Out, as in out of the building. Out, as in out of work.' Mitchell has froth in the corners of his mouth.

Jonathon looks with incredulity at each of us, like this is a clear injustice and we should all be standing up for him. When no one does, he gets to his feet abruptly, blinking, like he's about to cry. 'Mitch?' he says. After a horribly awkward silence, he whips open the door and disappears down the corridor. *Holy fuck*. I cross my fingers under the table in the hope that I'm not asked to take on any of Jonathon's responsibilities: namely analytics, contracts, and pretending to do more work than I'm paid for.

'Here's the situation. Encounter have just launched a subscription platform. It uses a patented matching algorithm that works in real time to schedule dates in a user's calendar without the need for previous virtual interaction.' *That's exactly what we'd planned to launch next month.*

'They've got there first, which means three things. One: our guys over in Bangladesh who were working on the interface have done six months' work which is now useless, but we still need to pay them. Two: MediaCell have suggested they'll transfer our funding over to Encounter if things here don't change. If they do that, we're toast. Three: we need to come up with a new, different, better idea that keeps us relevant. And we have to be making a *profit* from that idea within three months.'

The silence in the room is like a taut balloon. Since when did my breathing sound so loud? Adam coughs. We all look at him, expecting him to say something that'll deflect attention away from any of us. He drums his fingers on the table, which is somehow worse than before. A noise – a bit like a lawnmower chugging to life – comes from the end of the table. Mitchell is … laughing? He definitely sounds like he's laughing, but he looks more like The Joker just before he detonates a bomb that'll blow up a school, or a river cruise full of veterans, or something else equally disturbing.

'What's the matter with you all?' He laughs and rubs the three-day-old stubble on his chin. 'Why're you all so fucking miserable?'

Oh, I don't know, because you've told us we're going to lose our jobs in three months? Because you just fired Jonathon for making a bad joke, like he's done every day since I've been here? Because you look like you're going to chop someone's fingers off with a pair of bolt-cutters? Dear *God*, this man is unhinged.

49

This is a peak example of 'classic Mitchell behaviour'; it's like he rolls a dice and whatever emotion comes up, he goes with it, even if it doesn't match the situation. Just before Jules (his last PA) went on maternity leave, he told her to work from home for her last few days with us because he 'needed some time to process what she'd done' (she was eight months pregnant at this point). Then, on her last day he threw her a surprise party (costing hundreds) and gave a speech on the beauty of new life that was genuinely moving. He even shed a tear.

'Er, shall we ... come up with ... some sort of strategy?' Rhea says. After an extended pause, Mitchell jumps up with sudden alacrity and smacks his hand on the table.

'Yes! A strategy! I only had to wait a fucking age for someone to suggest it! Rhea, darlin' –' Rhea looks up, nervous '– you're getting a pay rise, my girl. This is what I want! Solutions! Not problems! That's what you're on the books for!'

Buoyed by this sudden validation, Rhea launches into a proposal, but Mitchell holds up a hand. 'Don't be fucking simple, Rhea, I've already come up with an action plan. I haven't been sat at home with me trotters up, twiddling me thumbs, have I?'

'No, of course you haven't. I just—'

'In three weeks' time, we're going to meet again, in here, and each of you is going to pitch a rebrand.' He draws his hands in an arc, as though he's a 1930s Hollywood director announcing his next big picture. I think I might have audibly sighed at this point, because Mitchell turns to me, bouncing on the balls of his feet.

'Don't think this doesn't concern you, Miss Evans.' *I'm shocked. I really didn't think he knew my last name.* 'You, Rhea, Bismah, Adam, and even Rodney over there will be pitching. Did you hear that, Rodders?' Rodney, who up until this point had been coding on a mini laptop at the other end of the conference table, looks up from his screen. 'Blink once for yes and twice for no, Rodney! You. Pitching. Yes?' Mitchell over-enunciates his words. Rodney stares back, completely devoid of expression.

'Fine,' he says.

'Three weeks. Two minutes each. Within the hour I'll decide who wins and everyone – and I mean everyone – is going to be working their backsides off to make it a success. Got it?' We all nod furiously and stand up, ready to get as far away from this horrible meeting as possible. Mitchell jabs at the keypad and swears under his breath.

'Can anyone figure out how to open this fucking door?!'

Chapter Six

I stay at work half an hour later than my usual clock-off time, which is something I do pretty frequently on Fridays. It's a semi-believable reason to keep my head down when Jonathon initiates a mass exodus to a bar round the corner. Occasionally, a mate of his invites me out of pity, which is an offer I can't accept, not since the 'cokecident'. Too frugal to buy beer, I'd once taken up an offer of Coke (thinking of the beverage) and ended up in a disabled loo watching Jonathon and one of the skinny girls from MeowCall snort lines of cocaine from the toilet cistern.

Back at the flat, the heating doesn't kick in until 6.30 p.m., so staying at work for a little longer means less time turning myself into a sad blanket burrito with a hot-water bottle shoved under my arse. I riffle around in my bag for my bruised and neglected banana and as I do, my fingers catch on the pointed edge of a card. Pulling it out, I bend the corners straight and see my name hastily scrawled along the envelope. Tom's handwriting.

Before I get too overwhelmed, I pull the card out to

find a sun-bleached image of a martini glass, the glue marks showing beneath patches of glitter that spell out 'Birthday Girl!' I'm so horrified by Tom's poor taste that it's a few moments before I realise where I've seen this card before: in the window of the corner shop below our flat, where it has sat for approximately thirty-seven-and-a-half years. Wow. Tom's hardly sentimental, but this? Inside, the message reads: 'Sorry I'm not there. Have fun. Tom.' That's it? It's so impersonal, I'm almost offended. I *am* offended. My throat feels thick. I pinch the skin between my finger and thumb and count down from ten, nine, eight ... a fucking martini glass?!

I steal one of Bismah's posh tea bags and make a cup of tea, using Tom's shit card as a coaster. On my laptop, I open the questionnaire I've been slowly adding to all afternoon and scroll down to number nine. *How much time would you be willing to dedicate to your ElderCare companion?* I'm not sure if this is a coded question. If I say, 'whenever I'm not at work because I can't afford to go out,' would that be seen as a red flag? Too desperate, perhaps? I go for 'most evenings and weekends, except for occasional nights at my partner's residence'. Partner sounds better than boyfriend. More ... mature. Under 'hobbies' I write, 'Baking, swimming, and nature documentaries,' which is well-rounded and wholesome enough to sound legitimate. After attaching a photo, I press 'send' and turn my screen off.

Tom is usually out on Fridays with the other venture

capitalists. I've met up with them a couple of times in the past, but unless you're out-of-your-mind-pissed, thumbscrews would be less painful than sustaining a conversation with one of his colleagues. Before he got promoted, I would say that Tom was too much his own person for silk ties and Möet. But when he won golf clubs from his office raffle and asked if I'd like a set so I could join him on the course at weekends, I knew he'd turned to the dark side.

As I'm waiting for my computer to shut down, I think forward to my prospective weekend and am engulfed by a wave of loneliness. I should be at the pub with workmates. I should be ordering £12 cocktails, or chipping in for a bottle of prosecco. I should be one of those dainty drunk girls you see slumped against the Perspex partition on the tube and secretly judge for their smeared mascara, but also envy. I'm twenty-six. It's my birthday. And so far today the most fun I've had has involved two strangers gaping at my vagina and a video of dogs pretending to play musical instruments.

I open my phone and ping a message to Maggie, copying the same text to Suki even though there's a very slim chance either will be free tonight. I should have made plans knowing Tom was away, but I think part of me left it late on purpose. At least if I'm stuck on my own, it'll be down to bad organisation. The thought of being cancelled at the last minute for a better Friday-night offering is too much.

When did it get so hard to socialise? When did I have

to start bargaining with myself to make plans? If you go and have a coffee with that snooty girl from your last job, you can read in a café by yourself for two hours afterwards. If neither Maggie nor Suki messages me back, I'll buy a bottle of wine on the way home and have a bath, even though there's a strong chance that it'll need a deep clean before I can possibly put my bare arse in it.

I hoick my tote bag up onto my shoulders and pick up my phone as it pings. It's a voice note from Suki:

'Yo, birthday bitch! Sorry I can't come out tonight. I've got a ceramics workshop. Forgot I booked it for my ex, didn't I? Long story short, Jazz now thinks I'm into romantic surprises, so might have shot myself in the foot, there. Snatch night tomorrow, though! Ah, that reminds me. A mate of mine is a curator at a gallery in Mayfair and there's a charity art auction in a few weeks' time if you fancied coming along. It'll be packed to the rafters full of tossers, but free booze, right? Let me know. See you soon, bud!'

I smile and play it again, listening to her shoes scuff the street amongst the guffaws of City boys who drift in swathes to Shoreditch for Friday drinks, having only worked two hours either side of lunch. The sound of Suki's voice drowns out as Pamela, the cleaner, starts dragging a Henry hoover across the floor. Why is it that his creepy cartoon eyes always look slightly ... mocking?

***

55

When I get to our flat, I hear the rumbling bass of a bloke talking and the distant chatter of a crowd. I tentatively push the door open to our kitchen-cum-dining-cum-living room as a swell of cheering swiftly merges into an incomprehensible football chant. Yaz jumps in front of the screen, which replays a goal I presume he just scored on a video game, and is about to pull his T-shirt over his head when he spots me.

'Oh, hey, Els!' he says somewhat sheepishly. The leather sofa creaks as his mates turn to look at me too. He pulls his shirt back down and makes finger guns with his hands. 'I got you a birthday present!'

He did? I didn't even know Yaz knew when my birthday was. He scoots past me to the fridge and pulls open the door. A sausage roll sits insipidly on a plate with a single candle stuck in the top. Sweet, really. I know we might not have exchanged much in the way of heartfelt discussions, but if there's one thing I haven't kept secret it's my love of 'so-cheap-it-can't-be-real' meat wrapped in flaky pastry. 'Oh thanks, you shouldn't have!' I say, feeling a tad embarrassed as his mates, exclusively wearing a combination of white shirts and 'nice jeans', start a rowdy version of 'Happy Birthday', with added fist pumps. Yaz scrabbles around in his back pocket and pulls out a lighter. I give it a second or two before I blow it out again and smile meekly.

'Look, Tom's checked in with me about everything that's gone on between yous two.'

This completely throws me. I think about what 'goings

on' Tom could possibly have informed Yaz about, because as far as I'm aware, we completely failed to talk about the impending reality of my being homeless before he buggered off to Vegas for a long weekend.

'Mmmm,' I reply, deciding to play it cool until I've got a single fucking clue what he's talking about.

'Yeah, so like, I wanted to let you know that you don't need to worry about finding someone to take the room, yeah? Tom mentioned that he was gonna let you find a replacement so we don't have to get the estate agent involved – save on those fees – you know what I'm saying?' Yaz thumps my shoulder and grins conspiratorially. It takes me a little while to process what he's said. If Tom isn't planning on staying, which is news to me, why would he expect *me* to advertise *our room*, all whilst figuring out how to avoid living behind the trolley stand at Sainsbury's? That total, total shit! *He's* the one who was funny about terminating the rental agreement early.

'Right! Totally!' I say. I must look psychotic, because Yaz looks a little scared.

'My mate Lance is looking for a place and he can move in as soon as you're ready.' A guy with a neat haircut salutes me from a beanbag on the floor. His aftershave is so strong I can practically taste it. 'That's him! So, we can keep it all between us, but just let me know when I can give him the green light, okay?'

I look down at the sad-looking sausage roll and bite off a huge mouthful. The candle hangs from a soggy flap of pastry. 'That's great, Yaz,' I say, spraying him with crumbly flakes of dough, 'in fact, tell him next weekend is just perfect. Fuck, if he wants to come earlier, he can top and tail with me!' Yaz squints, unsure if I'm having a laugh. 'I've actually got something lined up, so tell him he can start bringing his stuff round.' Yaz takes a small step away. *Come on, Elissa, resume normal human interaction.*

I swallow the wodge of beige mush and feel it slowly travel down my throat in an uncomfortable clod. This was a bad idea; I can barely breathe. 'So, you all off somewhere exciting tonight?' Yaz looks visibly relieved.

'Yeah, we're heading to a bierkeller near Borough. You know, two-litre pints, bratwurst, girls in Bavarian costumes …'

'Ah, beer and boobs, I get you!' I'm not sure I do get it, though. I've been to one of them before. It's basically a load of blokes who ironically wear lederhosen, whereas the girls have tits pushed up to their chin and pin plaits across their forehead. 'Have a good one,' I say to Yaz, who vaults over the back of the sofa and picks up a video game controller.

'You too,' he says, giving me a thumbs-up without turning around.

I take a tumbler and head to my room with a bottle of red that I'd hidden behind a bag of lentils, in case of emergency.

***

A few hours later, I hazily sit up in bed and kick off the blanket that I seem to have swaddled myself in. The flat is mercifully quiet, so I pad down the hallway and flick the central heating onto 'manual', ignoring the sign next to it, which reads,

LEAVE THE HEATING ON TIMER OR WEAR A JUMPER!!!

Shamaya, who is luckily spending the weekend at her parents', taped it up as soon as she moved in.

Back in my room, I plug my laptop in and slide under the covers. I clumsily stab at the play button and lunge at my half-drunk tumbler of wine as it slips off the bedside table. Ross Poldark (the greatest period drama hero of all time) is threshing a field topless and it requires my absolute attention. Does he need to be threshing topless? No. Is it a health and safety concern that he's threshing topless? Yes. Do I know exactly what 'threshing' is? No, but that doesn't matter. I take another swig of wine. It slips over my tongue like velvet, softening the edges of Captain Poldark's sweaty abs, which are now stuck with bits of straw and muck.

The doorbell rings.

I groan and swing my legs out of bed, pull my hoodie straight, and stand up. *Whooooosh*. My vision twists and the wall shunts sideways as I scrabble for the door handle and squint down the hallway. The nice fuggy feeling of red wine I'd had in bed with Poldark (I like the way that sounds) now throbs above my temples. As I shuffle down the corridor, the intercom rings again and I knock the phone off the stand by accident, my hand feeling paw-like as I swipe at the cord. From the receiver I can hear a woman's voice. Oh, standing is so hard. I solve this problem by sliding down the wall until I'm sat on the floor. The receiver swings in an arc near my head and I mentally congratulate myself for making the horribly difficult task of picking up the phone oodles easier.

'Hello?!' I shout at the dangling mouthpiece.

'Elissa? Elissa, is that you?'

'Yeah wodduwant?' I slur back.

'Elissa, buzz me in! It's Maggie!' A sharp bubble pinches my throat.

'Mags?'

'Come on, my love, buzz the door!'

'Okay, Mags,' I say in a quiet voice. I stretch and smack the wall above my head until I make contact with the buzzer. A light trundle of footsteps taps up the stairs a few seconds later. By the time she's squatting down next to me, smelling of the cool outdoors and jasmine perfume, I'm sniffing and crying in long-drawn-out sobs. She encircles me with puffy sleeves from her duck-down jacket. I want to slide my legs out and fall asleep with my head nestled on her chest.

I'm not sure how long we stay there on the hallway floor. I can vaguely sense Maggie cooing at me in soft tones, her hand rhythmically stroking my hair, but it sounds distant, like her voice is playing through a muffled train speaker.

60

'Come on then, up we go, one, two, three!'

She lifts me up to my feet and we stand there a while, swaying and hugging. It feels so nice. This is the first time I've been properly touched or held in weeks. Not in a sexy way, obviously. I feel as sexually appealing as Mr Bean, and Maggie is my oldest and most platonic friend. She gives off a very maternal, matronly vibe, which is something I did tell her once, but she didn't take it very well. I meant it as a compliment.

'Oh, you're such a pickle, aren't you?' she asks me after making me drink a pint of water.

I nod at Maggie, my head a little less cloudy now.

She smiles at me sadly, her red hair falling in a feathered curtain as it slips from behind her ear. She tucks it back. 'Come on, let's get you into bed. And if you drink the rest of that water, I'll bring through something nice for you.' Maggie walks me to my bedroom, her thumb moving in little circles on the small of my back. I climb under the covers obediently.

'How come you came here, Mags?'

'Have you looked at your phone? I sent you so many messages! I was going to come over here and surprise you! I thought you might need a cheer-up. And I needed some adult company. Just after I texted you this morning, one of the girls in Year Two got the pre-audition jitters and turned into a vom-cano during a rousing performance of "This Is Me" from that circus film.' She smiles through a grimace. 'Els, it was awful. Her bonkers mum insisted on coming in at breaktime to rig up these aerobatic ribbon things,' she gesticulates in front of her, 'and then plied her with Skittles before shoving her on stage.'

'Well, that's one way of encouraging talent,' I say.

'It's the "drama mums", they're worse than the "sports mums". Although I suppose in their way they're being encouraging and supportive. And they pay for the costumes,' Maggie says with a guilty smile.

'Sounds like child exploitation.' Maggie side-eyes me. 'What kind of show are you putting on? It all sounds a bit serious.'

'It's a musical version of *King Lear*,' Maggie says, blinking erratically.

'Is that appropriate for seven-year-olds?'

'Not entirely, but I had to chair the PTA meeting and my idea of *Hansel and Gretel* set in a dystopian future got completely shot down. You'll never believe this, Els ...' She shifts to face me and puts the plate down, looking mischievous.

'What?' I turn my head on the pillow towards her, a surge of affection tickling my ribcage. I don't want to be around anyone else right now or talk about anything other than the deranged parents of her students. I hug her arm and put my head on her shoulder, smiling contently.

'Giselle's mum – she's the self-appointed spokesperson – she actually said that the set design for a house made of biscuit could be triggering for some of the students with gluten intolerance.'

'Shut up.'

'Honestly! She did!'

'I'll come and watch it, Mags.'

She squeezes my hand. 'Ah, thank you, peach. Anyway, that's how Giselle ended up spraying us all with rainbow vomit. And that's when I decided that I'd had enough of anyone under four feet tall, so I decided to come here and hang out with you.'

'You're too good.' I put my head on her shoulder. 'This reminds me of when we used to get in after a night out, except no one's lost a shoe.'

'It's a bit early for that. We wouldn't have left for the club yet.'

'What?' I scrabble for my phone and see that it is, indeed, 22.04. Messages from Maggie dominate my notifications, including a public tweet asking after my whereabouts. Best hide that before work on Monday. 'Oh my God. I'm an embarrassment. I hope the next twenty-six years of my life aren't as pathetic as this.'

'Don't say that! You're doing great! You're a big-shot Twitter person who gets all the gossip on dating and love! You're pretty much a fairy godmother, except you have an algorithm rather than little mouse helpers!' I smile sadly. She's being so nice, I don't have the heart to tell her how unlike my life that sounds.

In a haze of incomprehensible spluttering, I tell Maggie about Shamaya wanting me to move out, but leave out the part where Tom does absolutely nothing to comfort me. I'm not ready to talk about it.

63

'If you want to get away for a bit, I'm sure Mum and Dad won't mind if you come to ours for a few days,' says Maggie.

'Thanks, Maggie. Honestly, that means a lot.' I take a deep breath and smooth the duvet cover over my legs. As nice as Maggie's parents are, they're very ... hands-on. My family thought it was a terrible idea when I moved to London. Impractical gifting of beauty treatments aside, Mum's favourite motto is 'what you can't do on your own isn't worth doing' and Dad's is 'happy wife, happy life', so there you have it. I need to keep up the appearance of independence, at the very least.

'I'll think about it,' I add. 'I'm going to try and figure something out with Tom. Maybe have a look at some new house-shares for us.' I look around at our unremarkable room and frown at a red-wine stain on the carpet that wasn't there earlier. Maggie's smile is a straight, thin line, and my heart hurts all over again.

Chapter Seven

It's still early when I wake up the next day. The universe is targeting every sense as a way to rouse me: the early Spring sunshine hits my eyes in a retina-scarring blast, my pyjamas stick to my back and legs, and a repetitive ringtone is trilling so loudly it's like rusty spoons are scraping in my earhole.

Maggie, an annoyingly heavy sleeper, is lying comatose beside me, her forehead dewy. My temples feel like they're clenched in a vice. Hangovers never felt like this before. What would my twenty-one-year-old self say if she could see me now? *Eurgh*. I can't even have a sad, drunken night alone successfully.

I lean over Maggie, who turns away from me and pulls the cover up to her chin, despite the sauna-like temperature of the room. I guess I forgot to turn the heating off last night. Shamaya would go ballistic. I groggily pick up my phone and see that it's a London number. To answer, or not to answer; that is the question (for anyone my age, so it seems).

I press the green button and clutch my forehead. 'Hello?' I croak. If this is an advert for PPI repayment, I swear I'm never answering my phone again.

'Hello? Is that Elissa Evans?' says a bright and offensively cheery voice.

'Yep, Elissa, I am her, I mean yes, Elissa talking. I mean, Elissa speaking,' I garble back at her. By now I've woken up Maggie, who blinks at me from under the cover with small, puffy eyes.

'Sorry!' I mouth at her.

'It's Alina from ElderCare. Sorry to call on a weekend! I've got the graveyard shift. How are you?'

'Alina! Yes, I'm great, thanks!' I lie. She must notice my voice, which sounds like Tom Waits if Tom Waits was into heavy metal and liked taking meth of an evening, because she says, 'I haven't woken you up, have I?'

'Ha! Not at all! I was just making pancakes, actually!' Maggie wiggles her eyebrows at me expectantly, and slowly pulls the duvet down from her face. I shake my head and shrug.

'Okay, so I've got some great news. Are you ready?' *Oh God.* Alina takes my silence as an invitation. 'We've found you a match!'

'Er, a match?' My stomach sinks. Have I signed up to some sort of geriatric dating service where homeless girls living in London can find a sugar granddaddy? I'm desperate, but not that desperate. Maggie sits up in bed. She's clearly eavesdropping and looks increasingly confused.

66

'Yes! A match! For the home share? I got your application yesterday and processed it straightaway. It really helped that you were so detailed. Usually I have to phone back and forth to get the right information before I'm happy to set up a meeting, but not this time! I don't think I've had an applicant tell me about winning the "biggest sunflower award" in primary school before. Hahaha!' Alina's laugh is gutsy and loud. I feel myself wincing. 'Just joking with you, sweetheart!'

In total, I spent the best part of four hours filling in the questionnaire, more out of boredom than anything else. I renamed it 'social metrics for unique user engagement by location'; dry enough to stop Mitchell from snooping on me from his office.

'I've had a lovely lady called Annie on my books for a little while now. We had her matched up recently, but it fell through – nothing to do with her, of course, just a slight issue involving her neighbour and a dog. You like dogs, Elissa?'

'Um, sure! Dogs are great!' I mean, dogs are dogs, aren't they? I can't say I've spent that much time around them, other than the occasional cockapoo at Brockwell Park.

'Well, that's great! I should add a "dog question" to the form ... Hang on, I'm just writing myself a Post-it note ...' I can hear a scratching sound as Alina jots something down. 'Right, what was I saying? Oh yes! Annie. She's a lovely lady. Eighty-three years old. Widowed housewife. Lives in Hampstead – great part of London. Do you know it?'

With wide eyes and a deep frown, Maggie yanks my arm to pull the phone away from my ear. I twist out of her grasp and hush her quiet, scooting to the other side of the bed where she can't reach me.

'No, I mean, I've heard of it, but I've never been,' I reply. I'm very sceptical about 'great parts of London'.

'Okay, so I know this might seem quick, but if you're happy to go forward, you can meet Annie this afternoon. I've already spoken with her and she's had a read of your application, so what we need to do now is put a face to the name and after that comes all the boring logistical stuff: DBS, references. How does that sound?'

'This afternoon?' I grab Maggie's arm and ignore her melodramatic reaction as I twist her wrist towards me. It's 11.08. So, practically the afternoon. My head throbs and it feels like my skull is cracking from the inside. I really hadn't thought anything would come from this, not this quickly anyway. I've barely had time to look into places for me and Tom, which would obviously be preferable to becoming a pensioner's skivvy, even if it was only for a few months. Alina charges on, oblivious to my pain.

'Annie has suggested 3 p.m. Craig from the ElderCare team will be there as well, you know, just in case he needs to pull your leg out of the dog's mouth!' She booms with laughter again. 'Joking, ain't I? I'll email you over the address now. Call if you need to, love! Bye, bye!' I look down at my phone and over to Maggie.

68

'What was all that about? You hardly said anything but you seemed to be agreeing to a lot.'

'Hmm. Yeah. I think I might have signed up to something really stupid.'

Maggie sits up and takes both my hands in hers. She's using her teacher voice, which is equal parts sympathetic and stern, but also a little bit patronising. 'I don't want to be nosy, and I'm saying this because I care ...'

Oh, my head. I want a little break from adulting now. I've done far too much of it over the past few days. I wonder how much it would cost to go in one of those sensory deprivation tanks. And then just stay there. For ever.

'If you're struggling for money, Els, I can lend you some. You don't need to do this,' says Maggie. I take a huge gulp of water and wipe my mouth with my forearm.

'I'm just going to go and see what it's like, Mags. Don't worry.'

'Well – and you know I'm just as much a feminist as you – I just don't think this should be your last resort.'

'Maggie.' I move my hands and wrap hers instead. 'It kind of is. Mum and Dad are on another cruise and stopped giving me handouts when I got my first student loan. The money Nan left me has mostly gone on my Oyster card, and my boss hasn't given me a single sign that I'm going on the payroll any time soon. Tom is ... Tom's got this issue with the lease. I haven't got a choice.'

'You always have choice. Women should always have a choice. I can't let you do this.'

69

Why is she being so self-righteous? It's all right for her! Maggie's parents won't hear of her leaving their river-fronted townhouse on the banks of the fucking Thames and they bloody well don't charge her rent either!

'Well, I am, and you know what? For the first time in ... ages, I feel like I'm doing this because *I* want to. And they might be really nice!' I climb over her knees and pull my stretched grey pyjama top over my head.

'When have you ever heard of them being nice, Elissa? They might treat you well at first, but I'm telling you now: intelligent, vulnerable people still get exploited.' Maggie takes a deep breath and sits up straight. 'This choice might *seem* right now, but it'll follow you every-where. It'll ruin sex for you. I know they say you can detach from it, but I know you; you're too sensitive.' Maggie looks like she's about to cry. 'I mean, it's your choice and your body, and of course, I'll still be here whatever happens, but I can't help thinking that you'll come to regret this.'

'Maggie,' I say slowly. 'What do you think I'm *actually* doing this afternoon?' Maggie's brow furrows.

'Well, you know ...' She looks hesitant now. 'I don't want to say it.'

'Did you think I was going to let someone shag me so I can pay the rent?' Maggie's expression smooths and she stifles a little sob.

'No. No ... that's not what I thought at all.'

'You did!' I jump up. Maggie shrieks and I jab her ribs

70

with my knuckles, laughing at how ticklish she still is. 'I'm bloody well not becoming a sex worker!'

'In my defence, you were in a very ... distressed state last night!' she says, between gasps. I stand up and shake the mass of curls out of my face. There's no time to style it. A topknot and a comb-through will have to do. I pick up my knickers and ping them towards her. She screams and pulls the cover up as a shield.

'I'm having a shower.'

'Hang on, what *are* you actually doing this afternoon?!' Maggie shouts at me down the corridor.

'I'll fill you in over porridge and coffee!'

***

I tell Maggie about ElderCare and the plan to go to Snatch that evening, but Suki has already messaged her (somehow) so she's coming along. A tiny part of me hoped that Suki had forgotten, or had double-booked herself, but she'd sent me a clip this morning: her head on a pillow with another girl's hand lazily draped across her collarbone. In it, she whispered, 'Snatch night, Snatch night, Snatch night' over and over again into the microphone, so I guess it's still going ahead.

Maggie has gone off to meet her boyfriend Martin, whom she met last July on a charity gig overseas. From what I gather, it's a scheme for overachieving teachers who don't feel exhausted enough by the end of the year, so spend their summer holidays training educators in India. I've met Martin once but haven't really formed an opinion of him yet. He laughs at Maggie's jokes and doesn't mock her for being perpetually upbeat, which is more than I can say for her previous boyfriend.

I'm due to meet Annie in a place called Evergreen Village at 3 p.m., which is around twelve minutes from Hampstead station and on the same tube line as me. Questions are swirling around my head about Annie and how this ElderCare thing might work, if I have to go through with it. I click through the website, which has the same garish branding as the flyer, and look at images of happy companions doing implausible activities: decorating a cake that I'm 99 per cent sure has been shop-bought for the picture; completing a puzzle and laughing as if it's the most fun thing in the world; and walking down a garden to point at a slightly dog-eared rose.

I smile at this last one. When I'd go back to Hereford between terms at university, my nanny would always say, 'Come and take a turn around the estate,' which was entirely ironic because she had a tiny back-to-back garden. She'd point out all the flowers that had bloomed since my last visit, or tut in frustration at the molehills that had appeared overnight. Her little two-up-two-down terraced house had once housed seven children and she barely spent a day alone, right up until she went into hospital for the last time. Loneliness hadn't been an issue for her. She'd had the same neighbours for decades and they swapped gossip over the garden fence about the new postman or 'her who's moved into Reggie's old place'.

A single bed and handrails in the bath, though? I mean, it's hardly the young professional life I'd imagined when I moved to London and got a job that didn't exist when I was at school. But it can't be worse than washing Yaz's pubes down the plughole before taking a shower. I wonder if old people are more gross to live with than guys in their twenties who ingest all their protein in liquid form?

I think of Annie and wonder at the kind of old person she might be. Uppity and posh? Making the kinds of jokes you have to apologise for afterwards?

I wonder if last resorts really are *last resorts* if you've said that about every living situation open to you? I click through to a rental website and move the sliders down to the cheapest bracket possible, a perpetually depressing experience. The map of London, initially obscured by little purple flags indicating available property, reveals itself at such speed it's like watching the opening titles for *EastEnders*. If I have to find a place by myself (and somehow manage to get upgraded from 'expenses only' to minimum wage) there are three. Three rooms that I could afford in Europe's biggest capital city. I skim-read the entries and am left feeling a bit sick and slightly creeped out. Of the options available, one was masquerading as London, but was really in Southend-on-Sea with a two-hour commute; one wasn't a spare room, rather a space in

73

a 'platonic double bed'; and the last was a shed. A shed. It was described as 'spacious for a single tenant, with privacy shield', but in reality it was a fucking shed shoved into a living room with a sofa propped up against it.

Chapter Eight

I get off the tube at Hampstead and follow the map on my phone down a street with rows of tall Victorian red-brick houses dotted with sash windows and dainty shop fronts. I weave between demure middle-aged women who march along the pavement with arms looped through boutique bags. Others walk and sip coffee, pausing occasionally to look in the window of an estate agent, all whilst a well-behaved dog sits elegantly at their side. The bakery near my flat in Stockwell, which struggles to charge more than 50p for a croissant, would look entirely out of place here. Instead, pastries glazed with crackled syrup and delicate pastel macarons line patisserie windows. As I head up the hill, the shops make way for houses pushed back behind iron railings and heavily pruned box hedges. I veer left where the road splits into a single lane that tucks between holly bushes and a patchwork brick wall that ripples with ivy. We're not in Stockwell any more.

On a final cobbled lane, blossom drifts against heritage-green garage doors and Victorian lampposts flank the entrance to austere-looking townhouses. This can't be right, surely? Where's the Sixties prefab with pebbledash walls and mossy rooftiles? The net curtains? The geraniums? This turreted stone gatehouse must be a portal to some sort of elfin village; it surely isn't a home for the elderly. The entrance, a pointed archway, is framed with a Latin motif that sits below two Grecian statues; one holds a scroll and the other a set of scales.

Partially hidden behind the waxy leaves of a budding rhododendron, a carved wooden sign states 'Evergreen Village'. I'd once flicked through a book called *Secrets of the Capital* and managed to skim-read a chapter on 'London's Villages' before the sales assistant sarcastically asked me whether I was going to buy it. I was pretty convinced that places like this had been swallowed up by modern developments, or were empty through foreign investment, but here, barely five miles out of London, was a Dickensian remnant of the past. And it was glorious.

I check the email Alina has sent me. Along with the postcode, she's written an instruction. 'Tell the porter at the gate you're there to see Annie and he'll walk you round to her cottage.' Tell the porter? I would if I knew what a 'porter' was ...

I push on the iron gate and it swings open with well-oiled ease. 'Um, hello?' I say, stepping quietly under the archway. My footsteps echo down the length of sand-coloured stone. I pass beyond the threshold and hear a frantic scuffle, quickly followed by the appearance of a uniformed man who pops up behind a half-open stable door, his arms by his sides.

'Welcome to Evergreen Village. You are Elissa, yes? Mrs De Loutherberg expected you five minutes ago. I'll walk you over. Come this way, please.' He unlatches the stable door, nods his cap as he walks briskly past me, and marches around the perimeter of an oval-shaped green that has been given a horticultural crew-cut, with ruler-straight lawn lines and metal edging. The man stops at an entrance between two hawthorn bushes and motions ahead with an upturned hand.

'Please, this way,' he says, before turning towards the gatehouse, leaving me alone in front of a lacquered front door. Annie. You can't be horrible and be called Annie, right? De Loutherberg, though. No one at my semi-rural comprehensive school in Hereford would have got away with a name like that without getting thumped in the arm. I'm imagining Dame Maggie Smith, an uppity dowager, all wide eyes and quivering jowls.

I look around for a non-existent doorbell and as I duck down to see if it's hidden between the vines of a creeping wisteria, a dangling rope knocks against the back of my head. I pull it hard and the shrill sound of a bell peals from a tiny tower above the porch. I jump back and look as it violently swings back and forth, then glance over my shoulder. An elderly man stares at me with his hedge trimmers poised over a juniper bush. In the cottage next to him a curtain twitches and a chunky

77

woman steps quickly behind it, nearly out of sight but for a protruding stomach.

'Hello, Elissa. How are you?' A moon-faced man answers the door and stands with his hands on his knees, like I'm a new puppy he's taken a liking to.

'Fine, thanks. Sorry about the bell,' I stammer, but he ignores it and beckons me inside onto a woven grass mat.

'Shoes off!' He points to each of my feet, like I didn't realise I had two of them, and stands next to me with his hands clasped behind his back in the manner of a slightly creepy priest.

'I'm Craig. Alina must have told you about me on the phone?'

'Yep, she did. You work for ElderCare too?'

'I do indeed!' Craig replies, rocking on the balls of his feet. I'm aware of his body in proximity to mine and subconsciously lean away from him. 'Twelve years as a warden for our ladies and gents in Hampstead. I also cover Kentish Town and round by Camden. Some would say that's a big area to look after, but I'm sure our residents are lucky to have me!' He spits out a laugh. *Poor sods.* 'I visit them once a fortnight, or more if they haven't got an ElderCare companion, which is what we're hoping you'll become.' He smiles at me without showing his teeth and juts his chin forward. 'This is a quick visit really – completely standard procedure – to make sure you two click and the like.'

'Yeah, of course. I mean, I could be an axe murderer or some sort of scam artist trying to steal the weekly pension!'

I laugh and pull at the ends of my scarf. Craig doesn't seem to get the joke. 'I'm not, obviously. I'd be a terrible axe murderer. I'm quite clumsy with sharp objects.' *Stop talking about axes, you total moron!*

'Right you are. Shall we go and meet Annie now?' Craig smooths his oily fringe over his forehead and I'm quite frankly insulted that he's the one who looks more uncomfortable.

Craig leads me through an archway into a light, airy living room that opens into a small kitchen at the back of the house. A pair of French doors are pulled wide open and the tinkling of a wind chime drifts in from outside. Sitting in a wooden chair, her legs stretched out and crossed at the ankle, is Annie.

'Ladies! Annie, Eloise—'

'Um, it's Elissa?'

'Right. There! Now we're all introduced!' Craig claps his hands in front of him and his blue polo-shirt rides up a couple of inches to rest on his hairy belly. I catch myself staring, so smile and turn to face Annie instead, but she's looking out of the window bobbing her velvet moccasins up and down. Oh no. I've been lumped with a senile. I do not have the benevolence for this.

'I'll let you ladies chat whilst I do the rounds. I'll be fifteen minutes or so, all right? Don't be naughty!' He speaks with palpable sarcasm, not that Annie has noticed. She's quietly humming to herself. I hear Craig close the front door. The noise of Annie's carriage clock thrums loudly from the living room and the sound of secateurs cuts the silence into awkward chunks of time.

Annie turns to me after a minute and lets out a sharp laugh. 'Thank Christ. I thought he'd never leave.'

Chapter Nine

'Now we can have a proper cup of tea. I don't waste the good tea bags on *him*,' says Annie. 'Come on, sit down, you don't have to look so worried.'

'Are you sure? I can make tea if you like,' I say, at once impressed and unsettled by Annie's sharp clarity that Craig is a total creep. Annie leans heavily on the arms of her chair as she pushes herself up, her forearms shaking a little. I'm about to help her, but she flashes me a look that makes me sit down again.

'You don't mind a bit of swearing, do you?' says Annie, her face entirely neutral.

'Um ...' Is there a right or wrong answer to this question? If I say I like swearing she might turf me out, but if I say I don't like it, she might think I'm some straitlaced loser who's trying to suck up so I can sleep somewhere other than the pavement. The corner of Annie's mouth twitches and there's definitely a glint in her eye. Here goes. 'Fuck no!'

Annie recoils and turns the tap off, clearly affronted.

'Chuffing hell, is that how you youngsters talk to each

other nowadays?' My cheeks flush with embarrassment. Of course she didn't mean 'fuck', you total idiot, she's eighty-three! She probably meant 'flipping', or 'bastard' at the worst. Well done, Elissa, you've just verbally abused an elderly woman.

Annie rolls her sleeves up to the elbow and I notice that she has a chunky ring on every one of her fingers. She's frowning at me the way Nanny used to when I refused to eat my mashed potato as a kid.

'I'm really sorry. I don't know why I said that.' I try and laugh it off. 'I don't even talk like that normally! Swearing is terrible. Really bad. I tell my brother that every time I see him. The youth of today! What are they like?'

She flicks the kettle on and giggles in a way that makes her torso shimmy. 'Christ alive, Elissa, your face! You look terrified! Oh, I'm sorry, I'm only mucking about. I'm a naughty old girl, much like the *lovely* Craig has suggested.' She walks over with two cups of tea that tinkle on their saucers. Her hands quake slightly as she sets them on the table next to a sugar bowl, plate of biscuits, and a small jug of milk. 'Here we go. I haven't used the proper crockery in a while, but you seem worth it. I have it up there on the dresser. Should have given it a wipe, really. 'Scuse the dust.' Annie sits down heavily and frowns at me. I try and gauge what she's thinking, but so far she's impossible to read.

'You don't fancy getting it out for Craig, then?' I smile at her and glug some milk into my cup. There's a clump of lint spinning on the surface of my tea, but I don't say anything.

'Am I horrible?' Annie's rings clink against her teacup as she lifts it to her mouth.

'Well, he's ... very friendly.'

'We're all ladies here, love. Call him what he is: a right sleazy bastard, is Craig. Something about him ... puts me on edge. I figure that if I pretend to go a bit doolally he'll stop coming round to eat my chocolate biscuits, but he still waltzes in and helps himself, along with leftovers from the fridge.' Annie catches my expression and continues. 'Oh yeah, he'll have the lot. I pretended I'd fallen asleep in the garden chair and he had a very nice time filling that gut of his with my food. Greedy sod.' Annie sips from her cup whilst resting her elbows on the table. She sucks her cheeks in and taps the table. Her rings clink against the wood and I sit up taller, trying to think of something to say. She fiddles with the thin gold chain around her neck, sliding the catch round to the back, and breathes out through her nose. We look at each other and I smile, but it's strained and Annie remains passive. 'Where are you from, love?'

Ah, this question. A lot of people, especially older people, don't quite know where to place me. Usually I can tell when it's asked out of curiosity and when it's phrased like an accusation. When I moved to the capital, I didn't stand out so much amongst London's patchwork community, so it stopped being the first thing I was asked.

'Well, my Mum and Dad were both born here; Mum

is half-Welsh, half-English, and Dad is technically from Tristan da Cunha, but his parents came here after the volcano erupted, so—'

'No, I meant whereabouts in London do you live. At the minute.'

'Oh, right! Well, I'm living in Stockwell at the moment.' *For the next week, anyway.* 'And before that I was in Kent.'

'And why do you want to live with an old bird like me?' says Annie.

I don't, is the long and short of it, especially if I'm always going to be this on edge. *Come on Elissa, you've been through enough interviews to figure out the correct response to questions like this.* I'm trying to gain experience in the field of geriatric wellbeing? I have dreams of becoming a carer? I'm on a mission to brew the perfect cup of tea and think that the elderly community is best suited to use as a trial study?

'My boyfriend doesn't want to live with me and I have nowhere to go because he was the one paying the rent.'

Annie blinks and her eyes crinkle as a smile pushes up her plump cheeks, revealing a row of starkly white dentures. 'I think we'll get on fine here, you and me.'

***

Craig returns a few minutes later and I'm sure I see him bridle when he spots the plate of biscuits between Annie and me.

'How have we got on, ladies?' says Craig. A small damp patch has spread across the top of his stomach from the exertion it took to visit the house next door.

'Perfectly fine,' says Annie, in her Yorkshire accent. 'You tell the people up at ElderCare that I'll have 'er'. My stomach twists uncomfortably. I take our cups over to the sink and turn the tap on, but Annie flaps her hands at me and gently pushes me out of the way with a bony hip. 'Go on, I'm sure you've got lots to be getting on with today; you don't want to be hanging round here with a bunch of old codgers on a Saturday!'

'Oh, okay, if you're sure,' I say as I wipe my hands on a neatly folded tea towel hooked through the railing of her cream-coloured Aga. 'See you, Annie.' The sun breaks through the window and illuminates wisps of her hair like she's been set alight. 'It was nice meeting you,' I say, fulling intending on this being the first and last time. Annie nods without facing me, so I turn around to pick up my coat and scarf, but they've disappeared off the back of my chair.

'I'll see you out, Elissa!' says Craig from the next room. Annie turns to face me, eyes narrow. 'Bye, love.'

Craig is standing next to the front door with my coat between his hands. I really don't want to put it on when he's holding it out like this. He's got a strange look on his face that could seem friendly at first glance, but the smile doesn't quite reach his eyes. I quickly jab my hands through the arm holes like I'm doing a bizarre karate move, but this makes my jumper gather around my armpits and I end up wriggling on the spot with Craig's hands pinned on my shoulders, which, it must be very clear to both of us, isn't helping.

I take a step forward, my coat half on, and lunge for my tote bag, which I've kicked across the floor in an effort to escape from his tentacle grip. When I've detached myself, I pull the front door open and step out onto the porch, turning back to say a brief goodbye. A flash of something akin to anger crosses Craig's face, but he paints a smile back on and strokes the door frame. 'Alina will be in touch,' he leaves a beat, 'about the outcome of today.'

'Okay, thanks, bye!' I mumble over my shoulder, stumbling as I cross onto the lawn with its perfect lines. Annie's right. Craig is a bloody pervert. Maybe she only wants me there to stop him from creeping about the place. I pause at the ridiculously ornate archway that leads out onto the cobbled lane and look back at the cottages that encircle the green.

What a weird experience. Imagine if I ended up living here? I don't belong, but then again, Annie doesn't seem like she does either. Not that it's unbelievable that a brash, wobbly woman from Yorkshire could live in a house with rooms that looked out onto the kind of garden you only see on TV when Alan Titchmarsh trundles around the Chelsea Flower Show. It's just that Annie didn't *seem* like the other people round here, with their trotting dogs and Burberry trench coats. She has absolutely zero pretension and wears a knuckleduster's worth of gaudy signet rings that I'm sure she didn't inherit. Her accent is rich and oddly entrancing.

I read somewhere that adapting your speech patterns is your brain's way of subconsciously assimilating within a community. I did it all the time when I first came to London, eager to shed my round country burr for a sharper accent that sounded more settled than I felt. Perhaps it hasn't been like that for Annie. I guess if you don't want to assimilate, you don't.

***

I walk back down the cobbled hill and turn right at a lilac café, then cross the road between two antique shops and head down the high street, which has largely emptied since I first walked up.

When I get to the station, I fish out my Oyster card and hold it against the sensor as normal, but the gate bleeps angrily at me and I bounce off the closed barriers. Already, a person behind me has walked into my back and huffed, like I've done it specifically to annoy them. I try again, but once more a red light flashes and the bleep turns into a continuous, ear-splitting alarm. There's an orchestra of sighs behind me and I hear someone say, 'Oops, rejected!' in a plummy accent. They must have assumed they were out of earshot. Or they're just an arsehole. The queue meanders around me to use the neighbouring gate and I try my contactless bank card as well. Another red light. *Fuck.* I was sure I had enough money. I got here, didn't I?

I check my account on the top-up machine and the worry worm in my stomach turns into a writhing snake. I don't have the funds to get back on the tube, and after dashing to an ATM, the prognosis looks bleak. If I squint *really hard*, it looks like I've got over £1000 in my account, but the minus sign in front of it says otherwise. I must have got my dates mixed up, because according to my statement I haven't had any money come in since last month. What Mitchell refers to as my 'expenses' works out to around £100 a week, but it's a completely arbitrary amount based on literally nothing, as he doesn't ask me to submit receipts. Essentially, I'm paid a quarter of the national minimum wage. I groan.

I go through a list of travel options in my head that all involve a level of risk or outright criminality, in order to get back to central London. I could order a car through an app and then bail at traffic lights before they charge me, but I don't trust my ability to do that without getting mown down on the North Circular. I could walk, but it'd take at least two hours and I'm wearing these awful shoes that rub my toes into raw nubbins.

Tonight, Suki is going to assume I'm up for a big night out and she's not wrong in the slightest. I really, really want to drink a whole load of vodka cranberry mixers and dance to Beyoncé in a place where you won't get bothered by men looking for an easy hook-up, but I have no idea how I'm going to pay for it.

I'd like to get through a day without crying in public.

I push down the familiar prickles in my throat and blink up at the sky. I've got one more option. My last option. Propped outside the station is a row of clunky bicycles locked into a quick release stand. I've got *just* enough money to take one out.

Chapter Ten

B y some stroke of fortune, after I tangled my bag in the spokes and veered off down the steps into Trafalgar Square to avoid colliding with a rickshaw, I end up in Spitalfields market. I clunk the bike into a free stand, thus ending my Tour de London and, with it, my heart palpitations. I walk past painted steel girders between empty market stalls and skirt around a queue of people lined up outside a posh chippie. Although Suki has said I can head over to her place before we go out, I'm not sure she's expecting me four hours early. Maggie is meeting us at Snatch with Martin, although I'm not sure he knows what he's letting himself in for. He's never witnessed a room full of women singing along to 'No Scrubs' by TLC. It's really quite powerful. I consider lingering in a bookshop, but at this point I'm dying to sit somewhere that doesn't come with an obligation to buy something. There's only so many places you can nurse a cup of tea for whole afternoons before you're blacklisted from the coffee shops of East London.

I reach a grubby glass door just off Falkirk Street, fitted with four long metal bars and papered with flyers for grime nights and a travelling circus (do they still exist?). I've never been inside Suki's place, although I've seen her slip down this road when I've veered off to meet Tom and his boring colleagues in the bars beneath the financial towers of the City. I'd always assumed it was one of those communal warehouse-living situations, where the walls are made from MDF partitions and polygamy comes as part of the tenancy agreement.

I double-check the address on my phone and examine the keypad. Someone once told me that drunkards piss on the 'wait' button at traffic lights and ever since then I've been slightly paranoid about touching buzzers. I pull my sleeve over my finger and press. No answer. I press it again, holding it in this time. Still no answer. Stepping back onto the pavement, I look up, but it's unclear which part of the building is office space and which is housing. I'm about to press the buzzer once more when Suki's voice echoes around the concrete alcove.

'Hello?'

I can't see where the microphone is, so I sort of shout near the buttons. 'Suki? It's me! I'm really early, sorry! Long story!'

'Elissaaaaaaaaaaaaaaa Evannnnnnnnnssssssss,' she yells, as though announcing a WWE wrestler. A group of puffer-jacket-wearing hipsters look over as Suki's voice booms into the street. 'Sure, babe, I'll buzz you up! I was sort of in the middle of something, if you know what I mean—'

'Suki!' interjects a voice from the background.

'Just pull the door, babe!' A whirring sound, like an amplified mosquito, cuts through. Hmm, maybe I should linger in the hallway to give Suki some time to put her pants on?

'Up here!' shouts Suki from the top of the stairs. She's waving at me from over the banister, an oversized T-shirt hanging off one shoulder. I plod to the top floor and when I reach the landing, she swings an arm across my shoulders, kicking open her front door with a bare foot.

'No trousers Saturday?' I say.

'No trousers Shag-er-day, my friend.'

I raise my eyebrows. 'Lucky you!'

'Oh yeah, lucky me! Jazz does this thing where she puts her leg round my ...'

We move into her flat and I forget to keep listening. Suki's place is just about the coolest thing I've seen outside of an Urban Outfitters. There's so much air and space and light; light that comes in at an angle through the three warehouse windows that line the wall. It's essentially a huge open-plan room with a bathroom tucked next to the front door and a bed space that sits on a split-level platform. A spiral staircase leads up to it and a number of trailing houseplants tumble from each ascending step.

A girl who must be Jazz (although it's never safe to assume) gently glides back and forth on a swing that's hooked to a ceiling girder, her toes brushing against the floorboards. Suki walks over and slips her into an embrace, smacking a noisy kiss on the girl's cheek that makes her giggle. 'This is Jazz. Jazz, Elissa.'

Jazz has a voice that tips one word into another, like some of the girls I knew at uni who studied art and took a lot of MDMA at the weekends. 'Elissa, hey! Cool scarf!'

'Er, thanks!' I'd knitted it, badly, about five years ago and I'm not sure it's ever seen the inside of a washing machine. Thank God for the trend of 'clothes so bad the charity shop won't have them'.

'Oh, hang on, you're the vagina girl, right?' She looks up for confirmation to Suki, who clenches her teeth in an admittance of guilt. I already like Jazz less than her predecessor.

'Sorry, babe, Jazz overheard.'

I sigh and drape my coat over the kitchen counter. 'I really hope that doesn't become my identifier.'

'No, no, it's funny! I thought it was hilarious!' Well, I'm glad the girlfriend Suki's had for five minutes knows about my 'hilarious' fanny too. Brilliant.

'I'm just gonna jump in the shower, be back in a min,' Jazz says, gently removing Suki's hands from her stomach and glancing coyly over her shoulder as she pulls a towel from the banister. When she's gone, Suki puffs her cheeks out in exhaustion and rubs her hands together in glee.

'Mate. She's wild.'

'She's something.'

'Beer?'

'Yeah, go on then.'

93

We sit on the sofa beside one of the windows where dusk, or more likely light pollution, has turned the sunlight into the beautiful pink and orange tones of early evening. Suki clinks the cap off a bottle of beer by smacking it down on the edge of her coffee table.

'Four pounds from IKEA and not a chip. Amazing,' she says as she passes the bottle to me. 'So, what's the deal with that twat Tom? And before you say "nothing", you've barely spoken about him in the past few weeks, so don't bother lying.' Suki tucks a leg underneath her and swigs, holding her bottle by the neck.

'I haven't heard from him since he left. I don't think I will, either. He's a thousand miles away and surrounded by girls who use glitter like body lotion. I doubt he's thinking about me.'

'Oh, that sounds dangerous.'

'Does it?'

Suki ignores my question. 'Are you guys okay, though?'

'Yeah? Like ... I mean, yeah. We're fine. Still trundling along. He's been out a lot recently and ... well, the next few months are going to be weird.' I sigh and trace my teeth with my tongue.

'Weird how?'

I tell Suki about Shamaya's thinly veiled eviction notice, and Tom's subsequent reluctance to move somewhere else with me. She doesn't interrupt but listens with her head tipped back.

'I don't want to freak him out and force him to live with me in a flat he hates. If we have to live apart for a while before finding somewhere new together, it won't be all bad. At least I'll *know* I won't be coming home to him rather than it being a surprise.'

I glance up at Suki, not knowing how to articulate what I'm feeling.

'I'm gonna be honest with you, babe: what you just said was really depressing. The way you talk about Tom? I've had stronger feelings for a houseplant.'

Tom and I never really spoke about our emotions, not towards each other, anyway. It was a norm we established at the beginning. He always struck me as the kind of kid who was never hugged as a child. He saved affection for special occasions, or performed it ironically. I met Tom during a temping stint at a literacy charity, in the long days of being ignored by my colleagues whilst the kettle boiled. I recognised him from alcopop-fuelled sports socials at university, but then he carried business cards, whereas I scanned the 'reduced' aisle at Tesco for sort-of-fresh food. His firm offered free consultancy to barely functioning charities, which is how I 'booked' him for a twenty-minute slot that mainly consisted of me staring at his sharp jawline. He has always been serious and assertive, so it was easy to say yes when he asked me out and easier still when he said it was 'okay if I wanted to move in with him'. He was radically consistent, which was wildly attractive to me. It's no surprise he doesn't want to break a lease.

'Truthfully, do you really love him?' Suki rests her chin on her hand.

I hesitate and swallow a mouthful of beer. My words are so close to my mouth, if I don't say it now they'll fight their way out later when I'm pissed and less coherent. 'What if the problem's not that me and Tom don't "love each other",' I say in a silly voice, 'because we get on great, usually. It's more that ... I'm not sure I can feel ... that. For anyone.' I drink some beer, my bottom lip quivering. Suki furrows her brow.

'Don't be stupid. Of course you can. If you haven't felt it yet, it's no big deal.' She sits up and pulls a cushion behind her back. 'Look, you and Tom ... I don't know, it might just be a thing you're going through, but it doesn't sound normal. I'm not saying he's a shit. Not a Patrick Bateman level of shit, but still. You fancied him at one point, right?' I nod pathetically. 'And when you move in with someone it feels like your relationship is moving forward, when maybe it's not. You are allowed to change your mind. How long were you together before you moved in?'

'Six months.'

'Exactly! That's no time at all! You're still shagging a couple of times a day at that point. Elissa, this relationship isn't something happening to you that you have no control over.'

She's right. She's completely right. And I think that's why I start bawling. Proper sobs that come right from the pit of my stomach. Suki takes the beer out of my hand and shuffles forward to hug me, which only makes me cry more.

'I'm really sorry, Elissa! Honestly, I didn't mean to make you upset! I'm a fucking idiot, I always put my foot in it.' The sharp little bristles of Suki's scalp rub against my cheekbone.

I draw a finger along my lash line, which is an old habit first taught to me by my mum. Apart from the really important stuff, like how to dab your eyes demurely in a toilet cubicle to stop your mascara from smearing, most maternal duties were delegated to my nanny.

'It's fine, it's fine,' I say to Suki, who looks unconvinced. 'Really. You're right. It's been niggling at the back of my mind for a while, I think. I don't know if that's why I'm being all sad and useless at the moment. I think I'm ... I think I'm just feeling a bit sorry for myself. When he comes back from Vegas, we can properly talk about it.' Oh God, that sounds so much lamer coming out of my mouth than I imagined.

'You do what you need to do, babe. This Snatch night has come at the perfect time! I've never left a Snatch night feeling anything other than fucking elated. You might come out with a UTI you didn't go in with, but that's nothing a bit of cranberry juice can't fix.'

'You make it sound so sexy.' I smile.

'There you go! There she is!' Suki smacks me on the arm, a little too hard, and thrusts my beer back into my hand.

'Do you want to hear about the next instalment in my lame life?' I say.

'Hit me.'

'There's a very slim chance I'm moving in with a pensioner in Hampstead.'

'For real?'

I tell her about Annie, the strange retirement cottages, the porter, and Craig the creepy warden.

'He sounds like an Operation Yewtree in waiting.'

'That's what I thought!'

'Men are trash.' Suki swigs her beer, pausing to burp over her shoulder. 'And it's no rent?' she says, wistfully.

'Nope.' I yawn and rub my eyes. 'Well, only a contribution towards the bills, but that shouldn't be too much. I'm not gonna do it, though.'

'Er, are you serious? Definitely do it! Annie sounds like a right laugh! It's a BBC Three sitcom waiting to happen!' Suki says excitedly. 'It can't be worse than living with boys and their gross pubes.'

'How would you know?'

'I just do. It's something you hear about. Boys leave pubes everywhere. It's a thing. Unless this Annie was a hippie in the 70s. She might leave gross grey pubes everywhere.'

'Please can we stop talking about the pubes of my maybe future housemate?'

'Do you want me to tell you about Jazz's instead?'

'No! No pubes talk!'

Suki stands behind the sofa and I hear the rattling of bottles.

'We may as well get started now. Fancy a Suki special?'

'As long as it's nothing sexual.'

'It's a cocktail! Which could be sexual, depending on your inclinations.'

She waves a bottle at me. Inside, gold flecks catch the light, suspended in a clear liquid. 'Mama's got her party juice in.'

Chapter Eleven

I wake up the next morning (just, it's 11.42 a.m.) and feel weirdly bright-eyed considering the time it was when I got in. My feet and shins throb from dancing and I'm desperate for a wee, probably from the huge bottle of water Maggie made me drink in the taxi on the way home. She turned up at Snatch about half an hour after we got there, with Martin trundling behind looking decidedly meek, an excessive amount of eyeliner smeared around his eyes. He'd taken her tongue-in-cheek suggestion of 'blending in' far too literally, giving him a Jack Sparrow look without the confident swagger.

What happened afterwards is a blur, but I do remember a largely empty dance floor filled with liquid smoke and disco lights that were just sparse enough to flatter the sweaty, gyrating attendees. My fitness tracker says that I burnt 503 calories, so I'll take that as a win. I was drunk in a way that I remember being as a teenager, when music sounds like it's coming from inside your own chest.

Suki's 'party juice' turned out to be a lot of vodka,

pineapple juice, and a slug of honey that she poured into a pint glass, garnished with a satsuma wedge and garish peacock straw complete with concertina tail. Thankfully, we had our first drink so early that I didn't spend any money on drinks at Snatch. That, and the promoter let me in for free because Suki roused the queue into a half-hearted rendition of 'Happy Birthday' that was so sluggish and depressing, I was taken pity on and waved inside.

The rest of the morning passes in a comfortable blur of period dramas in bed (a 1980s version of *Mansfield Park* this time) and frequent cups of tea. Predictably, as soon as she gets home, Shamaya notices that the heating has been on outside of our allocated allowance (apparently she could feel warmth in the walls). For the next few days I try and stay under Shamaya's radar by keeping to my room, only sneaking out to heat up a ready meal every now and then.

By 10.30 a.m. on Wednesday, I have approximately *zero* ideas for the meeting everyone is now calling 'The Big Pitch'. I suggested 'The Great Dating Pitch Off', but I guess I read the room incorrectly, because no one thought it was a good idea and Bismah gave me a withering smile that made me feel a bit stupid. I've tried drawing a spider diagram to help with ideas, mainly because I saw Adam do it first, except his was on a big roll of brown paper spread over an entire table, and mine covers a Post-it note. I feel this adequately represents our varying degrees of confidence.

I have no idea how Mitchell thinks this is going to work. Bismah, who has been here the longest, told me that in the early days, Mitchell used to change his mind about what kind of app he was developing all the time. Just before Lovr was born, we joined the 'matching market' and linked users with niche hobbies (like 1930s steam trains and Catalonian stamps from the Civil War era), which turned into a haven for weirdos with dodgy fetishes. According to Rachael on the front desk (who hears all the really good gossip because she has a trustworthy face and sympathetic voice), Lovr came about after Mitchell's wife left him for a long-standing business partner who made his fortune selling water in recyclable tin cans.

I tap my pen on the table and think. What do people want from a dating app? Options, right? Whilst filtering out the arseholes? But then again, if your first date was a good enough experience, would it matter if they moaned about their ex's poor music taste over a plate of dough balls?

I spend far too long watching the screensaver on my computer screen bounce from corner to corner before admitting defeat. I decide to let my ideas 'percolate' over an intense game of competitive Tetris with Hans from Rotterdam. Just as I'm about to swipe victory from under his nose, my phone buzzes. I jump in my chair, knocking my phone to the floor, but manage to accept the call just before it clicks onto voicemail, by lunging under the desk.

'Hang on, one second,' I whisper into the mouthpiece, which makes me feel like I'm orchestrating an espionage. Everyone is highly strung at the moment and Mitchell has been especially volatile. Yesterday morning he gave us all little nods as he marched through the room towards his office, which wasn't so odd except for the huge stack of A-level business textbooks he was trying to conceal under his arm.

I slide the courtyard door open and put the phone to my ear.

'Hi, sorry. Just had to go somewhere I could talk.'

'Elissa! It's Alina!'

'Alina! Hi!'

'We've had some great news! Annie thinks you two really clicked and she's happy to open her home to you as a companion. Exciting, eh?'

Oh my God. My stomach contracts and I'm not sure how to place the feeling. The night out at Snatch had made the whole 'granny roommate' thing seem distant and detached, like it was a fun idea someone else had and I was playing along with it.

Tom sent me a string of messages yesterday morning just as I got off the tube; a picture of him and the guys eating brunch, a WhatsApp saying that he missed me, and a short clip of a taught, lean stomach alternately flashing in pink and blue club lighting. When I looked closer, my name was written in lipstick just under the belly button of a woman whose face remained out of shot. It's a strange way of saying it, but I guess it shows he's missed me? Despite Suki's chastisement of my weak-willed approach to Tom's indifferent behaviour, I feel like it would be stupid of me to abandon our relationship. Deep, fiery, passionate romance is a farce anyway and makes me feel awkward. Unless it's Poldark, of course, but that's different.

'Elissa, you there, hun?'

'Yes! I'm here! Sorry, what did you say?'

'I said Annie's happy for you to move in whenever's convenient for you, but there's no rush. She isn't one of our high-dependency clients, so as long you're happy you can move in any time in the next month.'

I've googled the legal framework of tenancy agreements, and I'm pretty sure that it's not a big deal for Tom to leave and move elsewhere with me, especially if we find someone else to take the room, a problem Yaz has already solved for us. I've bookmarked the page to show him.

'Look, I'm really sorry, but I think I'm going to have to pull out. I've had a ... change of circumstances. I really appreciate what you've done so far, but—'

'She doesn't always make the best first impression, but she'll grow on you.'

'No! Nothing like that! It's just to do with my boyfriend, honestly.'

Alina barely disguises a sigh. On the line, I hear the weight of her fatigue. 'You're all right. These things happen. Bugger. Thought we'd solved our Annie problem. You sure you weren't put off? Because you're only obliged to offer fifteen hours a week in support.'

I eventually convince Alina that Annie had nothing to do with my withdrawal, although with her sharp, brusque demeanour, I can imagine she'd slip salt in my tea by Easter.

By the time I head home that evening, the awkwardness of the phone call makes way for something verging on a good mood. Mitchell and Rhea were out in meetings all day, the others ignored me to work on their pitches (allowing for an uninterrupted, two-hour YouTube binge) and Tom is back tonight. During the night, he messaged me a link to a beautiful beachside hut in Indonesia. Aside from a week gorge-walking in Wales, we haven't been anywhere remotely verging on exotic, unless you count an alumni university sports tour of Leicester, which I don't. Could this be him suggesting an *actual* holiday? The kind I'd need to buy mini shampoos and a neck pillow for?

The prospect of Tom getting back from Las Vegas is both exciting and a little anxiety-inducing. But that's normal. I don't know what kind of mutant girlfriend I'd be if I didn't feel *slight* trepidation at the thought of what happened in a place synonymous with lap dancing and poor life decisions.

***

As I walk up to the house, I can see our bedroom light on behind the scraggly branches of a crab-apple tree, so Tom must be back. I've missed him. I have missed him, haven't I? Yes, I've definitely missed him. I have enjoyed sleeping like a starfish in our three-quarter-size bed, but that doesn't mean I haven't missed him. I plod upstairs, avoiding the precarious stacks of leaflets and bills that line the communal staircase.

'Hey, you're home!' I call down the hallway, wiggling round his bag that blocks most of the narrow corridor.

'Yep, I'm in here.' Ouch. His voice sounds like a cement mixer. Must have been a heavy week. I push our bedroom door open and find Tom hunched on the edge of the bed. Part of me wants to laugh; he looks like an anxious football manager, more so because he's still got his 'going out' brogues on. I hover at the door, but when he doesn't get up, I go to sit next to him, my initial excitement deflating like a punctured balloon. I rest my head on his shoulder and slip my arm through his.

'Good stag? I want to know everything: who got a tattoo, where you put the tiger, how many times you said, "What happens in Vegas ..."' Tom smiles, but it doesn't quite reach his eyes. *Oh shit.*

'Yeah, yeah ... it was good. Really good.' He's not looking at me. Why isn't he looking at me? I feel like I've swallowed a scoop of crushed ice.

'So, that place in Indonesia looks cool. We could—'

'What place?'

'The link you sent me earlier? The place in Kuta, I think it was?'

'Ah, shit, yeah, that was meant for someone at work. Sorry.' Well, that was an anticlimax. Of course, why would he want his actual girlfriend to go on holiday with him? How completely bonkers of me. Disappointment sits heavy on my shoulders and I'm irritated at the feeling.

'Look—'

Oh God. No good sentence starts with 'look'.

'You know I said I wanted to go travelling. But, like, really go travelling. For a proper period of time?'

What is a 'proper period of time'? A month? Three months? A year?

'Mmmhmm,' I hum. Of course, travel! A surefire way to delay making any grown-up decisions. I could easily jack in my internship. I'm not sure why we haven't considered this before.

'Well, I've decided I'm going to do it. It's really exciting actually. Ben is moving out to Jakarta for work using this global hot-desking thing and I'm going to join him for a while.' A while. Another decidedly vague measure of time.

'Riiiiight.' I'm quickly realising that these plans don't involve me. He's nodding now, a sort of bouncy nod with his lips sucked in. Well, it's more of a grimace, really.

'When are you thinking of going?' I ask. A laugh creaks out of his throat but it's too loud. Too loud for him, anyway. He doesn't really laugh much.

'Well, that's the funny thing. There's this project I've been given at work that doesn't exactly require me to be in London. It'd be good if I was more mobile because there's stakeholders over in the Far East that need a bit of coaxing and it's always better to work on them face-to-face, so if I'm based there I can head up more of the client relation-ships, which is what I wanted to go into anyway, so this is a fast-track really ...' Tom lets his last few words trundle off with an upward intonation like he's pulling together the thin strands of an explanation.

The icy feeling moves from my stomach and rises up my throat, grating my words before they leave my mouth. I'm half hoping that I'll cry, so that Tom has the visual cue he needs to start apologising, or to touch me, or to do anything that isn't just sitting there spouting corporate buzzwords at me.

It's always been his backup, whenever we've talked about something awkward or difficult – the 'benefits', 'trajectory', 'risk', or 'value' of whatever it is he wants to do that requires me being out of the way.

Tom jiggles his foot up and down, making my knee bounce awkwardly against the bed frame. 'That's not really telling me when you're thinking of going,' I say. Oh, he's so uncomfortable. I know he's uncomfortable because I can feel how his body is tightly wound next to mine and yet I really, really don't care. I don't want to beg him to think about it and I definitely don't want to cry. I really want to cook some fucking ramen and eat it in bed with an episode of *Gilmore Girls* on my laptop. And for him to be somewhere else.

'Well, next week, actually, I've sorted out a lot of the logistics with work and I can stay with Ben until I figure out my own place. I'll be back and forth a fair amount. Work are paying for flights, so it frees me up a lot.'

He rubs his thumb across the bone at the top of my spine and it makes me want to slide out from under his hand, off the bed, and through the floorboards into the convenience shop below. 'So, you never intended to find another place with me? Last week, when I was trying to get my head around this stupid "I can't break the lease" malarkey ...?' I've added a very immature, thick-sounding voice to imitate him. It's not my finest hour.

'Not exactly, but yeah, I had thought about it. Talked it over.'

'With who, Yaz?'

'Yeah.'

'Ah, that makes sense.' I say, my words sharp. 'And where do I fit into all of this?' *Yes, Elissa – you can't be more direct than that. Good girl.*

'I don't know.'

'Right.' *Oh.*

We sit in silence, listening to the muffled sound of Yaz singing Jamiroquai lyrics as they mingle with a pulsing beat that only serves to heighten the painful awkwardness between us. He wants me to give him a solution; to tell him that it would probably be best if we weren't together; to tell him that it would be too hard to try and make it work in different time zones. But, I can't do it. I won't.

I always thought that break-ups would be full of rage and shouting, with someone unquestionably in the wrong and the other begging for forgiveness, then a vase would be flung against the wall and smash and everyone would reflect on how this was a metaphor for their fragile relationship. But, there isn't enough wall in this room to throw something against and the only thing Tom has ever bought me is a pair of bamboo chopsticks, which I like a lot, so I'd rather keep them intact.

'I'm going to go and stay with Mum and Dad for the rest of the week and then I'll head over on Monday morning to get my stuff. Look, I know this is awkward, El.' *Wow, understatement much.* 'But it means you're free to stay in the room until the end of the month, so it gives you a bit of time, you know.'

Time? Time for what? *Oh God, the rent.* I can't afford rent by myself. Well, I can't afford it *with* Tom, either, because of the dodgy conditions of my internship. This is how it's worked since we moved here; Tom pays the whole of our rent, then I feel bad about it and use my lunch expenses to buy us dinner a couple of times a week. It's the only reason I was able to take on the internship in the first place – his economics graduate salary was more than enough to cover both of us.

Now I want to cry. Bubbles prickle at the back of my throat and I can't stop thinking about how much of a fucking failure this whole thing has been.

I came to London wanting to make a difference, but couldn't land full-time hours; I've got a job that sounds exciting, but is shallow and actually makes me poorer through doing it; I barely see my friends because they're always busy in their – well-paid, I might add – jobs, and I can't even bring myself to feel sad that my boyfriend is dumping me because I'm not sure I've ever properly

110

been in love with him. He's stopped his anxious jiggling and we sit in the silence made by our refusal to state the obvious.

'Right,' I say. I can't break my gaze from his leather shoes. They're covered in sticky stains from spilt drinks. He hasn't mentioned me at all – how he's going to miss me, how he's essentially forcing me to move out, or if he's actually liked living together. Then again, I don't really feel like saying those things either. I sit up and scoot back on the bed until I'm leaning against the wall with my knees pulled in.

'I'll have Skype and stuff,' Tom says as he stands up, winding his earphones around two fingers, before sliding them into his back pocket.

'Yeah, well ...' I add lamely. We've never used it before, so I doubt we'll start now. Soon after Tom got headhunted a few months ago, he asked me to send calendar invites for joint social events, so he's not exactly going to cope with spontaneous video calls from a different continent, is he? 'Thanks for being so supportive about all this,' says Tom, standing near the door. I'm not sure what's happening. Is this a break-up, a hiatus, or something else entirely? He opens it and the sound of Yaz' playlist skips onto Chaka Khan's 'Like Sugar', which is so jarring a song in this current situation that it makes my throat close up again. He taps the metal doorknob, hovering. 'Maybe you could phone Maggie and see if you can stay with her?'

'Don't tell me how to deal with this shit show, Tom. I'll figure it out just fine.' Tom's eyes widen in surprise and

111

he gives me the tiniest of smiles, which makes me want to punch him in the throat.

'I'll be going then.' He holds the door open and looks at me.

He shifts his weight from one foot to the other and for a second I think he's going to walk over and kiss me. Despite myself, I lean forward to meet him, but he decides against it and awkwardly pats the wall below the light switch like he's soothing a horse. We lock eyes, which quickly turns into the worst staring contest I've ever experienced, until he shuts the door with a hard pull against its sticky frame. I wait until I hear him swing his backpack on and clump down the stairs before I get up to cook my noodles.

I stir the boiling water into a whirlpool and shrug off my coat. From the pocket, I fish out a severely crumped flyer, which has slipped into the lining through a hole I'd meant to patch up last winter. I smooth it out on the countertop with one hand and turn the hob down with the other. Water drips over the edge and hisses as it hits a lick of flame. Fuck it. I've got nothing to lose.

Chapter Twelve

'Shut. Up.'
   'Yep.'
   'I can't even ...'
   'Yep.'

Suki sits cross-legged on a stack of crates that have been
loosely fashioned into outdoor seating with the aid of a
cushion and potted palm trees. I take my boots off despite
the fuggy damp in the air and skim my toes across the
artificial grass. The pho noodles that dangle above Suki's
mouth now slip from her chopsticks, sending chicken broth
over the sides of her reusable tub. Most of us would give
ourselves a pat on the back for carrying round a glass
KeepCup, but Suki has an eco-friendly version of just
about everything.

'So, he's just gone and fucked off, then?' says Suki,
gesticulating to the place Tom has fucked off to with her
chopsticks, which is apparently over her left shoulder.

'Yes. Well, he's gone to his parents until his flight out
next week, but in essence, yes, he's fucked off.'

'I hope this is a stupid question, but he left you a key, right?'

'Yeah. Technically, I've got until the end of the month until I have to move out. Obviously he's not going to keep paying rent. Now I've calmed down, I'm trying not to be pissed off about it because he was really helping me out by paying for the whole lot in the first place.'

'Babe, that's not the point. He can't just change every-thing and expect you to be cool with it. There are a couple of major factors here. One, you're now homeless—'

'Wow, okay.'

'No, but seriously, this is what he's done. And he doesn't seem to give a fuck that you've essentially broken up. Actually, can we talk about how fucked up it is that he's just left his live-in girlfriend of six months to go on some sort of delayed fuck-boy gap year? That's savage.'

'The thing is, Sook, I keep thinking I'm going to get this wave of despair that things have ended but I just don't ... feel anything. I was kidding myself, wasn't I? You were right the other day. It was convenient, but sharing a sock drawer doesn't make you a good couple. Well, it was a lot more convenient for me than him. He was, quite literally, losing money because of me.' I pause and put my lunchbox to one side. 'When he went away, I didn't miss him. Not really. I missed rolling into the warm spot he left behind in the bed each morning, and falling asleep to a film on Sunday afternoons, and eating fajitas together.' My throat gets prickly and I have a lukewarm sip of coffee, which is

114

now too milky because all the foam has dissolved. 'Suki, there's nothing sadder than constructing a fajita on your own.'

'Oh, babe.' She leans over and rubs my knee. 'You can come and construct fajitas with me and Jazz any time. You know that, right? Jazz might even get off with you if you ask her nicely.'

'Thanks, Suki. I'll bear that in mind.' I smile despite how stupidly miserable I am, look up at the sky, and blink rapidly to dispel the threat of tears. 'You still haven't told me what happened to Fiona.'

Suki rubs her chin and skims a hand over her shaved head. She looks up at me with her bottom lip jutting out and I know instantly that she is putting on a facade of guilt; there's too much twinkle in her eye. I gasp and accidentally inhale a strand of my two-day-old spaghetti. My eyes water and I splutter from a momentary lapse of oxygen. 'Suki! What did you do?'

'Why would you think I did anything?' Suki bites a smile into the corner of her mouth, unable to keep up her kicked-spaniel act.

'Tell me you didn't then.'

'I didn't!'

I raise my eyebrows at her, using my best 'warning face' that I'd perfected during a summer as an au pair in Italy. When you speak zero Italian and have the authority of a flea, a 'look' can go a long way to stop one child trying to set the other's hair on fire with a stove lighter.

115

'Okay, I did.'

'I really liked Fiona! She made all those great cookies! I have dreams about the ones with the melty marshmallow middle. God, they were good. And that Lebanese breakfast thing she made after Pride?'

'All right, Greg Wallace, calm down. Anyway, she's single now so feel free to crack on.'

'Yeah, I'm not quite ready to give up on boys just yet.'

'Well, you keep saying that, but everyone's a bit gay, aren't they?'

'Are they? I don't think I am.'

'You think that now, my friend, but I saw how you backed up when Beyoncé came on.'

'Don't bring Beyoncé into this.'

Suki smirks and dangles her arm over the back of a crate propped on its side to serve as an armrest. 'Anyway, Fiona's fine. Well, she wasn't fine for a bit. She was really fucking mad actually. It was weird because I sort of felt like she didn't have the capacity for anger. She rationalised everything. D'you remember I told you about that night I got pissed with my brother after work and totally fucking forgot she'd booked a table at that posh place – what's it called? – the one with the mirrors that Piers Morgan is always in?'

'The Ivy?'

'Yeah, that's it!' Suki slurps, the steam from her pot twisting around a rope of noodles that hangs from her chopsticks. 'I turned up wasted and managed a couple of oysters before doing a tactical vom outside the front and then the doorman in his fancy fucking top hat wouldn't let me in again.'

'Suki,' I say, laughing, 'that is absolutely vile. Mind you, that's a Michelin dinner for one lucky urban fox.'

Suki snorts and folds her slender arms across her chest. 'Yeah, so that night I met her mum for the first time and Fi was like –' Suki imitates a deep, measured American accent '– "I know you work so hard and I understand that Fridays are your release, but it made my mom feel uncomfortable and I hope in turn that you appreciate that." It was a pretty dick move from me, but I wanted her to get mad at me for once. I fucking deserved it.'

Suki stands up and swings her arms like a swimmer warming up on poolside.

'Right, I better get back down to the pits. Louis wants to have some sort of foosball championship and the loser has to write the code for an interface patch on Sunday.' Suki is technically employed by The Butcher Works and is rented out to the five or six apps that are housed here. Louis is easily the wealthiest guy in the place, despite only just being able to legally drink in America.

'How can your day be so different to mine when we share the same building?' I wiggle into my shoes and pick a blob of sauce off my jumper. 'To my knowledge, our air-hockey table has never been plugged in.' I walk behind her as we clunk down the exterior metal staircase that leads into a communal courtyard. Suki turns around on the stairs and grips the railing, her eyes full of mischievous charm.

'That big meeting in a couple of weeks, you got a pitch ready for it?'

'Yep.'

'Liar.'

'I'll think of something. Eventually. Although, I don't see the point; Mitchell doesn't care what I have to say, especially if it's not what he wants to hear.'

'Oh, forgot to tell you, one of the coders on floor three told me—'

'Hang on,' I say, recognising the number on my screen with a little lurch in my stomach.

'If it's Tom, tell him to fuck off.' I wince and push the mouthpiece into my chest. She winks and takes the stairs unevenly, disappearing through a sliding door.

'Hi, it's Elissa.'

'Hi! I got your email, great news! That's it now, is it? No more changing your mind?'

'Nope. That's it. Definitely.'

'Okay, well I've submitted your DBS, so I can't foresee any delays. Like I said, Annie's ready when you are.'

'Actually, do you think Annie would be okay with me moving in some time sooner? Like ... this weekend?' I grit my teeth.

'If you get your documents back before Sunday, sure!' *Phew.* 'Let me see ... Craig's just submitted his rota and will be doing the rounds at Evergreen Village between 10 a.m.

and noon on Sunday, so if you arrive between those times, he can do a final briefing with you before you two become official ElderCare companions. Quick and efficient. I wish my other companions were as keen as you! Honestly, the dithering! Much less chance of me losing the paperwork between now and the weekend, know what I'm saying?' I laugh along. Not much chance of losing paperwork in a paperless office.

It all sounds great. And by 'great', I mean that I've run out of reasons to refuse the offer. But why did creepy *Craig* have to do the briefing? Hasn't he got a war veteran in Chalk Farm to steal military medals from?

'Annie will be thrilled. I guess I can tell you this now, seeing as you're both happy with each other, but you're the –' Alina pauses and I can hear her flicking through papers '– twenty-third match we've found for her since the last one with the dog allergy, and the first she's agreed to have after meeting them face-to-face. She doesn't let just anyone round for tea, our Annie!' Alina chuckles down the phone and rather than feeling comforted, I experience a swell of intimidation. 'You must have done something right, Elissa.'

'Ha, yeah, I guess so.'

'We'll get your forms sorted, you know – make sure you haven't tried to kidnap any grannies in the past – but we'll work on the basis that everything is fine for your move on Saturday. Any questions just call, all right, my love?'

I say goodbye and put the phone in the back pocket of

my jeans. Twenty-three matches? Annie's picky, that's for sure. What had I done that the other twenty-two hadn't?

Annie had been in the throes of second-wave feminism, where women were striking at work for equal pay and divorced mothers lived in communes to raise their babies together, and here I am whining about not being able to pay for rent because my rich boyfriend has essentially kicked me out. I mean, a pensioner's house is far from the loft flat in Camden that I'd imagined myself in when I first moved to London. I doubt I'll be able to invite a mate over for a movie night, but then again, I don't do that now, either.

Chapter Thirteen

'I don't know how much of this to leave,' I say. Maggie rolls her sleeves up and peers over my shoulder into the tiny room Tom and I have shared for nearly a year.

'Well, the furniture is the landlord's, right?'

'Yep. Everything except the lamp.'

'Oh, thank goodness,' says Maggie, leaning against the door frame. 'I thought for a second we'd have to find a way to get that chest of drawers in the Mini. I mean, I would have tried!' I put my arm around Maggie's waist and rest my head on her shoulder. We sway slightly, looking at the almost empty room.

'Let's get going, shall we? Anything last-minute to do? Did you want some help cleaning?'

I snort and balance a plastic container of shoes on my hip, some of which have mildew and mould from the damp patch in the corner. 'Absolutely bloody not. Tom can do it. He moaned that I never cleaned properly, anyway.' I put on a whiny voice, which, I'll admit, is very petty of me. *"You have to pick things up and hoover under them, Elissa!"'*

'I do that!' says Maggie.

'Hmmm. Well, I'll just write a quick note to Shamaya and Yaz. I'll be down in a second,' I reply.

The little bedroom, so often dark and dreary, looks almost cheerful. Sunshine sneaks through the branches of an oak tree growing on a strip of muck outside, dappling light on the gallery of absent memories formed by bleached shadows of Blu-tacked photographs.

'The parking timer is going to run out in a few minutes, Elissa!' Maggie calls up the stairs.

'All right, I'll be down in a sec!' I sidestep out of the room and prop the last of my boxes on the kitchen counter, which is strewn with grains of uncooked rice and a rogue pizza crust. I can't think of what to say to Yaz and Shamaya. I doubt we'll be meeting up to reminisce about the times we jostled for the bathroom before work. I use the marker dangling from a length of string next to the 'chore chart', and quickly scrawl a message on a pizza box. I settle on:

Good luck in the future! Hope the new housemate lets you eat their chicken nuggets too! (Yes, I noticed.)

I prop it up near the microwave. There's no conflict quite like passive-aggressive notes between housemates.

I come downstairs and wiggle the box behind Maggie's driving seat, which is a feat in itself. There's barely enough room for a passenger in her car. Maggie must notice I'm dithering on the kerb, because she winds down her window.

'D'you want a few minutes? I can do a lap of the block if you like.' I bite my lip and look back at the tatty front door, crowded with bin bags and marked with dents from people trying to kick it in, thinking it was the corner shop.

'No, it's okay. I'm done here.' I post the keys back through the letterbox and clamber over an IKEA bag of underwear and clothes I never saw the need to hang up. 'Let's go.' Mr Saleem gives me a little nod from the shop counter as the engine of Maggie's ancient Mini chugs into life.

'You okay, peach?'

I take a breath and nod. 'I am, actually.'

I'm not lying this time, even to myself.

We drive alongside Kennington Park and past the Imperial War Museum, where people pose below the branches of trees newly bursting with blossom, then over Waterloo Bridge. The path is thick with meandering tourists. Now I consider it, I don't think I've ever been through London in a car. It feels purposeful and undisputed, similar to the people with dogs in Hyde Park; there's no question whether they live here or not.

As we drive uphill, the chewing-gum-smeared pavements turn into wide avenues lined with gnarled trees and clipped hedges. When I first moved to London, I'd had delusions of grandeur, probably from looking at highly stylised Instagram feeds, so I'd bought a plastic window planter and a small bag of compost so we could have flowers on the windowsill. Someone had nicked it within a week and we weren't even on the ground floor. That wouldn't happen here, though. Some houses even have a tasteful wreath on the door, and not because they'd forgotten to take it down at Christmas.

'Is this it?' asks Maggie sceptically, pulling up in front of the decorative archway of Evergreen Village.

'Yep.' Blossom sprouts from an apple tree pinned against the outside wall and as I follow the line of its branches, I see a woman snap a picture of the ornate entrance, tugging a dachshund behind her as she rounds the corner.

'And you had doubts about this place?' Maggie asks, flicking up the sun visor to peer at the bell tower.

'Yeah. It's horrible, isn't it?' I say with a bashful smile.

'Swapping kebabs for pink wafer biscuits seems a small price to pay for this, El. It's beautiful!' Maggie steps from the car to the cobblestones.

'Well, I'm pretty sure it's the first and last time I'll ever get to call somewhere like this home.'

'I'll help you unload, but then I've got to get over to Grandma's – she gets quite upset when I'm not there on time. She has the tea poured at ten on the dot and if you're not there to drink it she won't make you another one on principle.'

Once we've unloaded the last box onto the pavement, I say goodbye to Maggie through the window and she drives away in a spluttering of fumes that make my eyes water. Nigel wafts his hand in front of his face and coughs. 'Miss Evans! So nice to see you again,' he says in a measured Nigerian accent.

'Sorry, I'm a bit early.'

'Not a problem. I will see to it that your things are brought over to Mrs De Loutherberg's home. Am I to expect another vehicle with the rest of your belongings?'

'Er ... this is it, actually.' Nigel raises his eyebrows. 'Minimalist living and all that – cluttered house, cluttered mind. Not that there's anything wrong with a bit of clutter if that's what you like ...' I laugh and feel my cheeks grow hot. Thankfully, Nigel leads me through the archway and around the green before I can say anything else.

I look over my shoulder at the sum of my possessions: two boxes, a suitcase, an IKEA bag, and a lamp. They look so small and pathetic sat out here on the kerb. Nigel mutters something to a bald man with a belly that bulges above and below his belt, and he disappears, reappearing a few seconds later with a brass luggage trolley that he wheels towards my things.

'Annie is out, but Mr Biggety is inside to welcome you.'

'Sorry, who?'

At that moment Annie's front door jerks open, revealing Craig standing on the doormat. 'A big hello to our new companion!' How can he be so sweaty already? It's barely ten o'clock in the morning. Nigel touches his cap and nods at us before slipping away to the porter's nook. Man's got the right idea.

'I rearranged my rounds just to make sure I could be here to see you settled in. Great, isn't it?' He stands next to the door to let me in, leaving barely enough room to inch past. When I do, I feel his knee graze my thigh, and from his breath I can say with near certainty that he had scrambled eggs for breakfast. 'Lovely,' says Craig, but what he's referring to as 'lovely' I'm not entirely sure. 'The room Annie's set out for you is upstairs at the end of the corridor. Shall we go and have a look?'

'Um, I think I should maybe wait for Annie?'

'No, best to get you settled in first. Our Annie gets a little muddled with all sorts of pernickety little things, so if we sort you out she won't have to worry, will she?' Craig says, his voice bright and sickly. 'I'll follow you up the stairs.' No bloody thanks! I'm not going to have creepy Craig scoping out my arse the whole way.

'No, after you.'

He surveys me for a moment before shrugging his shoulders and smiling, his eyes tiny slits in a pudgy face.

***

The room he takes me to is small but flooded with sunshine. A wooden single bed is pushed up against the wall by a window that looks down onto a magnolia tree that shades the kitchen window. Annie has left the drawers of a chest and bedside table open to show that they're empty, and a wardrobe is neatly hung with flocked hangers. I walk over to the drawers and look inside. They're lined with lavender-scented paper which is patterned with tiny bees. A new pair of sheepskin-lined slippers sit next to the bed with a pink envelope balanced on top.

'For you, Elissa. The floorboards get cold at night. X'

My chest pangs with the thoughtfulness of Annie's gift, and it makes me even more annoyed that Craig is standing around being gross.

'I think I'll be fine now, Craig,' I say. He widens his stance in the doorway, shoulders hunched.

'Annie won't be long. You know what ladies are like. They gabble away and forget to check the clock.' Craig smooths his hair down over his forehead and then clumps down the stairs, his footsteps muffled on the rich burgundy stair runner. I listen for the door. *Click*. Thank God for that.

I spend some time unpacking, pausing briefly to send a message to Suki who asks how the 'granny pad' is going. After I hang up my clothes, I shove the IKEA bag into my empty suitcase and slide it underneath the bed next to a shallow wicker basket stacked with neatly folded linen. I look around the room that's to be mine for … I'm not sure how long. A varnished dado rail splits the walls in two, the top half painted sage green and the bottom half wallpapered with old-fashioned illustrations of duck ponds and farm animals. There's a small fireplace too, on which I've put a framed polaroid of me and Maggie on our graduation day, her beaming and beautiful, me wincing and clutching my head as the tasselled cap I'd thrown a second before lands on me.

I don't know if Annie would think it rude of me to be

127

upstairs when she gets back (in my experience, older people are funny about doing things 'the proper way'), so I head down to wait for her in the kitchen. Not long afterwards, there's a scratch in the lock and Annie walks through the hallway with a bright pink yoga mat under her arm. I stand up by way of a greeting, faltering when it comes to verbalising a 'hello' because she looks surprised to see me.

'You all right, love? I wasn't expecting you until later!' She props her mat against the table and slides her feet into slippers. 'I told Craig earlier in t'week that I'd be here from the afternoon. They must have got it wrong.' She looks a little frazzled and her cheeks are pinched pink.

'Oh. I'm so sorry, Annie, Alina said to come from ten. Craig seemed to be expecting me ...'

'He what?'

'He was here when I arrived. Like, in here. In the house.'

'Was 'e now?' Annie looks triumphant. 'That sneaky bastard. 'Scuse my French, love.' She scowls and looks towards the door. 'I have a feeling ... I tell you what, if he comes creepin' round here when I'm out again, you let me know straightaway, all right? I don't trust him. He's the sort whose picture'll come up on *Watchdog*, you mark my words.' She hangs up a padded gilet on the coat stand, walks over to me, and puts a chilly, soft hand on my cheek. 'He ever say anything ... odd to you, you go over to George and Margaret's. George is a sweetheart, and Margaret ... well, she's always got a face ache, but she'll do right by you. They live over the other side – the house with all the roses growing at the front – okay? I've tried reporting him before but they said being a git wasn't grounds for dismissal. I reckon they put me on his rounds every week as punishment. They think we exaggerate, us old folk.' Annie sighs and she waves like she's shooing a fly. 'Anyway, I haven't asked you how you are, my love. You don't talk much, do you?' she says.

Considering the impression I had before meeting Annie, it's clear she's as far from quietly doddery as it's possible to get without being Cher and filling your face with a litre of botox. She grins. 'I'm only messing, Elissa. I know I don't half go on. Used to put such a face on my Arthur. Tea?'

'I'll make it!' I jump up and scoot around Annie as she walks towards the kettle, opening and closing cupboards to find the mugs. When I turn around to ask, Annie brings over two cups and saucers, the china rattling as her hands shake. I take them off her.

'Bloody hands. Might as well chop them off,' she says, rubbing at her thumb joints. 'Could never get used to mugs. Big, bulky things ...' She trails off and looks a little embarrassed.

'That's okay,' I say, 'these are lovely.' It's true, they are. I mean, the pragmatist in me is thinking about how you'd have to boil the kettle again after the first cup because there's no way that the amount of tea in this *Alice in Wonderland* crockery is enough to satisfy me. Maggie only just persuaded me to leave behind a huge, chipped pint-sized mug in the old flat because she thought it was 'a bit too studenty'. *Old flat.* It's a nice thought.

We sit at the kitchen table and Annie puts down a small bowl of white sugar cubes, a tiny flowery jug of milk, and a plate with four Jaffa Cakes on it.

'Doctor would smack me hand for this,' she says, motioning to the plate, 'but if you can't have a couple of packets of Jaffa Cakes when you're eighty-three, what's the bloody point?' Annie puts one in her mouth whole and closes her eyes in delight. Her skin is so thin and pale you can see blue veins traced underneath. She pouts her lips to meet the wobbling cup and sips. When she smiles, her eyelids crinkle into concertina wrinkles.

'I once ate a whole multipack of Kitkats during an episode of *Gogglebox*, so I'm the last person to judge. They weren't even mine.'

'You didn't!'

'Not that I steal, or anything! I went to the shop and replaced them. I don't often eat other people's food.'

'Not that regularly, anyway,' says Annie, popping a sugar cube in her mouth. She traces the handle of her cup and looks out of the window. 'I never used to get away with eating treats like this when I was married. Or before, actually. Arthur always expected scones, or a teacake when he got home from work, but he'd make a comment if I ate it too. You know, about how I'd get fat or something.' She tuts and rolls her eyes. 'Blokes. Double standards, in't it?'

130

'I know, tell me about it ...' I say, in an attempt to sympathise.

'Your fella like that too?'

'Um, well ... not really.' I pause. It's too soon to unpick what me and Tom are now. 'He gets a bit disgruntled when I eat his cereal bars. Most of the time he doesn't notice.'

'Good for you,' says Annie, although I didn't say it to make Tom look good. He wouldn't notice if I gained a few pounds because he barely notices when I've had a haircut.

We chat about how long Annie has been in Evergreen Village (since her husband took up lecturing in the Sixties), how she likes Hampstead (she loves the Heath, but hates how many people let their dogs crap on the path), and some of the other residents of the village (Gwen, George, Margaret, and Gloria. They play boules together, but Annie doesn't join them).

'Why is it called a village, Annie? If that's not too stupid a question?' I ask, filling up the kettle again.

'Well, Hampstead was a village itself before the city kept creeping closer and closer to meet us up here on the hill. I haven't got a clue why we're called Evergreen Village. Posh people, in't it? It's a way of keeping out the riff-raff. I managed to slip through, somehow.' She winks and takes another Jaffa Cake.

'You're not from round here?' I ask.

'Nope. Sheffield. I met Arthur at a dance when I was studying engineering at the university. He was in the last

131

year of a doctorate in medieval theology. Different tastes, you could say.'

'Wow, that's really impressive,' I say, and I mean it.

'Ended up a professor at UCL. Buried himself in documents and scrolls at the archives. Slept in the library, some days.' She smiles sadly.

'I meant you, being an engineer. I couldn't do that.'

'Oh, I never ended up an engineer. We got married straight after I graduated and moved down south. That were the way things were, back then.' Annie stands up from her chair on a second attempt, her forearms shaking as she slowly shifts her bodyweight. 'Got me books though,' she says, patting a squat shelf below the mirror lined with dozens of clothbound books in hues of navy and green. 'Got to keep the ol' brain ticking over.'

***

Every time I think I see Annie a little clearer, she reveals something totally different to what I'd expect. First, the bold Yorkshire accent I'd only ever heard horrible people use as a parody of someone stupid, then the library of engineering books that may as well be in Mandarin for all I understand. From the sound of it, both Annie and her husband would have been great lecturers.

By the afternoon I get a sense that Annie wants some time on her own. I tell her about my job (she finds it very hard to grasp what social media is, let alone how it could be someone's job), but twice mentions that *Gardener's*

Question Time is coming on and that I'll probably find it dull. I mean, she's not wrong.

I go upstairs to work on my re-branding presentation and jot down a few lines in my notebook. I read back what I've got so far. It isn't a pitch, as such, but it's ... something – a loose marketing idea with a heavy emphasis on social media, so I can at least justify the need for my job in the future. I throw in a couple of statistics too, which sound good because you can't dispute numbers, even if the survey size was seventeen (a detail I choose to omit). I time myself and read through what I've got so far, but when I get to the end of my page and glance at my phone, barely a minute has passed. Bollocks. I tear the page out of my notebook, fling myself back on the bed, and shove a pillow over my face to muffle the sound of a barely restrained scream.

Just before nine o'clock, Annie taps on my door and peeps around the corner. I stop staring at the ceiling and invite her in.

'Would you like an Ovaltine?' She doesn't meet my eye and instead glances around the room, rubbing the joints in her hand. 'I always have one before bed.'

'Er, yeah, sure. That'd be great.' I feel like a kid again. It's at once jarring and extremely comforting, like re-watching a favourite film from childhood; the dialogue is like a lullaby, but you notice things that once weren't important. 'Hey, Annie?'

I hear her slippers scuff the carpet as she walks back to my room. 'Hmm?'

'What made you choose me? Over the others that ElderCare wanted you to take on?' I tap my notebook with the end of my pen.

Annie scrunches her mouth to one side and pops a hip.

'The others were all right. Bit ... vanilla. I thought you seemed different. In a good way, mind. If nothing else, it'll be an experience.'

Chapter Fourteen

Annie is at geriatric chair Pilates, so I thought I'd bake something as a surprise to commemorate our first week as housemates. So far, Annie has cooked dinner for us twice, we've had Caribbean takeaway once (her idea), and one night I boiled up some tortellini and covered it in passata. Annie added some fresh basil leaves at the end, which made it at least 80 per cent tastier. I'm not entirely sure if she's keeping me out of the kitchen on purpose, so I thought I'd use her absence as a good excuse to make something from scratch.

I rub my nose with the back of my hand and accidentally inhale a line of flour. Together with my red cheeks and flustered appearance from standing over an Aga with a leaky rubber seal, I look like a Home Counties girl just back from a heavy night out. I open kitchen drawers with my elbow and try to find a utensil of some kind that will make my crumble ... crumblier. The dough has turned sticky and warm, which I'm pretty sure is the opposite of what it's supposed to be like.

I chop the dough up into smaller chunks and shove it in the oven. That's as good as it's going to get without scrapping the lot and starting again, which I can't do because I only bought the ingredients for one attempt, such was my level of confidence. Baked stuff always looks weird before it's cooked, right?

The spring sunshine filters through Annie's warped windows and steadily warms the kitchen to tropical levels, so I throw open the double French doors and walk barefoot onto the paving stones that are still cool in the shade. I can't remember why I thought baking was a good idea. I'd googled 'easy recipes for people who can't bake' and yet I'd still managed to fluff it up.

I used to bake with my nan, back when she was still trusted with an oven. However, she claimed she'd been baking so long she didn't need to weigh anything, which was a complete lie, because she consistently produced rock cakes whether the original recipe was for scones, buns, or bread.

I sit down on the back step and use my knee as leverage to twist sideways and stretch my back, which clunks somewhere near the base in a way that is both deeply satisfying and a little nauseating. As I turn the other way, something sharp pokes me through the material of Annie's apron. I pull the front pocket open and take out a crumpled envelope, the seal heavily worn and hinge-like, with a slick of glue long hardened and yellow along the paper's edge. I flip it over and read the rounded cursive of Annie's name and a handwritten date in the top right-hand corner, but there's no evidence it was ever in the post. 1962. Jesus, that's a while ago.

I try and smooth out the creases, no doubt caused by my leaning over to peer into the kiln-like oven, prodding at my unconvincing bake with the wrong end of a wooden spoon. I flip the letter over, but just as I'm about to open the concertina paper, I notice a kiss on the back page, bigger than the rest of the writing and dashed off at speed. If that 'x' was real, it'd be a brazen peck on the lips, I'm sure of it. I flip the letter back over and run my nail along the fold, but it's so worn I'm terrified of tearing it.

When I glance over my shoulder towards the house, the scene isn't how I left it. Curling smoke winds through the branches of the magnolia tree next to the kitchen window, and as the fire alarm starts shrieking, my stomach falls to the base of my spine.

The smell of burnt sugar hits the back of my throat when I get closer to the kitchen and makes my eyes sting. I slide the letter back into the envelope and shove it in the apron's pocket. Smoke billows from the sides of the oven door. I cover my mouth with the crook of my elbow, fumbling for a tea towel, and pull the ceramic dish out from the top shelf, swearing loudly as a globule of molten apple pulp lands on my thumb. I thrust it onto the counter and the singed pudding slides along the bench until it bounces off the tea and coffee tins and comes to a halt with a loud clatter. I'd only been out in the garden for ten minutes. How is it possible to start a house fire in such a short time? I squat down below the smoke that hangs at chest height, and squint at the temperature gauge. I'd never seen an Aga before, let alone used one. Annie did say which was the 'fast cook' oven and which the 'slow', but as there weren't any numbers on the thermometer, it was impossible to tell.

Apart from a lava-like substance that has hardened on the bottom of the oven, there isn't much damage that I can't disguise. I'd clearly been too liberal with the sugar, because the crumble has formed an impenetrable crust that refuses to budge, even when I stab it with a kitchen knife. I try and plunge down double-handed, but my fist slips off the handle and down the blade. 'Motherfucker!' I yell, dropping the knife in the sink. It speckles the white ceramic with blood.

Oh, shit. I don't do blood. It makes me feel weak and woozy and yep, that's my knees sliding down onto the floor. I put my head between my legs and breathe deeply. I wonder if I've got the strength to call 999. Either the ceiling and floorboards are actually blurring, or I'm about to pass out. I rest my cheek on the floor, blowing away dust particles with each breath. If I die, at least it was in the pursuit of approval from an eighty-three-year-old.

'Elissa? Oh, Jesus Christ. Gloria! Gloria, go and get Shaunae. Elissa, love, what's happened? Sit up for me.' Annie wiggles my shoulder and I lever myself onto my uninjured hand. Did I actually faint? Annie pushes a mass

138

of hair out of my face and I blink up at her and a woman wearing floaty trousers. They each hook me under the shoulder and pull me to my feet, which takes a couple of attempts because my knees feel wholly incapable of holding my body weight.

'Annie, the girl's gone and cut herself,' says the woman, who looks extremely concerned now my vision is sharper.

'Come on, let us have a look, chicken,' says Annie. I shakily open my hand to let her inspect the wound and squeeze my eyes shut, drawing in a big shaky breath as Annie runs her warm fingertips over my palm. 'Chuffin' hell, Elissa, is that it? I thought you'd chopped a finger off!'

'What?' *Oh*. It's tiny; hardly bigger than a paper cut. It definitely felt more life-threatening when I first did it.

'Panic over, Gloria. She'll live.'

Gloria clutches her chest and laughs wheezily. 'These young 'uns! I delivered my own baby, child. You try staying conscious doing that!' I try and smile, but my brain isn't quite communicating with my face and I twitch instead. 'You've got a soft one here! I'll make her a tea. Extra sugar,' says Gloria, shuffling over to the kettle.

'Honestly, I thought it was way worse than that,' I say, as Annie walks me over to a chair.

'I knew something were wrong when I came in and it smelt like a bonfire. What've you been up to?'

'This?' Gloria asks, grimacing at the charred mass that now features Jackson Pollock style droplets of blood.

139

'It's an apple crumble,' I say, taking a scalding sip of the sugary tea that Gloria has just put in front of me.

'If you say so.' Annie squints, bending down to look at the blackened oven dish. 'Well, Gloria, now you've met Elissa. She makes apps about dating.' Annie's overtones of pride, combined with the effects of the tea, put some colour in my cheeks.

'Ooh, apps, is it? I've got one of those for my knitting patterns. Shaunae, my daughter, set it up for me. She does our yoga class as well. Very good girl, is my Shaunae. She's taking me for lunch today, so I'd best be going.' Gloria delicately picks up her yoga mat, which is rolled up neatly in a drawstring bag. 'I hope you make a full recovery from your injuries, Elissa,' she says with a hint of irony that feels unnecessary.

I hear the door shut behind her. 'Let's have a look, sweetheart,' Annie says to me tenderly, peeling back the damp kitchen towel that she'd previously placed on my palm. She's so gentle, even though her hands shake more violently the more delicate she tries to be. 'Gloria is a bit of a boast. It becomes white noise after she's told you her grandson's won a French-speaking spelling bee for the fourth time in as many days. Not one for a two-way conversation,' she adds, wiping the pads of my fingers clean where the dried blood has turned copper-coloured. 'You best let that air, love. Try and keep it dry.'

'Leave the crumble dish for me to sort out. I don't know what happened. I must have put it in the wrong oven. I forgot which one does what.' I feel a bit tearful and that in itself is so infuriating I want to cry from frustration. I can't seem to do anything right at the moment. I'm flailing at work and can't convince them to pay me, Tom thinks I'm useless, and I've fucked up a recipe so easy they don't even bother including it on *The Great British Bake Off*.

'Oh, Elissa, stop flapping. I think it's lovely you wanted to make something. I want you to think this is your kitchen just as much as mine. You've got to learn to cook some-where, haven't you? Even if you said your skills were a *tad* more advanced on your application.'

'Was it that obvious?'

Annie tilts the dish up towards me and grimaces.

'Fair point,' I reply. She's wrangled a smile out of me.

'I know this isn't very enviro-eco-friendly or whatever you call it, but I'm going to put the whole dish in the wheelie bin. Arthur gave it me on our fortieth anniversary. This and a wooden spoon.'

Oh God, I feel horrible. I've nearly set fire to the kitchen and destroyed a gift from Annie's dead husband in a single morning. 'Annie, I'm so sorry. Please let me see if I can salvage it.'

'No, I wouldn't let you, Elissa.' She picks up the dish and twists it round in her hands. 'I've always hated it. Now I've got a good excuse to get rid of it.' Annie slips into her garden shoes and disappears around the corner. When she returns, she walks straight over to the fridge, pulls open the door, and hides something behind her back, knocking the door shut with her elbow.

'Lucky I've got a plan B, eh?' Annie reveals two ramekins topped with foil. 'Melt-in-the-middle chocolate pudding. I know it's all made by machines, but they're so good they make your teeth hurt.'

'I haven't even had breakfast yet.'

'I won't tell if you won't.' She winks and puts them in the microwave.

I look around at Annie's kitchen and through into the living room. Apart from the mass of engineering books from the Sixties and Seventies, it looks like any old person's home. I mean, the high Victorian ceilings and wood panelling are leagues apart from my nanny's two-up-two-down council house in Hereford, with its polystyrene ceiling tiles and textured plaster. There's the same winged armchair, stacking side-tables, and talcum powder in the medicine cabinet. But Annie's house lacks something that my nanny had in abundance. Here, there isn't a single photograph on display.

My whole family frames and displays photos in the same way teenagers upload onto Instagram. There's barely a surface in the house that doesn't have a picture frame on it. They're tacked to the back of the bathroom door and they dangle from key rings. Walking up the stairs is like experiencing a flipbook of your own face ageing in yearly increments from reception to sixth form. It was stifling, at times, to have that many versions of yourself presented back at you, especially the dodgy teenage years where cheap, thick foundation dominated the scene.

I pull my sleeves down over my hands as the microwave pings. 'Annie, did you and Arthur ever have children?' Annie peels the film off and turns the puddings upside down onto fluted porcelain plates. 'Yes. Richard. He lives in Australia. My two grandsons are there as well.'

'Have you been over to see them?'

'No.'

'Oh.' We both dig into our puddings. Chocolate sauce oozes out and pools around the cake. Annie puts her spoon down, but I put mine in my mouth.

'I want to. I'm desperate to meet 'em. I've seen a picture, from when they were babies. Codey – he's a big lad. Chubby little arms and legs.' She smiles. 'Just like his dad.'

'Why don't you? Go and visit them?'

Annie twists a ring round on her finer. 'Oh, I can't manage travel at my age. And I'm not sure they'll ever come here. Do you want to finish this?' she says, motioning to her plate and the half-eaten pudding on it.

'No, better not. I already feel a bit sick. Not in a bad way! Like when you've eaten a big Christmas dinner and feel like you've earnt a nap.' I've scraped my plate clean and if I was on my own, I would have licked it too.

Annie is definitely being a bit weird about her family. Why would someone move to Australia and never come back to visit their mum, who, as far as I can tell, is a treat of an old person?

Annie is busying herself around the sink, carefully

143

washing up jars for the recycling bin. I'm going to poke a little bit more.

'You could borrow my phone to video call Richard if you like.'

Annie stiffens, her shoulders hunched. 'No, no, he doesn't do that sort of thing. The time difference is awkward. He's very busy. Works in a bank in Sydney and flies out to Hong Kong a lot. No, I shan't.'

'But I'm sure we could figure something if—'

'He's his father's son, Richard, always was.'

'I could send him an email if you like—'

Annie puts a plate down hard on the draining board. 'I said no, Elissa.' She clutches her hands together as though she's hurt her fingers. 'Don't waste your time worrying about me, all right?'

'Oh. Okay.'

The tea towel, held tight in her hand, dances as her hand shakes. 'I'm sorry, love. I don't mean to snap.'

I stand up, scraping my chair noisily across the kitchen tiles. 'No, I'm sorry. I shouldn't have kept going on about it.'

'You don't have to fix me, Elissa. I'm fine. I'm doing just fine,' she says as she scoops a glass up with the tea towel, turning it round in her hands to dry. She places it on a shelf and puts her hands on my arms.

'Come 'ere. I've upset you, haven't I?'

'No, no, of course you haven't,' I lie, letting her pull me into a hug. She smells of lavender and a delicate mustiness from clothes that are worn too irregularly to wash that

144

often. 'No offence or owt but I think you need a bath. You smell like Guy Fawkes after Bonfire Night.'

I nod and turn to go upstairs.

'Elissa?'

I stop at the doorway. 'Mmm?'

'Thank you for the crumble. I mean it. And for getting it out of the oven before it burnt the place down.'

I laugh weakly. 'Any time.'

***

I shut myself in the bathroom, wrapping my hand in a flannel to twist the taps of Annie's coral-coloured bath, set in the corner amongst flowery tiles in shades of brown and mustard. Whilst it's filling up, I sit in a king-size bath towel and scroll through old pictures on my phone. Talking to Annie about her family has clearly touched a nerve, which is weird, because I swear older people normally can't stop spouting off about their grandchildren.

As I scroll through my phone, I find sad reminders of how colourless my life has been of late. My diminishing enthusiasm for London is there in my camera roll, as New Year's fireworks and sun-soaked beer gardens flick to a picture of Tom holding a burnt pizza, looking slightly pissed off, a strange-shaped banana, and the feet of a man on the tube who wasn't wearing shoes. Then, a flurry of blurred pictures of the back of Suki's head and a selfie of Maggie kissing me on the cheek – the first night out I'd had in months. Like Annie, I'm not sure I'd invite questions about my life either.

I have to wipe the screen every couple of minutes to clear the steam that's slowly filling the bathroom. Eventually, I pull the window open and a cool spring breeze tempts the steam outside. I get in the bath and feel the hot water loosening the strain I'm holding in my joints and spine. Lifting my knees up, I let my head drift below the surface of the water. My hair looks like a mushroom cloud when I open my eyes and look up. I barely last ten seconds before I break the surface and gulp breaths like a goldfish. There must be a reason why Annie got so funny about me asking questions about her son. I mean, of the people I know who don't like their grandmas, it's either because they're horribly racist or keep asking why they haven't got a boyfriend. Annie doesn't strike me as either kind. Then there's the totally unbelievable list of reasons why she barely speaks to her son. And that comment about Richard being 'his father's son', what did that mean exactly? From the sound of it, Arthur liked having a clever wife at home, but then again, weren't most husbands like that back then?

I run a hand along my leg, where the stubble has grown and is so rough it could pass as Velcro. I really need to sort it out; you could light a match on my knee. I lean back, my lips bobbing on the water line. Old people always seemed so ... pedestrian to me before. My nanny was a nice, uncomplicated type: milky tea, *Countdown* on telly, dinner at 5.00 p.m., that sort of thing. It barely crossed my mind that she had once been a young woman, perhaps with different ideas about how her life would end up. Clearly, I hadn't been as insightful as I could have been.

Chapter Fifteen

As I wait for my eyes to adjust in the early morning light, I squint at my phone, alarmed that Mitchell sent an email at 3.47 a.m. reminding us about The Big Pitch this morning. Like I could forget. During the night, hours were spent staring at the ceiling, mentally rehearsing lines. In a weak moment, I messaged Tom and lamely asked him to wish me luck. If it goes tits up today, I'll know why. He never messaged me back.

When we were packing clothes on Saturday morning, Maggie and I found £2.65 in a pair of jeans, as well as a handful of coins in the 'odds and sods' drawer of the bedside table, so today I piss off the Hampstead commuters yet again by topping up my Oyster card with coppers and a stack of 20p pieces.

I arrive at The Butcher Works half an hour later. Rachael narrows her eyes from the reception desk as I push through the revolving doors.

'You're in early.'

'I am!' I say proudly.

'That's unlike you,' she states, drumming her acrylic nails on the table.

'Oi! I'm not that bad,' I say with feigned disbelief.

'Oh, I know. Sorry, did that sound bitchy? Too many late nights.' Rachael blinks rapidly and rubs her brow bone. She picks up the phone, which flashes with a call. The phones don't actually ring here; it's seen as too corporate. 'What's up! Butcher Works here, Rachael speaking, unless you don't want me, in which case I'll transfer you ...' I close the door to her laughter and walk into Lovr's space, which is busy with movement and noise for the first time in days.

Mitchell is completely electrified. He's got a very loud purple shirt on and is walking around the office with his sleeves rolled up. I scan the room. I'm still the last person to arrive. Adam is rolling up his brown paper and Rhea is, for once, not at the treadmill desk. She's wearing an incredibly tight tailored dress that rings with 'don't challenge me or I'll crush your skull between my thighs.' I look down at my too short floral trousers, the result of a one-time trip to the laundrette last winter when our clothes refused to dry in a windowless living room.

Oh, shit. I've completely underestimated this, haven't I? Why is everyone looking so ... professional? Bismah doesn't seem to notice me as I turn my laptop on. She's walking back and forth, practising her pitch from an iPad that she's using as a scrolling autocue. The only person who doesn't look bothered is Rodney, who is uncharacteristically visible, placidly typing out lines and lines of code. I open up my drawer and put on a bit of emergency eyeliner, which isn't usually something I do unless I'm bored or procrastinating. We've reached desperate times.

I pretend to nip outside so I can run over my pitch, but instead furiously wipe my hands on my jeans, panic setting in. After a few minutes spent pacing the artificial grass, I unlock my phone to make a call.

'Hello?'

'Hi. It's me. It's Elissa.'

'Oh, 'ey up. You all right?' says Annie, brightening.

'Yeah, yeah. I've got five minutes at work and thought I'd check in.' There's a pause and I hear the muffled sound of Annie crunching on a biscuit.

'Bees still buzzing. Same bloody adverts on telly. All as normal. You?'

'Er, yeah. Sorry to just call out of the blue. I dunno why, but I've got this really weird feeling.'

'Dicky tummy, is it? I should have checked the date on that tin of salmon. I've been fine, but I've got a strong constitution, mind.'

'No, not like that. More of an ... overwhelming sense of dread?'

'Right. Go on.'

'I'm about to go into this big meeting at work and I'm terrified.'

'Why? You about to be sacked?'

'No! I don't think so.'

'Well, that's already better. What's the problem then?'

'I'm not prepared. I've got to pitch this big, grand idea, and every time I try and say it out loud, I sound really simple.'

'If it's your idea, you should be the most confident one in the room. I know you work with technology and I won't pretend to understand it, but it's all the same. Bullshit.' Ah, nihilism. How encouraging. Unaware of my increasing sense of dread, Annie continues. 'Bullshit your way through. If you've got an inkling that your idea is good, take that thought and ramp it up. Bullshit until they're on your side and it's over, then work out the details. You've got to believe in it yourself first, otherwise why would anyone else?'

A rapping sound comes from the glass doors of our work space, and I turn around to see Bismah pointing and mouthing 'upstairs'.

'Thanks, Annie. Honestly.'

'S all right.'

***

When we get up to the conference room, Mitchell is already there, along with an unfamiliar, clean-shaven man with high cheekbones. For some reason, all the tables have been moved out and a number of mismatched stools, chairs, and other pieces of furniture have been pulled into a circle. With Mitchell's restless leg bobbing up and down and his companion stony-faced and silent, it feels like a very unsupportive support group.

'How are we all?' he asks. There's a little chorus of replies. 'I didn't hear anything, did you, Vlad?' The other man shakes his head, looking awkward. 'I said, how are we all, team?' Bismah does a little 'woo' and Adam smacks his thigh as though he's at a rugby match. Rodney remains silent and I give a half-hearted thumbs-up.

'Okay, let's get this show on the road, shall we? Before we start, this is Vlad. He's representing the board of investors and gets to decide if I can pay my mortgage next month.' Mitchell laughs and slaps Vlad on the back, who doesn't seem to understand the joke because he blinks and does a dry cough. In an attempt to lighten the mood, Adam jumps in with a strained laugh and mimes wiping sweat off his brow. On a scale of one to fist-swallowingly-awkward, we're already at a seven.

'Good man, good man,' Mitchell says. 'Rhea is sending over meeting notes, so I won't bore Vlad over here with the details –' it's just as likely Mitchell hasn't actually read them '– so I'll just say this before we start.' He pauses dramatically. 'This app means everything to me. Not just as a business, but as a passion. I know we get pigeonholed within the dating industry and it's easy to chase the whys and wherefores of swiping, keeping users engaged, and monetising the platform. But, what are we really trying to do?' He looks around at us all. Bismah raises her hand, but Mitchell gives her a withering look and she quickly folds it into her lap again. 'We're in the business of love,' he continues. 'Of compatibility. Of happiness. And that's why we need to constantly adapt and change, because that's the nature of love, isn't it? It's transitory. It's fluid.' If I put to one side that Mitchell's talking complete bullshit, it's a speech worthy of Richard Curtis. Christ, Mitchell's all misty-eyed. Whatever he was hoping to achieve, it's clearly worked on Rhea, because she's gazing at him like he's just rescued a disabled kid from a quarry.

'Adam! Start us off, mate.'

Adam stands and pulls his polo shirt straight. It's one I've seen once before, on his birthday – a designer brand with a huge embroidered logo stitched on the front. He runs a hand through his fluffy hair, which makes it stick up stupidly.

'Okay, so you're a sporty guy ... or girl –' he motions to Rhea, who flicks her ponytail at him and smiles '– and you're sick of your partner always moaning about you going to training, or matches.' He puts on a whiny voice: '"*Come and watch a film with me, let's go ice skating, pleeeeaaaase!*"' I wince. 'And for once, you'd like to date someone who won't only come to Twickers with you, but will get the beers in before the half-time rush! My app has preference settings for common sports or fitness interests, a strict "gym-wear only" profile picture, and we can work with partner companies to book the first five dates at fitness classes. You know, check her out while she's lifting a tractor tyre. See if he's skipping leg day ...' The men in the room nod enthusiastically, except Rodney. 'So, yeah. That's it.'

Mitchell nods, making a few notes. I look sceptically

around the room and start to feel a lot better about my pitch.

'Biz. You're up.' Bismah drags a stool into the middle of the circle, props her tablet on it, and taps the screen to set the script running. The clock ticks loudly as we wait.

'So, you know this idea of offering something reciprocal, right? Like a service? People, especially millennials, don't want to commit unless they're getting something back. Well, from my research I've discovered that our users aren't just too busy to date organically, they're looking for someone who can slot into their life and maybe ... their dog's life!' She pauses and catches my eye. I give her a little nod, clueless as to where this might be going. 'My idea is to be the first app to involve pets in the dating process. Users will only see a picture of the dog on the app, not the owner themselves. If they think their dogs would look cute together, they can swipe for a match!' Oh God, Bismah is so engrossed in her autocue that she can't see Mitchell's tightly clenched jaw. 'It bases the compatibility of two owners on how much their dogs like each other upon a first meeting—'

'How do you know if the dogs like each other?' interrupts Adam.

'See how many times they sniff each other's arse?' Mitchell replies. Bismah's smile wanes.

'Um, hang on, I've got some information, just bear with me,' she says, looking flustered as she scrolls through her script.

154

'Would you use the same metric for when the owners meet?' Adam continues.

Mitchell smirks. 'We'll leave it there, shall we, darlin'?' Bismah nods frantically and sits down, locking the tablet. I try to catch her eye, but she's staring at a spot on the carpet, her eyes glassy.

'Rodders!' Mitchell booms. Rodney blinks. 'Vlad, you're gonna love this one. Rodders, Rodney, Ronaldinho.' It is very clear that by now we have entered the danger zone. Mitchell has got a manic look of excitement in his eyes, but his face is drained of colour. Why couldn't I have gone first, when he was all placid and sentimental and making speeches about human nature?

Rodney walks into the middle of the circle and pushes his glasses up his nose. 'Hello. My name is Rodney—'

'WE KNOW YOUR FLIPPIN' NAME, RODNEY, GET THE SHIT ON WITH IT!'

Unfazed, he continues. 'When a couple who share a kind and tender love for each other come together to consider the future, they think of a home.'

Hello, Rodney! Dark horse, much? I knew there was something romantic hidden behind the beige clothing and complete lack of expression.

'My thought surrounds the idea of "building a home together". When users match, they co-design a house. What view do they wish to rise to each morning? How many seats around the dining table? How many rooms are required to house the fruits of their love?' Oh my God, I think I'm

155

in love with Rodney a little bit. 'Once they have finalised their design, they must press their screens at the exact same moment.' Rodney has a distant look in his eye. He takes off his glasses, cleans them on the bottom of his T-shirt, and puts them back on again. 'Then, the algorithm I have created will test the structural integrity of their house. This represents the relationship's potential for longevity.' Rodney gives a slight bow and returns to his stool. His idea sounds like *Grand Designs*, but for the emotionally stunted.

'Rodney.' Mitchell is having palpitations. 'If I didn't have a strong reason to keep you locked at the back of the work-space in a cubicle with only a FUCKING TAMAGOTCHI for company, I have one now. Get out, Rodney, get out!' yells Mitchell. Rodney hops up, blinks, and leaves.

'Er, boss?' Adam says.

'What?' replies Mitchell.

'Is Rodney fired too? Only he was working on a patch that was due to go out today and—'

'OF COURSE HE'S NOT FUCKING FIRED! WHY, DO YOU WANT TO BE?!'

Adam shakes his head emphatically. 'Nah, cool, cool.'

Mitchell is stoic and silent through Rhea's pitch (an idea about matching based on preference for facial hair). When she finishes, Mitchell refuses to acknowledge that she's even spoken and I'm not convinced Vlad the Investor is even awake. He's put dark sunglasses on, which seems entirely sinister. When the room is thick with silence, Mitchell thumps the table with the side of his fist.

'One more left!' Between the feelings of personal humiliation and self-preservation that have permeated the room, the faces turned to me aren't dissimilar to those of the poor bastards who organised lifeboats on the *Titanic*. Mitchell turns to me but doesn't meet my eye. 'I swear to fucking God, if you mention dogs or beards, I'll choose Rodney's structural disaster idea and make him the poster boy.'

I flick open my notebook and half stand up, but my scarf catches on the side of my chair and pulls me down again. It's okay, I didn't need to stand up anyway. I fold my legs one way, then the other. *Deep breath. Come on, girl.*

'My pitch isn't so much a fully formed idea—' I hear Mitchell sigh, so I look down at my notes to see how quickly I can get to the crux of it all. The rhetorical questions I wrote down in a panic seem really stupid now, but I plough on regardless. 'How has technology affected the way we connect with each other?' I'm instantly annoyed because I can hear my voice wavering like I'm a self-conscious teenager who has to read aloud in class. 'What does "connection" actually mean?'

'Is this a pitch or a fucking TED Talk, darlin'?' interrupts Mitchell.

'Hang on, just give me a chance.' I can feel my heart beating in my throat. He bristles and folds his arms. 'Please.' He motions me to continue.

'When I thought about what people really want from a dating app, I thought of a million different things, but it's actually dead simple.' I catch Rhea's eye, but she looks away. 'There's too much choice nowadays – we're completely drowning in choice.' I pause and glance up. No threat of an eruption yet ... 'People under 35 – especially those living in London – are reporting higher rates of loneliness than any generation before. Why? We have hundreds of new ways to communicate, but somehow it's not working. We are more connected but more alone than ever. Take our app, for instance. Our users take an average of 1.7 seconds to decide whether to match with someone or not. They won't waste even half a minute on a person, because who knows who might be around the corner? In real life, that wouldn't happen. Of course we don't want to waste time on the "wrong one", but how can we know who the "right one" is if we never give them a chance?'

'So what are you trying to say, darlin'? That we should all give each other a kiss on the cheek and lock the doors up for some other silly sod to have a go at this business?'

'No, no, that's not what I'm saying. I don't have the answer for that.' I'm not explaining this properly. *Come on, think, Elissa!* 'So, like I said, I don't have a pitch, really.' Rhea whispers something to Adam and he stifles a laugh. 'But I have an idea. We match users depending on their interest in community and charity projects. The idea is they meet whilst volunteering.' I think back to last week, to the comment Annie made about taking me on as a companion. I'd thought it was a bit rude at the time, but when she said, 'whatever happens, it'll be an experience,'

I had a lightbulb moment. Where had playing it safe got me? Where had it got anyone?

'People today don't want to have drinks on the South Bank and dinner in Prezzo every Thursday night. It's textbook, dull, and boring. But I think we can help them a little, to get past the fluff and chit-chat. This way, they share an experience that is valuable, even if they don't go on a second date. We can launch a campaign that focuses on just *one* of our users. We expose the whole process – good and bad – and use social media to document their "community dates". Only then do we open the new platform to our user base. Build excitement, you know?'

'Like incentivising a relationship?'

'Yeah, I guess …' I agree hesitantly. Is that what I'm saying? I can't really tell. I stopped reading from my notebook after those hideous opening questions. Mitchell nods slowly.

Vlad rouses himself from a self-imposed coma and pushes back his chair, followed by Mitchell, who clicks his fingers as everyone looks for a way to slip out of the room. Rhea looks up immediately. 'Down in my office in five, all right?' he says to her. Mitchell looks gleeful. *Holy fuck, we're not going with the beard idea, are we?* That would severely limit the type of YouTube videos I can get away with watching in a feigned attempt at market research. God, at least it's over. There's half a cheese twist sitting on my laptop charger that's asking to be eaten.

***

159

The day passes uneventfully after the huge anticlimax of this morning. I wrote a blog post, pinged off some tweets, and ate my warm but slightly sweaty cheese twist. Mitchell has been in his office with the blinds pulled down all day and Rhea has gone in and out like an indecisive puppy, dutifully filling up Mitchell's glass teapot with hot water and fresh peppermint leaves, something she is vastly over-qualified to do.

Just as I'm shutting my laptop for the day, Suki steps off the metal staircase in the courtyard. When she spots me, she pushes through the door into our office space.

'So, what am I coding this week? Redirecting the ugly ones to a rival app? New interface that features a "sex position of the week"?' She hops onto the edge of my desk, swings her legs back and forth, and shrugs her jacket off one shoulder.

'Absolutely clueless. They're still in there working on it.'

'Who?'

'Mitchell and Rhea.'

'Oh, *are* they?' she asks knowingly.

'Oh my God, *definitely* not,' I say in response to her suggestive eyebrow waggle. 'Have you *seen* Rhea? She's inhumanly attractive, like a Kardashian, except with an ounce of intelligence.'

'Just an ounce?'

'Maybe two ounces.' I pull the drawstring on my ruck-sack closed and swing it onto my back.

'I'm going to have a look,' says Suki, looking towards

Mitchell's glass cube. 'Just a little one.' She slides off the desk and pins herself against the far wall. She looks from side to side then rolls on the floor like a poor man's James Bond. 'Do you dare me?' she hisses.

'No!'

'Okay, I'll do it.'

'Suki! No! Suki! Stop it!' I hiss at her, bobbing down behind my desk chair. 'You can't!'

She shrugs and flicks the hood of her coat up, pulling at the toggles until it's tight around her face.

'What are you doing?' I laugh, but am genuinely appalled. I peer around the chair and see her crawl towards the door, where there's a gap in the blinds from inside Mitchell's office. She moves closer until she's all but pressed up against the glass.

'Suki, come back! This is weird!' I say in a whisper so forceful it hurts my throat.

'What are you doing?' a voice says from behind me. I recognise it as Adam's – a public-school drawl that rasps from drinking too much and sleeping too little.

I whip around so fast I twist my ankle and end up on the floor in an awkward cross-legged position. 'Ouch, fuck! Er, nothing! I dropped my earring!' I don't think he's noticed Suki, who's doing a good job of resembling a squidgy ninja as she lies face down on the carpet, her shaved head covered by her hood. Adam leans from one side to the other, inspecting me. I try and pull down my hair but it pings up above my ears again.

161

'You're wearing two already?'

'I mean my other piercing. I've got another one. Not an ear piercing. Somewhere else.' Ha! That's shown him.

In the week or so since he's been without Jonathon, Adam has become distinctly less of an arsehole. In fact, he actually asked about my weekend plans the other day without a hint of irony. Maybe he'll be able to talk to females soon, without relying on innuendo.

'You're going to like the new campaign,' says Adam cockily, as I stand and hoick my trousers up by the belt loops.

'What? How do you know about it already? Mitchell and Rhea haven't left his office all day.'

'Yeah, it got sorted about an hour ago.' He taps his nose. 'Top secret until next week, I'm afraid.'

I groan. 'So we're going with the app for people with beard fetishes, are we? Brilliant.' I have no idea how I'm going to get a six-month social media campaign out of stubble and waxed moustaches.

'Er, not quite ...' says Adam. He peers over my shoulder in the direction of Mitchell's office. 'Rhea not left yet?'

Suki pops up next to me. Adam jumps and splashes water down his shirt. 'Nope! And I think I know why,' she says. 'Anyway, bye, Adam. Els, shall we go?' She grabs me by the arm and steers me out of the door and onto the street.

After Suki drags me to the end of Hoxton Square, she spins me round under a streetlight and bursts into laughter, causing a man in the public urinal opposite to stumble and piss on his shoes. She tries to talk, but each word splutters, a fat tear rolling down her olive skin.

'I'm ... I'm gonna piss myself, honestly. Tell me to think of something sad,' she blurts out, before tumbling into hysterics again.

'Floppy willies? Hairy bollocks?'

'Oh, babe, I said sad, not disgusting.'

'Thought that would work.'

She hooks an arm through mine and we turn onto Old Street. 'Do you want the good news, bad news or the absolutely hilarious news?'

'Er, bad first. Then you can tell me the hilarious news to make it better.'

'I'm not sure it's going to, babe.'

I stop in the middle of the path, which causes a round of expletives from other pedestrians, many of whom are jogging to catch a bus.

'Okay, okay! So, the bad news.' Suki rubs her knuckles along her bristly scalp. 'I wasn't at the Lovr meeting so I'm not sure what this is about, but it looks like you're going to feature in some sort of campaign, because your name was all over the screen in Mitchell's office underneath a huge picture of your face. I couldn't see exactly what was written, for reasons I'll explain in a sec, but the phrase "go for the experience, leave with a Lovr" was up there. Look, I took a picture.'

Suki pulls out her phone and passes it to me. We both hunch over the screen. *Oh God, she's right.*

163

'What the fuck? Why am I up there? That's what I pitched this morning! I mean, it was more of a loose idea, the whole "community date thing", but I was just rambling. I definitely didn't say, "Make me the face of the fucking campaign"! Suki! Why are they even assuming I'll do it? They don't know I'm single, do they?' That's the first time I've actually said it out loud. Declaring it is like trying new food; it tastes strange and foreign in my mouth, but I don't hate the experience. I'm single, even though I didn't explicitly get dumped, just swapped for global hot-desking and cheap Indonesian rent.

'I think everyone knows,' says Suki, squeezing my arm.

'How? I haven't told anyone at work except you.'

'Babe, you're a social media manager. How do you *think* everyone knows? I was getting a macchiato last Friday and I overheard Adam talking to Rhea about it. Adam was on about a mate of his who plays hockey with your Tom in Southwark. Apparently, Tom was talking about leaving London and they made the connection with you, somehow. Also, you've deleted every picture of you as a couple from your profile, so it's kind of obvious, babe.'

'Yeah, well ... nice to know he was mouthing off about ditching me with all his hockey mates. I bet they're all gutted to lose a completely average hockey player from South London's division-five team.'

I'm quite conscious that I sound bitter. Tom was obsessed with that hockey team, despite the fact they were terrible and never won anything.

164

'Ready for the hilarious part?' She points at the screen again.

'More hilarious than me fronting a dating app?' I zoom in on the picture to try and read the presentation slide, but there's a couple of figures blocking out part of the screen, who look vaguely familiar ...

'Holy fuck! No! This can't be real!'

Suki erupts into laughter, quickly fiddling with the settings of the picture to brighten the photograph's contrast.

'Oh. My. God. No! My eyes. They're burning!' My jaw aches from holding it open in shock. 'How? *Rhea*? I mean, I can see why she's in Lycra all the time – that position looks like it needs ... flexibility.' I'd been so distracted by the picture of myself in the background that I'd completely ignored the fleshy frames of Mitchell and Rhea, who look like they're wrestling except for the fact that Rhea's dress is hitched up around her waist and Mitchell's wrinkly bum is slapped pink and tense, the outline of a brown ball sack dangling between his legs.

'I full-on freaked out when Adam came in,' Suki says. 'They definitely heard and, well, let's just say Mitchell didn't get a chance to finish in a way that anyone would class as dignified.'

'I'm in shock.'

'About your boss shagging the PR girl or the fact he clearly wants you to front some sort of rebranding campaign?' She tries to keep a straight face but almost chokes through stifled laughter.

165

'Good question. This is too much to process.' I look at the picture again, which looks filthier and filthier the more Mitchell's gross climax face bores into the back of my brain. 'Rhea, though?'

'I know! She's fit! What is she doing getting stuffed by him? What a waste.'

'This is mad.'

'Right! Did you know I got off with her once? Last year. Christmas party.'

'Not that! I mean me! My pitch! It wasn't even a proper idea, more of a ... saddo ramble. The only thing I deserve to be the face of is eating too many biscuits.'

'Well, looks like that decision's been made for you, babe. I'll see if I can find out anything else tomorrow. Good thing about having remote access to the work files, you know? I've got to get going. Jazz has a burlesque performance at an open cabaret night and I've got to wrap her up in bandages before she goes. She's doing a reverse Egyptian mummy routine.' I must look confused, because Suki elaborates. 'It's a sexy comedy thing.'

'Right. Of course.' It does sound like a laugh actually, but before I ask if it's the sort of thing anyone can come to, she puts her phone in her pocket and says goodbye, waving me off with a three-fingered salute.

Chapter Sixteen

'One more time, love. I still don't get it ...' Annie pauses as we walk over a cobbled driveway. A car turns to pull in and beeps us. Annie puts her hand up and quickens her short steps to meet me on the pavement.

I've been trying to explain my current work predicament to Annie as we walk to the shop, but apart from her surprisingly brilliant advice last week, it's proving more difficult to explain what it is I actually *do* at Lovr. So far, I've had to peel back the whole idea of what a social media campaign is, to the concept of an app, to why people my age won't just ask someone out if they like the look of them. I actually laugh aloud at that last one. If someone asked for my number in a bar (when I accidentally end up in one) I'd assume they were a serial killer.

'Do you remember that show that was on TV ages ago, *Blind Date?*'

'Oh yeah, that were good Friday-night viewing,' Annie says, hooking her hand through the crook of my elbow.

'Well, it's like that, except rather than three guys to pick from you have hundreds. Maybe thousands.'

'Bloody hell, really? That's too many to choose from! Why would you ever pick one when you might meet Johnny Bedeale round the corner?'

I have no idea who Johnny Bedeale is, but it's probably best not to bring him up again in case he's a pop star pervert from the Seventies. 'Well, yeah, that's the main problem really. People aren't given a chance. They swipe someone—'

'Eh?'

'They pick someone. Someone they like, but it's usually based on pictures, not personality. If they don't hit it off instantly, that's it. They try someone else. And it's exhausting. Everyone is so busy they don't have time to go on rubbish dates. It's pretty cutthroat.'

'And you use this swipey phone thing, do you?'

'Well, er, actually, I don't. I haven't thought about it. I don't know if it would be appropriate. I'm only just single so ...'

'Can we sit down?'

'Oh, sure. Are you okay? Have we done a bit much?' I say, feeling a strange sense of pride as Annie's hand tightens around my elbow for support.

We reach a shelter at the bottom of the road with a wooden bench nestled inside, the slats worn smooth with wear. Annie grips the arm rest with white knuckles as she lowers herself, emitting a wheezy breath as she tips backwards against its frame. Maybe I should have called a taxi, or gone myself. Once I'd convinced her that we could watch *Nazi Hunters* on catch-up, I felt compelled to follow through on my idea to 'nip to the supermarket together', even though she'd taken an age to find the right shoes and even longer to get them on, since she wouldn't let me help. What ensued was a tussle with the shoehorn that ended in Annie stubbornly sitting on the stairs until I'd promised to put it away.

'I'm fine,' she says, unzipping her bodywarmer. 'I'm a smidge concerned, that's all.'

'About what?'

'About you. And this bloke. What you said just now ... mull it over for a second. I'm not being funny or owt, but it seems like you and your fella have been apart for longer than two weeks. You haven't mentioned him once, and, well, you don't seem too bothered by it, love.'

'I am. But it's not as simple as that.'

'Isn't it?'

I sigh and scuff the ground with the toe of my boot.

'Are you thinking about getting back with him, love?'

'Fuck no. Sorry, Annie,' I quickly add.

''S all right. I'm getting used to your effin' and jeffin',' she says, nudging me with a sharp elbow.

I pull a loose ringlet straight, letting it bounce back once, twice, three times. 'It sounds really stupid, but ... I guess I don't know how to *move on*. I don't feel compelled to work my way through a tub of Ben & Jerry's and watch romcoms. I'm angry, and embarrassed, but not really with him.'

169

I push my hands deep into my pockets and roll a ball of lint between my fingers. 'It's like, what's wrong with me? I convinced myself that we were a "normal" couple for ages. I think I wanted to feel like I was special to someone.' My throat feels tight but I'm not upset – more frustrated that I'm articulating myself so badly. 'It felt real at the time. But the way he's left without looking back? I feel like a kid who had a playground boyfriend. It felt adult, but it was play-acting.'

'And have you tried talking to him? It might help. Give you a bit of closure.'

'No. I'm not sure what there is to say.'

Annie tuts and glances over her shoulder, as though she's looking out for the bus. 'It sounds to me like you're waiting for permission.'

'I don't know what you mean,' I say, crossing my ankles.

'Well – and I'm sorry if I'm speaking out of turn – but I don't know what you're waiting for.'

'Nothing,' I snap back in a tone I know sounds whiny. 'I know he's gone off to have this "big adventure" and it's all exciting for him, but I'm hardly living the best version of my life. No offence,' I quickly add. 'But when he left, I was so bloody confused about how I felt – if I felt *anything* – that I let him go. And now ... I don't know. I wanted to be doing something really cool before I properly cut him out, so his memory isn't of some pathetic saddo who trundled after him for the best part of two years. I want him to realise.'

Annie's face has softened. She twists one of her rings up over a knuckle, her skin pale and silken in the gap left behind. 'Realise?'

'Yeah. That I was enough. And if I wasn't, then he should have told me a bit fucking sooner.' I'm past feeling sad. I'm angry now, at how stupid my own words sound coming out of my mouth.

'Can I tell you something?' Annie says. I nod.

'You owe it to yourself to take some ownership of this relationship of yours. Because it won't just happen. I promise you. If he made you feel ... less than, that ain't right. The more you sit with the idea that someone else has the ultimate say-so over your identity, well, it'll get to you in the end. If it hasn't already.'

I get up and pull my scarf tighter. 'Shall we keep walking?'

'You know what I mean though, don't you, love? I'm all right, I can manage,' she adds as I reach over to offer my arm for support. Annie shuffles forward a few small steps, reacquainting herself with balance after the unapologetically hard bench.

'I think so. It just feels quite ... "meh". I thought I'd get a chance to rage a bit, but I think the whole relationship has more to do with me than I thought. Does that make sense? I haven't got an ex-boyfriend to compare Tom to. The only long-term relationship I've seen up close is my parents, and, well, Dad always taught us to cope with stuff on our own. I don't think I learnt how to deal with problems properly. I just ignored them instead. With Tom, the bar was so low from the offset, anything supportive he did beyond existing beside me was a reward. He could buy me a packet of Monster Munch and I'd be thrilled for a week.'

Annie breaks into a wheezy laugh and immediately, the mood around us lifts.

'Better than when I was young. You lot have trial runs. We never got that chance. I'm not saying Arthur was the worst husband in the world, but he never *saw* me. Not in the way that ... someone could. I did my best as his wife. But marriage is bloody long, especially when you've had a taste of something good, and pure. When I fell short of whatever "idea" he had in his head, my punishment was silence. Years of it.'

'Here it is. Have you ever been here before, Annie?' Thank God. That's about as much geriatric therapy as I can handle for one day.

I'd like to say my reason for coming here was entirely selfless, but to be honest I'm not sure I can last another weekend of long days with nothing to snack on. This morning, I thought an alien was about to burst through my stomach going by the grumbles it made every few minutes. Over the week, I've realised that there isn't much to Annie beneath the big scarves and padded waistcoats. She's tiny. I've never been skinny, exactly, mainly because you'd have to prise my Gregg's loyalty card out of my cold dead fingers, but in the past week I've felt like a naughty kid who's been sent to bed without supper. On Wednesday I ate the dry end-slice from a loaf of bread that I'm ashamed to say I found in the top of the compost bin.

After a couple of hours of my heavy hinting that we could go to the shops together, and Annie's strong opposition to this (they'll all be closed on a Sunday, they won't have the fruit juice I like, it doesn't feel right food shopping at the weekend), she finally admits that she struggles to walk with groceries because holding the bags makes her wrists seize up. She said it like I was a detective forcing a murder confession. I can see why carers have a reputation for being pushy and patronising when they talk to older people; it's easy to think they're being difficult on purpose when, at least in Annie's case, it's a matter of pride.

It's still a sticking point for us, this whole 'companion' role. Apparently, ElderCare took requests from those in the community who thought they'd benefit from a companion, but from the sound of it, Annie didn't want one. Eventually, ElderCare must have worn her down, probably because a companion is a lot cheaper than sending a proper warden round. Either that or she just wanted to get rid of creepy Craig, which I don't blame her for either.

'I'm just saying,' continues Annie, squeezing past me as I hold open the door to Osman's, 'things are different now, for you lot. You've got choices. Too many, going by what you've said about your app, but you know what I'm getting at? It's what we were brought up thinking. You followed your man. Got on with it. But it only works for so long.'

Annie hasn't looked at the shelves yet, but absentmindedly runs her hand over the puckered skin of a swollen orange. 'Second chances, Elissa. Don't take 'em for granted. Ooh, courgettes, let's have one of those.'

Chapter Seventeen

Deciding that I absolutely cannot leave it any longer, I tackle a job I've put off for weeks and go through the unpacked bin liners that I shoved under the bed as soon as I moved in. The jumble sale hoard that has followed me from one rented room to another hasn't truly been sorted through in years, yet I'm reluctant to chuck anything out, such is my sentimental nature. I'd save a crisp packet if the sell-by date fell on my birthday.

Tom and I had our first proper argument about the amount I'd brought down to London when we'd moved. He couldn't understand how you could have so many similar types of clothing, and to be honest, he has a point. I once got told I dressed like 'an Amish person forced out clubbing', which, after googling the Amish, may have been in reference to the amount of long-sleeved tops and ankle-length dresses I own.

I shove the lot into an IKEA bag for the charity shop. Wow, this feels great! I'm going to clothe the poor and care for the old. I am Mother Teresa. Or Angelina Jolie. Where's my Nobel Peace Prize?

I pull out a drawstring bag containing a gym kit I'd carefully folded, packed, and subsequently never used. I had intentions of joining in with the office 'Fun' Run, led by Rhea and Adam on Tuesday lunchtimes, but they took it too seriously and tracked times on a leader board, which put me right off.

Since then, I'd half-heartedly thought about jogging in the evenings, but as it got darker, the chance of being attacked in the park increased, so I settled for a speed-walk to the tube as my primary form of exercise. I think I've actually jogged once, involuntarily. Tom forced me to go with him, and despite his largely sedentary lifestyle, he barely broke a sweat whilst I heaved myself along behind him. In the end, I sat down on a bench halfway round Clapham Common in a sulk because he said my form was embarrassing. Well, he can stuff his comments, because today is the day I'm going to bloody well run 5 km.

I wriggle into my Lycra leggings, roll a pair of patterned socks down to the ankle, and twist my mass of hair into something resembling a bun with an elastic band. I stretch in the corridor (I'm not quite ready to perform a lunge in public) and bolt out of the door with one earphone in (just like the internet told me to do) so I can listen for the footsteps of a potential attacker.

I feel *great*. My boobs are strapped down in a very tight sports bra and I can't quite expand my rib cage, but generally, I feel *good*. When I get to the entrance of the Heath, a middle-aged man wearing a singlet and sweatbands gives me a nod as he passes. I'm in the club! The club for fit people who find running fun! I speed up a little, dance round a yappy Pomeranian, and sprint past a group of men playing touch rugby in a kaleidoscope of coloured jerseys. I try to pick up the pace but my lungs feel spiky and small. That's okay. I've just set off too quickly. *Come on, Elissa, think of 'the tortoise and the hare' and all that stuff you hear at primary school about 'it's the taking part that counts'.* I look at my watch. I must have been running for half an hour by now. *Nine? Nine minutes? How?!* I've got a stitch. Or it might be my appendix bursting, I have no idea. It definitely feels like something is *very* wrong. I bend over, put my hands on my knees, and try to take in breaths that are shallow enough to reach my lungs without slicing at the sides.

'Are you okay?' A man with soft, almond-shaped eyes pats me on the shoulder. He taps his watch twice and his timer pauses, flashing persistently.

'Um, yeah, I think so,' I say, squeezing out the words in between gasps.

'Have you got any water with you?' he asks, looking me up and down. Despite my brain fog, I hover my hands over my crotch so he doesn't notice the offensive camel toe I've somehow developed between my bedroom and here. There's Lycra so far up my bum I'll need tweezers to pull it down again.

'No. Er, it must be the distance, this is my, er ... fifth lap.'

He guides me to a bench and sweeps a scattering of mushy blossom to the floor before lowering me down. 'Hold on, I'll be back in a second.' He sprints off into the distance and I use the time to flex my spongy hands and feet. Surely this is my body rebelling against the unreasonable demands I've made of it. A minute or so later, a bottle is thrust beneath my head, which I've put between my legs. I blink up at the outline of his broad shoulders. He moves to sit at the other end of the bench and unscrews the cap, handing me the bottle. 'Here you go.'

'Thanks,' I say, inelegantly draining it in one go. Those years spent downing cider at the SU bar have come into good use.

'Oi, I was saving some of that.' He grins at me. *Oh*. He's got an angular jawline, like an edgy model who gets booked because their prison mugshot was so good. I guess he's a bit rough around the edges, except for those eyes that crinkle with kindness. My vision becomes sharper and I see that my skin has gone clammy, not unlike corned beef. Nice. I must have forgotten to reply, because Mystery Running Man jumps in again.

'I'm joking, obviously!' he says.

'Ha, I know. I mean you could have some, but you'd have to lick it off my face. Hahaha!' I reply, wiping a dribble off my chin with the back of my arm. *We're inviting strangers to lick our face now, are we, Elissa? Cool, cool.*

'I mean, if you're asking ...?' Mystery Running Man

178

says. Jesus, Mary and Joseph, did that actually work?! All those years spent reading flirting advice in *Cosmo* as a teenager, and almost passing out from a light jog is the method that does it? I open my mouth, about to wrap things up so I can't embarrass myself further, but he starts talking. 'That's not what I meant. I was joking. Badly.' He looks up at the sky and shakes his head. 'Feeling better?'

'Yes. Loads. Thanks.' I smile at him in a way I hope comes across as coy but charming.

'It's probably low sodium levels. Marathon runners get cramps and feel dizzy all the time because they're sweating all the salt out.' *Less talk about sweat and more talk about how you want to lick my face, please.* He taps his watch again and the timer starts up. 'I'll see you around. What's your name?'

'Elissa.'

'Nice to meet you, Elissa.' He puts his earphones in and ... was that a wink? He winked at me! It wasn't a big wink, but it was clearly a wink.

I wonder if there's some sort of app that allows you to see if you run the same routes as Mystery Men who rescue women with diminished cardiovascular ability? Could be a bit dodgy; I'm 99 per cent sure it would end up getting used by stalkers who like to flash their willies from beneath a trenchcoat.

As I limp back to Evergreen, I remember Tom, red-faced and angry at how terrible I was the only time we went jogging together. In fact, he jogged off and left me clutching a silver birch sapling for support. Normally I feel guilty when I think about seeing someone else. Today? Not so much.

Chapter Eighteen

The following Monday, I manage to get in and out of the bath in a record fifteen minutes, including the time it takes to fill it with three inches of water. Annie is up early, sweeping soggy blossom from the patio into a dustpan. I make her a cup of tea in her favourite china teacup and put it on an upturned terracotta pot in the greenhouse as I leave. I walk around the oval green, even though every fibre in my being wants to take a shortcut over it. I did that once last week and there was a Mexican wave of curtain-twitching.

George and Margaret are sitting on a bench in the early morning sunshine, and as I pass their gate, he smiles and waves at me with big, swooping arms. Margaret scowls. The sky is clear and blue, except for a criss-cross pattern of jet streams from planes heading into Gatwick airport. The dogs who trot on loosely held leads, the petals caught in the wind, the smell of sourdough as I pass the posh bakeries near the tube station – it's all a beautiful distraction from what's waiting for me at work.

During days on the underground when the noise of the wheels grinding around corners is too loud for my motivational Beyoncé playlist, I like to play a game called 'Spot the Hipster'. It basically involves predicting which people in my carriage are going to get off when we arrive at Old Street. The biggest clues are: man buns, bum bags worn across the chest, and very severe fringes. But this morning I'm far too distracted. I'm tempted to avoid going into work altogether by just … not getting off the train.

Even though Annie struggles to understand what it is my job involves, I've had to accept that she (infuriatingly) made total sense when we spoke about what the 'community dating' campaign could mean for me. Last week, I described the secret photograph Suki had taken of the presentation (I left out the details of Mitchell and Rhea to save her from an early grave) and she doesn't understand why I'm reluctant to lead a campaign that was my idea in the first place. She also gave a rousing speech, whilst gesticulating with some sticky baklava pinched between her fingers, about how women should own their own accomplishments, rather than let a bloke re-fabricate them as his own. She's very modern for a pensioner. Obviously, she's right, and whilst the petty side of me wants to remind her that she gave up a career for her husband, I know she's telling the truth.

Even though I truly believe that I made a decent – if improvised – pitch, I would happily let someone take that away from me if it meant I could stay anonymous. What

182

if the whole thing fails miserably and I end up blacklisted from ever working again, because I'm the one who stuck my neck out? I think about what I'd say to someone else in the same predicament as me – Maggie, for instance. I'd absolutely turn all Sasha Fierce and tell her to work it, own it, sell it, and take a fat payslip home at the end. I'm a totally upstanding feminist, except when it comes to me.

I try and keep a low profile when I get to work, expecting everyone to look at me with collective cynicism, but the mood is instantly bright and ... sweet Jesus, cheerful? Mitchell can't have announced the Pitch Off results yet, otherwise I doubt there'd be this much festivity. A table has been pulled into the middle of the room and on it sits a hot plate with a steaming jug of coffee, a tray of assorted Danish pastries, and sliced fruit arranged in aesthetically pleasing concentric circles.

Mitchell still has the blinds pulled down inside his glass cube and Rhea is once again missing from the walking desk. They've either gone straight back into his office, or alternatively never left it at all.

I take a few slices of kiwi from the fruit platter and lick my chin as the juice dribbles over my bottom lip. Adam takes long, lolloping steps over to me.

'Why'd you have to eat it?' I go to spit it back out into my hand, purposefully to annoy Adam, but he grimaces and looks away. 'Me and my girlfriend do a food blog. Circles do well. Circles and hands, that's what the algorithm likes. But you know that, eh?'

I nod along, pretending that, as the social media manager, I've got a clue as to what he's on about. Food and circles? Why do people care? As for algorithms ... well, that's an ongoing mystery.

'Haha, yeah, sure!' I reply as Adam precisely rearranges the fruit with the end of a pencil.

I hang up my jacket and scarf and pull a face at my coffee cup, which has grown a crust over the weekend. As I turn back to the kitchen to rinse it out, Suki walks in. She winks at me and slides down the banister into our work space, her yellow-stitched Doc Martens clumping as she reaches the bottom.

'Heard there was free food, so thought I'd come and say hello.'

'How do you know about things like this? I've only just got here myself.'

'You're not on the right email lists, my friend,' she says, giving me a lopsided smile. 'Is all this in honour of your big campaign launch?'

'Shhhhh! No one knows that we saw—'

'Mitchell and Rhea shagging in the romantic silhouette of a dusty projector?'

'I knew,' says a monotone voice from behind us.

'Holy fuck, Rodney! You can't sneak up on people like that!' says Suki. Rodney blinks. How he manages to move with silent precision in an office made largely of glass is beyond me.

'How long have you been standing there?'

'I knew,' he repeats, his face empty.

Suki spins round in surprise and drops half a cinnamon swirl on the floor. She kicks it under Adam's desk and puts one hand on each of our backs, shoving us forward into the kitchen. There's no one in here but the cleaner, who has earbuds in and hums tunelessly to a beat of late-Eighties soul music.

'Er, context, please, Rodney?' I say. He looks at me and blinks twice. Suki runs a hand over her bristled head impatiently.

'Mitchell and Rhea. They've been making love every Thursday evening between 6.15 and 6.45 p.m. And sometimes between 6.50 and 7.20 a.m. on Tuesdays.'

'Well, if that isn't disturbingly specific, Rodney,' says Suki.

'They think I've gone home. But I haven't. It is rare for anyone to notice when I have left.' Rodney sniffs and wrinkles his nose to push his glasses back up.

'Oh, er, I'm sure that's not true, Rodney,' I say, trying not to catch Suki's eye. She is standing out of Rodney's eye-line, biting her knuckles in awkwardness.

'I don't say it to inspire guilt. I prefer it that way.' Rodney shrugs and smiles meekly. I try and paint a look of friendly encouragement on my face, but it's like building rapport with a mannequin.

'Well, we sort of knew they were, you know—'

'Banging,' interjects Suki.

'Yes, er, that. But do you know anything about the new campaign?'

Rodney squints, which I interpret as confusion.

'Basically, Elissa needs to know if she's going to become a *Diary of a Call Girl* type "girl-about-London",' says Suki. Rodney's squint deepens.

'I don't know about the new campaign. I just write the code,' he says, clasping his hands.

'Right, well, great chat, Rodney, we've er, got to get on,' I say, walking over to the sink. I find a fork to chip out the hardened coffee granules in my mug. Rodney clearly doesn't feel it necessary to respond, because he's already halfway out of the door.

'He's lying. He knows something.' Suki looks through the kitchen window at Rodney's receding figure, or what there is of a figure beneath a magnolia T-shirt that's at least three sizes too big.

'He doesn't. You're paranoid,' I say over the spluttering of the hot water tank as steam fills my mug. I'll 'let it soak', which, of course, is every lazy person's reason for letting mouldy crockery linger.

'Honestly, he does. I just know it.'

'You're acting like he's a serial killer, Suki.'

'He might be.'

'Sook!'

'What? I'm just saying! He's weirdly chill about this whole thing, don't you reckon? I mean, I know you think he just does the code round here, but Frank on the third floor saw him chatting to Amy – the one with the funny ears? – and both of them were proper spooked when Frank interrupted. Just saying.' Suki chews the corner of her lip and folds her arms.

'I've never seen him chat to anyone down here. I mean, I've tried, but—' I break off as Adam taps on the window and points to an invisible watch on his wrist.

'Bloody hell. Suki, this is it.'

'Calm your tits! Look, I'm coming in with you. It'll be fine. Well, it might not be if Rodney really is a serial killer ...' She drops to a whisper as we head back into the office and upstairs to one of the smaller meeting rooms. Mitchell holds the door open as people walk past and I can see he's got sweat patches already. He's either as nervous as I am or hasn't quite recovered from last Friday's rendezvous with Rhea. Suki bounds in behind me.

'Sook, you in with us for this?' Mitchell asks, rubbing his chin.

'Yeah, got a calendar invite last night. Tech streamlining for the new campaign? Oh, thanks, I'll have one of those, Bismah.' Suki pulls a chair out and swipes a hulled strawberry from the fruit platter as Bismah places it on the table with a wobble. Bismah smiles and flexes her wrists. She's such a tiny human, it's a wonder she manages to hold up an iPad without toppling over.

'Tech streamlining? For what?' I hiss at Suki as she pulls her leg up onto her knee and leans over.

'Chill out, I made it up. I'm meant to be working from home. Couldn't leave you to face this lot alone, could I?' Suki winks and pops a grape into her mouth.

'Thanks,' I say, feeling a little prickle in my throat. 'That means a lot.'

'Eh, it's nothing.' She shrugs.

'Right. Sure.' I fiddle with the elastic on my notebook, which I have no intention of writing in.

I've just got to remember what Annie said. I can't keep dancing away from opportunities because I get freaked out and assume someone else could do it better than me. *Come on, Elissa. You've got this.*

'Okay, chaps. You all know what this is about, so let's just cut to the cock and bollocks of it all, shall we?' Mitchell theatrically taps the screen, but nothing happens. 'For fuck's sake, Rodney! £43 an hour and we can't work a flat screen? Give me your iPad. Give it to me. The iPad, Rodney!' Mitchell cricks his neck from one side to the other and flares his nostrils as Rodney inputs the passcode with floppy fingers, eventually mirroring the presentation onto the screen.

Mitchell nods as we look at the images displayed in gargantuan HD, then turns to me and winks. In the corner, under the title 'Community X Lovr' is a picture of me that I recognise from my ID badge. In it, I'm wide-eyed and so shiny I look like I've had an accident with a vat of chip oil. Wonderful. A murmur of acknowledgment drifts around the room, made worse when Mitchell starts to clap. Adam points double-handed finger guns at me and the others look decidedly relieved that they're not the ones who are now responsible for the app's success.

188

'Now, Elissa,' Mitchell says as the noise of clapping diminishes. 'No pressure, darlin', but myself and Rhea over here –' he squeezes her shoulder and she flashes a smile down at the table '– have been working all weekend putting in the final details of a campaign inspired by your pitch.' Rhea clears her throat and Suki kicks me under the table with the toe of her giant boots. I wince in pain and feign surprise. Mitchell slides his glasses on top of his bald head and adopts a pose of intense speculation, fingers interlocked under his chin.

'A little birdy told me that our lovely Els here is single. That right, sweetheart?' Mitchell raises his eyebrows and looks around the room. Oh God. This is so much worse than I imagined. It's one thing to 'own the campaign', but I didn't sign up for a budget Cilla Black experience. Does he actually want me to answer?

'Well ...'

'She's keeping her cards close to her chest,' Mitchell says, grinning. Thankfully, everyone else is starting to feel as uncomfortable as I am, because eyes are going in all directions, except towards me. 'If Elissa chooses to accept, which I hope she does, as you lot won't be paying your bills otherwise ...' Mitchell coughs out a laugh then flicks all expression from his face '... seriously though, we think you're right, Els. About the whole "community dating" thing. It's the best idea we've got.'

I take a moment to ignore the fact that I'm in Mitchell's unenviable Short Name Club and instead mentally log the compliment. *My idea was the best one.* I should probably say something at this point instead of blinking into the middle distance.

'Um, thanks. I mean, it's got some holes in it. I didn't spend a huge amount of time working on –' I bite my lip. I'm doing it again. Why am I giving reasons for why I don't deserve this? *Think of Annie, Elissa, think of Annie.* '– the pitch, I guess. But I honestly believe that this has potential, you know? And before you ask, I'll do it. I'll be your poster girl, I'll face the new campaign, whatever. I came up with it, so I should see it through, shouldn't I?' My breathing is shallow and beside me Suki leans away to cast an appraising look over my (slightly clammy) frame.

'Right. Well, this meeting is going to be significantly shorter than I thought. Els, I like your enthusiasm. Feisty. Just what we need to promote. Rhea, you making notes?' Rhea nods as her lacquered fingernails clack on a propped-up tablet.

'Everyone got their listening ears on? Sitting comfortably?' says Mitchell, eyeing us all around the room. A few sit a little taller and shuffle in their seats. Rodney pinches his earlobes, as though he's taken Mitchell's request literally. 'Okay, so we'll begin.' Mitchell clasps his hands and pouts over his index fingers. It's astounding how quickly he can switch from patronising to pensive. 'Experiences. That's what we're in the game of, here. I won't parrot what Elissa told us all last week, but in a nutshell, youngsters

– and I do still class myself within that bracket – don't want a "shag and see how it goes" type situation. That's the measure of it, right, Elissa?' It's absolutely not the bloody measure of it.

'Um, well, yes, and no, I mean—'

'London is thriving,' says Mitchell, cutting me off. 'It's full of people from everywhere in the world, but we're all too caught up in our own heads and our own screens and then, BOOM! We realise how fucking selfish we are and all of a sudden, we've got a generation that could empathise with a blood-starved gnat. So, rather than book ourselves an orphanage tour of Southeast Asia, we can get them doing wellness workshops and community work here.' At this, Rhea bridles. I've seen her pictures on social media: bikini-clad, giving out fizzy sweets to children with mucky clothes and swollen bellies. She called it a 'philanthropic cultural exchange'. I call it exploitation, especially when the next picture is her in neon body paint drinking from a bucket of cheap cocktail and ketamine at a Full Moon Party.

'We've got six weeks. Each week, we're going to curate a unique date for Elissa to go on with a bloke.' My stomach lurches. I haven't dated since Tom and I first got together. Back then it was Netflix, takeaway pizza, and sex in a cold flat with the duvet pulled up to our ears. The thought of Mitchell having a hand in my breakout dates makes life in a convent sound incredibly appealing. 'It is blokes, isn't it?'

'Yeah, yeah it is.'

'And that date can be anything from a craft workshop, to a one-off yoga session in a skyscraper, to a charity day getting rid of needles on the Hackney towpath ... I don't know. I've got some contacts to pull in, and Big Man over here –' Mitchell motions to Adam, who casually salutes the room '– is gonna be on the blower to connect us with agencies and events. Rhea?'

Rhea cranes her neck as she types. 'Oh, right. Bear with me.' It's clear that half of what Mitchell says is too inappropriate for the official minutes. She finishes her sentence with a flourishing tap of the keyboard and flicks her ponytail over her shoulder, folding her arms. 'So, Elissa, our social media guru, will go on these "experience dates" each week.' Her voice is a tone higher than usual and ripples with sarcasm. Maybe I'm imagining it? Oh, no, she's just done air quotes. She clearly isn't happy about something. 'Suki's team will be developing an algorithm, but for now I'll manually match Elissa from our database, which is still active, although not operating with optimum user levels. Okay?'

Oh no. Reading between the lines, this means we've barely got anyone signed up to the app. I thought that at the very least I'd be choosing the guys? I've seen some of the slicked-back, silk-pocket-square stockbrokers she's been out with. Maybe I could get Suki to fiddle with the system to generate me a friendly, slipper-wearing, Sunday-afternoon-film enthusiast. I've really spent too much time at Evergreen Village, haven't I?

I think someone's asked me a question, because everyone is staring.

'Sorry, what?'

'Your first date. It's tonight. You wanted this, so it's all systems go now, sweetheart.'

Chapter Nineteen

It was a stupid plan. I thought 'owning my idea' would mean, like, publicising the community dates, not actually going on them. You know, weekly meetings with tea and a plate of digestives where I interview users about the process, the app, whether the 'experience' was experiential enough, that sort of thing. Maybe I could use a pseudonym? But that would only work if I was disguising my face as well as my name, which I can't do because Bismah's already uploaded my profile onto the bloody website and Rhea has written my bio. It currently reads:

I'm a 26-year-old pottery enthusiast with a big heart and a penchant for slow walks along the Thames.

Of course I bloody like slow walks. What other kind of walk is there?

I was being truthful in the meeting when I said I hadn't thought about the details of the pitch too much. I really hadn't. But, there's something about living with Annie that has made me feel close to content for the first time in ... I don't even know how long. I want more of that, in other areas too. Last week I didn't do a single quiz on the internet like 'which European city is most like your teenage self?' Not one! I even bought a red notebook and have written night-time affirmations in it all of three times whilst Annie watches *University Challenge*. We hide in the kitchen when creepy Craig wanders past the front lawn. Well, I hide, Annie shuffles behind the coat rack as fast as her dodgy back can cope with. She asks me about 'that horrible boss' and 'lovely Maggie the teacher'. We say things like 'You made the last one, I'll put the kettle on'. Annie is undemanding. Annie squeezes my fingers to say thank you. Annie still won't talk to me about why her bloody son won't speak to her, but I've got a plan to help with that.

It's pushing six o'clock and I've got to meet my first match – David Meldrew – at eight. Considering it takes me thirty minutes to get up to the Village and then another fifty over to Knightsbridge, I barely have time to get ready. I break my self-imposed rule of 'never run unless your life is in danger' and jog every other step on the hill up to Evergreen. I look like a drunk gazelle hobbling over cobblestones slick with rain and soggy blossom. When I get in, a clump of mud lands on Annie's thick rubber-soled slippers and I flick it off as she comes through the doorway.

'Did they announce your campaign today, love? You give 'em what for?' she says, her eyes wide with anticipation.

'Annie, I'm freaking out,' I say, dashing past her up the stairs two at a time.

'What d'you mean?' she calls from the hallway. 'They didn't go for that dog swap app, did they? I thought your idea was lovely. Really well thought through.' Her voice muffles as I turn down the carpeted hallway and open my bedroom door. 'They're bloody idiots, Elissa, you hear me?' she calls up the stairs.

'It's not the dog one. It's mine. Mine won. My idea – we're doing it. But they want me to actually *be* in the campaign, not just design it. I've got to go play crazy golf with some City worker in ... about an hour.' I can hear her coming up the stairs as I flick through my sparse hangers for the third time and regret my decision to drop a bin bag of lacy, sparkly clothes at the charity shop. I didn't think I'd be at the 'jeans and a nice top' stage for months. The thought of deliberately dressing to attract someone makes me feel clammy. Is the rule still boobs, belly, or legs on show, but never at the same time? What if this campaign gets the traction everyone hopes it'll have and I'm outed as a deceptive, amoral polyamorist? What if Louis Theroux makes a documentary about me and my unconventional lifestyle and people on Twitter troll me?

'I don't want to go on a date,' I say, flopping down on the corner of my bed. I fiddle with the edge of a pillowcase printed with tiny cowboys and Indians. The sight of them makes me irrationally angry. Annie is hovering at the door. She stands at a crooked angle and pushes the base of her palm into the curve of her back.

'He might be all right, love,' Annie says. 'Seems like you're casting him off before giving him a chance.'

'He won't be all right. He'll be some finance tosser with daddy issues who Rhea has paired me up with because for some reason she hates me and thinks this'll be funny. Everyone is going to laugh. Because it's hilarious, isn't it? Me having to tweet about all the shit dates I'm going to go on.' I rifle through the chest of drawers and blink my eyes clear so I can see whether the bralette in my hands is acceptable as outerwear. 'I'm going to be known as the saddo who can't make someone love her and plays Scrabble with a pensioner at the weekends.' Annie doesn't meet my eye when I look at her and I bite my lip so hard I taste old pennies.

'I didn't mean it like that. I mean ... I don't know what I mean. I like playing Scrabble, it's just—'

'Put this on.' She carefully takes a black T-shirt off its hanger and lays it on the bed. 'With a big necklace and jeans. You can dress anything up with a good necklace.' She smiles, pats me on the arm, and turns to leave.

'Annie?'

'What, love?'

'I didn't mean it. About the Scrabble thing. Honestly. I do like living here. Even though I'm rubbish at spelling and you always get the triple word score.' I laugh. Annie doesn't.

'It's fine. I understand. It's not ideal, this, is it? I was married with a new-born at your age. I'm not saying that's ideal either, mind you. Being here in London when you don't know many folk and only a little one for company … it's hard. Not the worst kind of hard there is, but still hard. You get used to it.' She twists a ring around her finger and rubs the joints on her left palm. 'I shan't prattle on any longer. You get yourself ready now. I won't put the double lock on the front door, all right? You can come in when you fancy, that way.' She gives me the smallest of nods and shuffles back down the corridor.

Oh God, I feel terrible. I want to go downstairs, make tea, watch *Pointless*, and talk to Annie for hours and hours so she forgets how horrible I am. I look at my phone. *Shit*. I should have left by now. I quickly change and dig out a long necklace that Mum brought me back last year from a stopover port in Sharm-el-Sheikh, before squeezing into my battered brogues.

'See you, Annie!' I shout through into the living room. I linger for a minute, but she doesn't reply.

By the time I get to Hampstead tube station, my back is clammy from speed-walking. As I walk down the escalator, my phone buzzes.

REMINDER: Pick up tortillas and spice mix (not hot) for fajita night!

198

Fuck. We had plans. We had plans and I'd completely forgotten. Here I am, travelling to a sodding crazy-golf date when I'm meant to be making dinner for Annie. Why didn't she say anything? A memory pings to mind of a chat we'd had this morning whilst I was chopping cherry tomatoes for my salad. She was looking forward to it. She'd been chatting about a disastrous attempt at Mexican food in 1994, where she'd sliced up a whole habanero chilli and the poor woman she'd asked round for tea was left with an inflamed oesophagus and swollen eyelids. She hadn't had the nerve to try it again since. I'll make it up to her. I've got to.

I feel a bit sick wondering what she thinks of me – that I'm a scrounger who only spends time with her because I'm contractually obliged to for four evenings a week. But, that's not true. I feel attached to Annie – her home, her world, her life, her bizarre neighbours. Even the ones with standoffish wives. The thought of going back to that front door, dripping with wisteria, to find my slippers warm on the radiator is the closest I've felt to belonging in years. It's worlds away from the days I'd walk home with crossed fingers in my coat pocket, hoping that I'd be alone in the flat. Now, I *want* to be around the person I live with.

I get to the end of the escalator and stumble as the tread flattens under my feet. An elbow bumps into my back and a flurry of tuts flit around my ears as I step to the side and blink away the tears that are making my vision foggy.

What am I doing? If my date has a thing for bloodshot eyes and bad posture, he's in luck tonight.

***

The crazy-golf bar looks like someone designed it with a Las Vegas theme, but only ever saw the budget replicas on the strip in Great Yarmouth. Once I figure out where the entrance is (through a door disguised as a Smeg fridge), I stand on tiptoes to look over the heads of two dozen men and women who laugh at the mini-golf clubs they've just picked up from the stand.

Right, what am I actually looking for here? Dark hair. Slight stubble. The self-confidence of a man who sings in Latin when drunk. That must be him, the one who's just given me a salute and a lopsided smile. Of course. He's halfway down a pint of beer when I reach him, and lurches forwards to plant a kiss on each cheek.

'Eloise?' he says, eyes just about focusing on mine.

'No, not Eloise. Elissa.'

He nods and pats me on the shoulder with a heavy hand. I guess that's an acknowledgment, of sorts. This is when I need to say his name, isn't it? Except I don't know it. I've barely looked at the profile Rhea sent me and despite trying to hook into the Wifi each time the tube stopped for thirty seconds on the way home, I only managed to load up his profile picture. I can hardly get my phone out to check now. *Think, Elissa.*

The man looks at me with his chin pulled in as he sways and squints with concentration.

'Er, how do you pronounce your name again?'

'How do I pronounce it?' he says, stumbling over his words.

'Yes, your name, is it said the normal way?' Please don't be a biblical name, please don't be a biblical name, please don't be a—

'David. Said the normal way.' *Shit.* He tips the glass up towards his mouth and a dribble of beer rolls down his chin.

'David ... ahh, right. I've only ever known a "Daveid", said in the Spanish way, you know? Hahaha. David. Nice to meet you.'

David, who is clearly not Spanish, mumbles something and shakes his glass to catch every last drop of beer in his mouth. I tug my top down from the back so the material shifts up and over my bra, which I've just noticed is on full display, as is half of my areola, clearly visible through thin grey lace. I must start washing colours and whites separately, but honestly, who has the time?

'Hmm?' I say, distracted. David leans to talk into my ear and I step away from him. He smells of stale beer and an overwhelming peppery aftershave.

'So ... how does this work, then?' David asks, swinging his mini-golf club in the direction of the blinking and shrieking putting course behind me.

'Er, well, it's golf, isn't it? Fewest hits wins? Or is it most?'

201

'No, I mean, this date thing. To be honest I thought you were going to be Rhea.' He guffaws in a way I've only ever heard on *Prime Minister's Question Time*.

'Oh, right.' *Thank God*. Overlooking the thinly veiled insult, *I'd* rather it was Rhea here too.

'Yeah, we played lacrosse together back at Christ's. Great girl. You're all right though. Not my usual type, but you've got good eyes.'

'Thanks, I can see out of them and everything.'

'What?'

'Nothing.'

I drum my fingers on the table. This is painful. David goes to drink from his empty glass and looks confused when nothing comes out.

'I think the idea is that we look on this as an "experience". Like, it's a date and everything, but it's more about the whole thing. So that it's not a waste. Of time.' I emphasise the last few words. I am aware that I'm coming across as a massively uptight bitch, but I'm annoyed at Rhea for luring this poor sod with the false promise of an evening with her and her perky boobs. This isn't what I had in mind when I thought of 'community dates'. I imagined planting a herbaceous border around a community centre whilst getting to know a philanthropic man who can hold a conversation without a beer in hand. Crazy golf with a charity tin on the tequila bar is a stretch. But it's hardly worth thinking about that now. I may as well try and make this worth his while. I'll have to write it up, after all.

First, I've got to remember what it's like to flirt. I try and think back to uni, to lingering eyes and walking hip-first across dance floors sticky with sambuca. I pull my shoulders back and push my tongue behind my bottom lip to make it look fuller (something I saw in *Cosmo* as a teen and always remembered). But David is looking over my shoulder at a group of giggling women with bums so peachy I'm sure they came out of the womb in active wear. Seeing as I'm being ignored, I physically move to stand in front of David's eyeline.

'Shall we ... start the game?' I ask.

An hour later, David has sobered up a bit, quite possibly because the queue for the bar is now eight people deep, but the upside is that I got a good lead before he was able to focus on the ball properly. He's also not as awful as I first thought. Whilst we wait for others to chase a neon golf ball round the AstroTurf, David works his way through a number of conversation points. These include: his regrets concerning Rhea; his loneliness post-university when he lost touch with rugby mates; his older brother who works remotely on a banking start-up in Goa; and his plans to adopt a pet from Battersea Dogs Home.

He crosses his wrists and props them on the end of an upturned golf club. He looks quite jaunty now, like he's going to kick it in a circle and give me some jazz hands, except his eyes have gone watery and morose and I'm led to think it would be a very *sad* dance. Oh dear. I've got to steer towards something more joyful.

'Have you ever had a dog before?' I say.

David sighs. 'No. Actually, yeah. When I was eight. But it did a liquid shit in Dad's study. Leaked between the floorboards. Ringo lived in the shed after that. When I came back from boarding school at Christmas, Dad said he'd run off.' I snort. David's eyes narrow. I can't help it. I'm trying desperately hard not to, but I'm barely disguising my laughter as a coughing fit as it is, so I turn around, shoulders shaking, to swallow it back down.

'I'm really sorry. It's not funny. It isn't.' I breathe out sharply and turn back, but I sound like a canal boat chugging along. David stands tall with his shoulders pulled back and a huge grin spread across his face.

'It's not funny, is it?' he says, lopsidedly smirking. He runs a hand through his hair and laughs too, in a pitch much higher than his regular voice. 'It was quite devastating, actually,' he says with mock sincerity.

'I don't doubt that. I lost my hamster when I was ten because his testicles got caught in the bars of his cage, so, you know, I'm no stranger to childhood trauma.'

He laughs and knocks my club to the floor by bumping into me with his hip.

'Um, are you guys gonna move on, or, like, should we wait?' a woman says, holding her lips in a silent 'o' of red lipstick.

'No, go on ahead,' David replies. *Oh.* He wants to keep talking to me. Maybe I'm not the subpar date I thought I was.

'Do you want to see a picture? Of my hamster?' *Smooth, Elissa.* That line didn't work well even at primary school.

'Not if he's got his balls stuck in a cage.'

'No! I didn't take a picture of that. I just wrapped him in bandages and poured some perfume on him, so if someone in the future digs him up they'll think he was worshipped like an Egyptian deity. Obviously.'

'Yeah, far more normal ...' he says, nodding.

'Look, you'd have done the same thing. He was the gladiator of rodents. I'll show you.' I smile and my eyebrows strain from the effort of making my eyes look wide and alluring. David sits down on a bench surrounded by fake Monstera and ivy vines. I pull my phone from my back pocket.

My lock screen (up until recently a selfie of me and Tom on the Thames, now replaced by a particularly great poutine I ate last year) is busy with notifications. Five missed calls, all from a number I don't recognise. My stomach twists and I feel like ice cubes are rattling around in my chest.

'Brought back bad memories? The hamster?' says David, drumming his fingers on his knee.

'What? No. Sorry, David. I've just got to check something. You can keep going if you want, just knock my ball about, will you? I'm the purple one.' I prop my club up against the wall and apologise over my shoulder as I weave around the spinning blades of a miniature windmill and accidentally kick a golf ball into a pit of rubber snakes.

Outside, my phone buzzes in my hand as I move past the bouncer.

'No return of entry if you're leaving, madam,' he says, scanning the queue as he talks.

'But I'm just taking a phone call.'

'That's the system. If you leave you can't re-enter.'

'Why?' I say, unusually annoyed.

He waves in another couple, clicks a counter inside his pocket, and looks at me with decided boredom. It's Monday, and drizzly, but beyond that I don't know why he has a reason to be such an arsehole. My screen lights up. Six missed calls. Either my Mum and Dad have fallen off the back of a cruiser somewhere in the Mediterranean shipping channel, or my brother has taken some dodgy MDMA and is in a coma. Why else does anyone ring six times in a row?

'Fine. But I've left someone in there, can you go and tell him I'm stuck out here and can't come back in?'

He winks at me and flashes a gold tooth so shiny I can see my head in bulbous reflection. 'Sure thing, princess. I'll just toddle in and find him, shall I? He'll be one of the ones playing golf, will he?' My phone buzzes again. It's a London number. No cruiser or drug incident, then.

'Hi. I've had a bunch of missed calls from this num—'

'Elissa Evans?' a clipped voice says over the background noise of phones ringing, squeaky trolleys, and the odd incomprehensible shout.

'Yep, speaking,' I say, plugging my other ear with a finger.

206

'Mrs Annie De Loutherberg has given us your name as next of kin, is that correct?'

'Annie? Is she okay? Has something happened?'

'Are you happy to act as next of kin?'

'Yes. Yes, yes, of course. Is she okay? What's happened?'

'Annie's had a fall. A pedestrian found her. We've brought her into the Royal Free.'

Chapter Twenty

As I run from Hampstead station, Alina from ElderCare calls and I'm 99 per cent sure she's going to kick me out because I'm irresponsible and can't be trusted to adequately look after an old lady. I bailed on dinner with Annie and now she's fallen over, in the dark, on her way to the shop. But Alina doesn't mention it. Instead, she runs off a list of things to put in an overnight bag for Annie in hospital.

Even though my stomach is so far up my throat I think I might gag, it's like there's a sturdy hand on my back shoving me around the house with an emotionless pragmatism I've only ever seen in mums who pick screaming toddlers up from the floor like they're a bag of potatoes. I go into the kitchen and open the pantry door, unhook a floppy carpet bag, and wrap a slice of Victoria sponge in cling film to pack in a Tupperware alongside a stack of Yorkshire tea. She won't drink the NHS stuff, I know it.

I lean against the fridge and close my eyes for a second to take a couple of deep breaths. Even though Alina said,

'Don't worry, love, she's not the first of ours to bugger a hip this week', I'm not feeling any less guilty. I don't know what I'll say when I see Annie, other than apologise over and over again. I give myself a little slap on the cheeks, change out of the flimsy bralette I'd had the poor judgement to wear, and hover on the precipice of Annie's bedroom. I haven't been in before. I place the half-packed bag on her feather-down duvet. The bed sheets are crisp and tucked into precise hospital corners, like Nanny used to do. When I stayed over as a kid, she'd tuck the sheet across my chest so tight I couldn't roll over.

I pack Annie's pyjamas, dressing gown, slippers, flannel (a coral colour very popular with the over-seventies), a spongy shower puff, and a crossword book. What else? Medication? I can't remember if Annie takes any. I squat down next to her bedside table. It's where I keep my contraceptives, even though it's pointless taking them because a) I don't have a boyfriend any more and b) I'd have to be comfortable bonking someone within ten feet of a pensioner, regardless of the partition wall. The good thing is my pill gives me the libido of a Benedictine monk, so the chances of option b occurring are fairly slim.

It feels a bit ... taboo, looking in someone else's drawers. But I'm not going through them, I just need to grab prescription boxes, and maybe a bit of night cream, then I'm out. The drawer gets stuck on the larger of two jewellery boxes, so I squeeze a finger round to wiggle it free again. The box shifts to one side and the force of the drawer's release tips me backwards onto my heels, the contents strewn in my lap.

I pick up the larger box, but as soon as I touch the lid, it springs open to reveal dozens of letters stacked and squashed inside. On the corner of each envelope I notice tiny inked numbers. I turn over one, then another. I've seen this before. Back when I made the Once-and-Never-To-Be-Repeated crumble. The looped writing is identical; bloated vowels and neat, angled letters. A quick flick through tells me they'd been arranged by date and go back to ... 1960.

On every envelope, in ink that has bled into the paper, is Annie's name, but just like before, no address, or stamp. I flick through, glancing at scrawled handwriting as a letter slips out onto the bed, but by the time I've reached 1965, five minutes have elapsed. I glance at the loudly ticking carriage clock on Annie's bedside table and swear, tearing an envelope in my haste to slot them back in the box. I hope I haven't ripped the note inside. I carefully slide my finger under the flap, but it's so worn and the paper so creased, it flops open like tissue paper.

The letter, an A4 sheet with browning ink on both sides, looks passably undamaged, apart from a small hole in the middle of the page where it's been opened and refolded – countless times from the looks of it. As I'm about to inch it back into the torn envelope, I see that it's signed off with the initial 'H', and another single kiss. Are these love letters? Christ, Annie's lucky. The only thing I've got to commemorate the big romances of my life (Orlando

210

Bloom in *Pirates of the Caribbean* aside) is an MSN chat from 2004 when Jacob in the year above said I was fit and then asked to see my boobs on a webcam.

I should be at the hospital by now. I'll sort out the letter explosion when I get back. I scoop them into a rough pile with both my arms and swing Annie's bag over my shoulder, doing a mental checklist of anything I might have missed before closing the door behind me, the powder-soft sensation of cheap, worn paper on my fingertips.

***

Falling over on a gritty playground is such a staple feature of being a kid, but when you're old, it's not just your ego that gets bruised. You hear about it in snatched, sombre conversations: 'Did you hear Sue's mum had a fall?' Maggie's gran (not the scary one) went into hospital after a fall and didn't come out again. Not Annie, though. It can't happen to Annie. She's a bit wobbly and can't hold more than half a cup of tea without her hands shaking, but she isn't old enough to, you know, die from falling over.

I text Maggie on the bus:

On my way to the hospital. Annie's had a fall. Don't know what this means. Think it's bad? Terrified it's my fault?? Isn't it my job to make sure things like this don't happen???

I unzip my coat and rub a patch of condensation from the window to see if we're close. I haven't been to a hospital in London before, but I've heard stories. Not great ones, either.

I get off the bus and cross a narrow car park to the main entrance, which is all concrete on the outside and shiny, wash-down walls on the inside. A receptionist points me in the direction of the geriatric ward and as soon as I start walking away, I forget which '-ology' department I was meant to turn left at. Eventually, an auxiliary takes pity on me studying the hospital map and escorts me to the third floor, leaving me at a curved reception desk. It's a place of contrasts: a bunch of daffodils on a Formica table top below a poster for norovirus; a nurse gossiping with a phone tucked into his chest whilst an elderly man ambles down the corridor, shouting incoherently at a calm Malaysian nurse. All the chairs around me could be pissed or bled on without worrying about stains. It's all plastic and pleather.

'Um, hi,' I say to the nurse behind the desk. 'I'm here to see a patient. She was brought in earlier. Annie? Annie De Loutherberg?'

'One second,' he replies, almost before I've finished speaking. I stand there for another couple of minutes, unconvinced that his frantic typing on the computer is anything to do with what I've just asked. I wait a little longer and glance at the clock behind him.

'Is she here? The lady downstairs told me this is where

212

she would be?' He slowly drags his eyes to meet mine and flicks me another smile.

'That's what I'm looking up,' he says in a monotone. Crikey. I don't dare move, in case he sees it as a deliberate act of provocation. 'Two-one-three,' he says, moving to pick up the phone, which rings again.

'Is that the room? Which direction? Sorry, I know I'm asking lots of questions,' I add, even though I'm not sure exactly what part of hospital etiquette I'm getting wrong here.

'Two-one-three. It's behind you?' he says, swivelling back round on his chair to wipe a name off a whiteboard attached to the back wall. Sure enough, a door behind me opens onto a small ward, with half a dozen beds inside. At the end, looking out of the window with her hands interlocked in her lap, is Annie. I walk into the room and stop at the end of her bed. I can't help it. My face scrunches up before I can even say hello and I cover my eyes. I feel guilty and embarrassed and ashamed and now I'm worrying if my breath smells like the vodka screwball I drank two hours ago.

'What's this, love? Come on, come here. What're you about?' I blink up at the ceiling and wipe my eyes on the sleeve of my jumper. Annie holds a hand above the bed sheets, so I reach out and take it, sitting on the edge of a high-backed chair.

'I'm so sorry, Annie. About tonight. I should have remembered I was doing dinner. I forgot and there's no

213

good reason for it. I should have been there. I shouldn't have left you to go out in the dark. I was so distracted because of this stupid dating thing that everything else got knocked out of my head. Honestly, I'm so, so sorry.' I can feel the thick bands of Annie's chunky rings run across my hand as she coaxes me into silence. A fat tear rolls off my chin and onto my jumper. A bruise, deep mauve and angry, has spread from Annie's cheekbone to her right eyebrow, seeping in bloodshot threads across her eye.

'Stop with that. It's not your fault. I don't want you going around blaming yourself. It were soggy blossom, love. I went to cross the road and couldn't see the bloody kerb for all the mulch that's there. I went at them at the council for the same thing last year, and do they do anything? Pffff.' She taps my hand and chuckles, but it turns into a wheeze that sounds like her lungs emptying. I push her pillows further down behind her back to prop her up. 'Bloody gas they gave me in the ambulance. Dries your insides up, it does.' She looks over me. 'Your makeup looked nice before you cried it all off.' Now it's my turn to laugh, and with it the knot in my stomach loosens.

'Yeah, well. It wasn't horrendous, but I wouldn't repeat the experience.'

'Poor lad. I wouldn't let him hear that review.'

'No, but he might end up reading it by the time I've written about "the date experience" for our website. I'll just have to lie. Try and put a positive spin on it. The good thing is he was so drunk to begin with he kept missing the golf ball, so I won. If you abandon a game halfway through, but you were in the lead, that counts as winning, doesn't it?'

'You left him high and dry?'

'Well, I don't think he was high, but he *definitely* wasn't dry. I left as soon as I heard about you.' My voice catches and I bite my lip to stop myself crying again.

'Look, Elissa,' Annie says, impatiently. 'We're doing all right, you and me. But I don't need to be followed around with a crash mat.' She catches me as my gaze flickers onto her bruise, and scowls. 'Do you know what I would have done if you hadn't been living with me for the past month? Getting me outside and printing recipes off the internet? I wouldn't have left the house, love. I would have had a brew and maybe a digestive, if there were one. But I wouldn't have eaten, not properly. And I might not have next morning, neither. I know that a bash on the hip and a bruised face is a bit of a pain, but I'd rather feel like I can do something as simple as get up and go to the shop when I want some dinner than sit at home clock-watching and feeling sorry for myself. Do I need to say it again, sausage?' Annie squeezes my fingers when I don't look up from my lap. 'This weren't your fault. I know I look like the devil's arsehole, but I feel better than I have done in years. Up here.' She taps her temple.

'Language!' a snooty voice barks from behind a paper curtain.

'Oh, bore off,' Annie mutters, winking at me.

I lift the bits I've packed for Annie out of the bag, placing

215

her face cream and flannel on the table. The teabags and cake are heavily side-eyed by the other oldies in the room.

'When'll you be out?'

'Not sure. Not long, I expect. They'll need the bed.'

'Well, I'll make sure I'm home when you're released.'

'Discharged, love.'

'Yeah, that.' I tuck the carpet bag under the bed, careful not to hook it over any handles, buttons, or levers that could unexpectedly catapult her out. I wonder whether to bring up the letters. If I say nothing but she notices something has changed, it'll surely be worse. I'll play it down.

'Oh, I had to go in your room to pick up a couple of bits. I left in a hurry, but I'll tidy up the drawers and put everything back in the right order.'

'Put what in the right order, love?' Annie asks, raising a wobbling cup of water to her mouth.

'Oh, some envelopes and bits. The drawer was a bit sticky, so—'

'You leave them for me, okay? I'll sort it. It's not a bother. You've been such a help, Elissa, just leave the room for when I'm back, all right?' Her voice has a slight edge to it, so I don't say anything else until the nurse comes in a few seconds later to steer me out for the night.

Back at Evergreen, I stop at the porter's gate to tell Nigel that it'll just be me at number seven for the next couple of days. After suggesting the word 'flapjack' for a mobile Scrabble game he's got going with his mum in Nigeria, I plod around the green to Annie's front gate.

Seeing lamplight through the kaleidoscopic stained glass in the late-night darkness makes me realise how much has happened since I left this morning. I step inside, pull the chain across the door, and lean against it. My head is thick and heavy with tiredness.

As I go upstairs, I pause at the entrance to her bedroom. It's worse than I remember. Paper is scattered all over the carpet and the pile I stacked on the duvet has toppled over, some letters open, having fallen out of envelopes grown loose and flimsy with age. If I lay them all out on the bed with the dates facing up and scoop those out from under the bed, I can put them in the right order again and Annie won't have to know just how many I've seen. I glance over the pages to check that the handwritten date matches the front of the envelope, but when I see the phrase, 'kiss the photograph you enclosed' my heart jumps and I'm torn between a desperate urge to read more and to fold it up like I never touched it in the first place. I feel a bit dirty, like I've seen Annie's underwear drawer.

I know I've been sitting reading for an inappropriately long time at the point when my foot grows hypersensitive from being tucked under my bum. I rub the sole and wince as the feeling comes back, sharp and prickly. Some of the notes are quickly dashed off and journal-like. Others made me blush. Hands in hair, lost buttons, torn stockings. No, this is definitely too much now. It doesn't seem to make sense when I think about the man Annie's described as her husband – the austere, old-fashioned academic who barked at her for serving dinner too late, or didn't come back to eat it at all.

I run my finger over the deep folds of the letter. Hang on ... I'm sure Annie's husband was called Arthur. I open another of the letters, this one from 1976. Again, there at the bottom, is the initial 'H' followed by a singular kiss.

I sit back against the bed and look around at the room: a single crime magazine on the bedside table, quilted jacket on a hook, mirror, lamp, and magnolia bedsheets. On the wall, a framed picture of a poppy-strewn field looks sun-bleached and overlooked. It could belong to anyone, really. The letters around my feet? They tell a different story. It's a relic, that's for sure, of a life that sings with experience. So, where did it go?

218

Chapter Twenty-One

Bismah and Rhea accost me as soon as I walk through the doors, taking my bag and yanking my coat off my shoulders as they fire questions at me about the date last night. Honestly, it's like I've been asked out by the first in line to the Lichtenstein throne, not a banker from Berkshire who has a turbulent relationship with his father. I'm decidedly vague about the details, which seems to be enough to knock them off the scent of failure.

Throughout the morning, I schedule a thread of tweets about the date that'll go out tonight, as though it was happening live. We had discussed the option of posting in real time, but decided it might have been a bit odd to keep nipping off to update my social media. 'Inauthentic', Mitchell called it. Unlike what I'm doing now, which is fine. I've omitted any features that are specific to David, so what I'm essentially writing is a fantasy retelling of a golfing date with a charming but subdued entrepreneur, who demonstrated a zest for life and a 'go-getter' personality.

My mind is half-focused on my tweets and half on the letters that I, admittedly, read a few more of last night. Dylan Thomas would struggle to come up with better affirmations of love than 'H' in his letters to Annie. 'H' can't be Annie's husband, the academic who, from what I can gather, patronised and belittled her into giving up a career in engineering. A phrase that I read last night flits round my head: 'I go to bed exhausted, but my heart is conscious of you always.' Surely this isn't the Arthur who wouldn't let her eat a bloody bourbon without making a snide comment? I stare at my screen, brow furrowed.

#LovrLive I'm winning golf! Who knew my perfect sporting environment is neon bulbs, fake vegetation, and poorly mixed cocktails!

If you think about it, why would Arthur be writing letters to Annie when they lived together? I mean, Annie has talked about his work at the university and the weeks he'd spend in archives up and down the country, but he doesn't seem the type to describe her hair as 'sunset woven strands'. I shouldn't have memorised the phrases, but they're stuck in my head like song lyrics I can't shake.

'So,' says Rhea, perching on the edge of my desk. She has a 'business' dress on that's so tight I can see her hip bones poking through the fabric. I can't remember the last time I saw mine. Maybe I'll give up pastries for Lent this year.

Rhea folds her arms. 'David messaged. Said you ditched

him.' She doesn't give me any sign that she's annoyed, embarrassed, or impressed by this information, so I just nod in confirmation. Rhea pinches the bridge of her nose and closes her eyes. I'll go with 'annoyed', then. She lowers her voice to a hissy whisper: 'Look, if this campaign is going to give us any traction, you can't leave halfway through a date, Elissa!' She glances over her shoulder in the direction of Mitchell's office. 'We've got to turn all this'—she waves her hands in my direction like an amateur magician—'into content for our users. They need to see that you're getting something out of it. Isn't that what you said? And bailing halfway through doesn't exactly inspire confidence.'

'I know. I'm sorry, it wasn't because of him, or the golf,' I add, lamely. Rhea pushes her ponytail over one shoulder and folds her arms.

'Well, you'd better stick around for the next one, okay? The guy's all lined up, but I've had to pull some serious strings at the O2 Arena and we're using a fair bit of what little capital we have left to—'

'You don't need to, Rhea. I've got the date sorted.'

'You have?'

I nod furiously. By 'sorted' I mean 'will sort', because I can't let this campaign fall any further from my original idea. At this rate, it'll look like every other novelty night out advertised in Friday's *Metro* supplement. Yes, last night was a disaster, but I've got to step up now, because I can't bear the thought of admitting to Annie that I let someone else take credit for my idea and then pulp and pound it into something I don't recognise.

'Yeah, there's this charity thing in Mayfair. I'll send you the details in the week.' That's it, Elissa. Keep it nice and vague so you don't have to describe a non-existent date.

'Well, you better let me know soon, because I'll need to tell Oliver. Or Niko. I haven't decided yet.'

'Any chance I can choose them this time?' Rhea makes a noise partway between a goose honking and air leaving a balloon.

'No. Not with something this important. I've got your profile, anyway, that's more than enough to work with.'

'You wrote my profile.'

'Look.' Rhea twists her hand, inspecting an immaculate French manicure. 'You do the venue and I'll find the man.' Coming from someone shagging Mitchell, who looks like the love child of Steve Jobs and a chicken egg, this doesn't fill me with hope. 'Anyway, there's a potential new investor in today, so if they ask you about the new app, say that it's going really well and throw in the word "community" a lot. I know Rodney's still working on the coding for the new matching algorithm, but they don't need to know that it's essentially me making the decisions at the moment. Got it?' She squeezes my forearm and for a moment I think she's going to give me a Chinese burn, but instead she laughs and flashes me a smile so toothy I can see her invisible braces.

'Got it.'

As Rodney finishes sticking loose cables to the skirting

board with masking tape, Mitchell bursts through the door, laughing and slapping the back of a man in a crisp open shirt and light grey blazer, followed by two others.

Bismah springs up and stands beside her desk, hands clasped behind her back as though she's about to meet the queen, whereas Rodney has wheeled the whiteboard half a foot to the side, which is the closest he's come to greeting a stranger. Mitchell jogs into the workspace and the others follow the line of his arm as he motions towards each of us. Rhea nods, arms crossed, and Bismah holds out a hand even though they're much too far away to shake it. Adam brings up the rear of the group, wearing suit trousers, a T-shirt, and sockless boat shoes. Ah, he's tried. I refresh our Twitter feed and try to look focused and purposeful, but a clip of a racoon attacking a broom starts playing and I slip into a goofy smile.

'Working hard?' a voice says from behind. I exit the browser with lightning speed, but it wasn't quick enough. Grey blazer man is smirking at me from the air hockey table and I feel warmth rush into my cheeks from the pit of my stomach.

'Haha, yeah, it's research. I'm looking for a way to—' I pause and lean forward. 'Hang on, we've met, haven't we?' Chiselled jawline. Soft eyes. Cropped hair.

'How's the training going?' he asks, slipping his hands into his pockets, smiling.

'Heath man! Er, man from the Heath. You got me some water,' I garble.

223

'I did,' he says. 'Nice to see you again.' Thank God I'm in normal clothes today. I tap my cheeks to see if they've returned to a normal colour and they burn under my fingertips. Ah, still as red as the last time we met. Wonderful.

'I haven't seen you about. Are you still running?' He glances down at his shoes and scuffs them softly against the carpet. Has he been looking out for me?

'Yeah, yeah, but I got an injury. In my leg. So, I've been more into swimming recently,' I lie.

'Swapped the Heath for the ponds?'

'Yeah, something like that.'

'You and Theo know each other?' I swivel my chair back round to face Mitchell, who's resting his forearms across the top of my computer screen. He's joined by the other investors, who now hover around my desk.

Theo jumps in. 'A bit. We've spotted each other running.' Crikey, he's being very generous.

'Running, Elissa? You've kept that one quiet, haven't you! You should be out there with The Butcher Works Run Club! We like seeing our employees getting involved in the social side of a community work space,' Mitchell says over his shoulder to the crowd. 'Rhea over here never misses a week, do you, sweetheart?' he adds, as Rhea pushes through the doors with a plate of fruit in one hand and macarons in the other. Theo's eyes widen at the comment and he turns to look out of the window. Honestly, when you hear it so often, it's mad how much of Mitchell's throwaway sexism becomes white noise.

224

Laughing and entirely oblivious, Mitchell steers the group away from my desk and stands with his hands in his pockets, his gaze tracing Rhea from behind as she arranges the lunch nibbles. Disturbingly, this public perve must have triggered a thought about me, because he turns on his heel just as Theo leans down to speak in my ear.

'Oh, nearly forgot! Elissa is our social media manager, but she's also heading up the trial for the app's rebranding. We're taking beta testing to another level here. I tell you, if you want anyone's job here, fellas,' says Mitchell, ignoring the two women stood either side of Theo, 'it's Elissa's.'

'Why's that, then?' asks Theo. His eyes are green, cat-like, and bright. I swear it's impossible to look good under fluorescent strip lighting, but somehow he manages it.

'Well ...' Mitchell rubs his hands together as though he hadn't expected anyone to ask. 'Elissa isn't only on the team here at Lovr, she's one of our users too.' Noises of curiosity come from the group and I swear I lose the ability to use two senses at once. I'm concentrating so hard on the blinking cursor of an empty blog post that all I can hear is a rushing noise throbbing in my ears. A hard rapping of knuckles on my desk breaks the feeling that a high-pressured balloon is about to burst beneath my rib cage.

'When's the next lucky bloke getting a chance for an "experience" with Elissa?' *Oh God.* Not only has he used air quotes for 'experience', but he's addressing me in the third person.

'Er, Saturday. Yep, I'm pretty sure it's Saturday. I'll have to check the app. All the details will be there,' I say, tilting the iPad up so the gang can't see that it's broken. Theo drifts to the back of the group, just out of Mitchell's eyeline, and rolls his eyes in mock scepticism, grinning. Is it that obvious I haven't planned anything yet? He's obviously seen through the defunct iPad, but he also seems ... on my side? Great for me, terrible for the pantomime that Lovr is attempting to perform.

'Okay, folks. We'll take lunch upstairs in the Cleaver Room. Leave these guys to hold the fort. Rhea, get Rodders to help you carry the plates. Make sure to take him on the outside staircase, though. The little fella could do with seeing the sunlight at least once today.' Mitchell laughs and shakes his head, leading out the group, who are tittering along a lot less enthusiastically than they were earlier.

I spend the afternoon in a distracted haze, in which I attempt to write a blog post for the site. Fifty per cent is exaggerated and 50 per cent underplayed to try and level out my ultimately disastrous date with David. I could have had it finished in time for a good read around the 'Love & sex' section of the *Guardian* website before I head to back to Hampstead, but every time someone passes the glass doors I nearly pull a muscle flicking my head round in the hope that Theo will come past.

Ultimately, it's pointless. I know his type. I fancied someone like him at school – a guy who shared a packet of Maltesers with me under the table in Maths but laughed when I asked for his number. He *seems* nice, but the power

226

balance is all wrong. If he knows he's good-looking (which he must if he's ever looked in a mirror) he'll have a Rolodex of girls he's talking to, ones with eyelash extensions who holiday in Bali. I won't register on the league table.

With Mitchell elsewhere in the building, I pack up just before five and step into the stream of commuters heading down Clerkenwell Road. A voice message pops up on my phone. It can only be from Suki. She constantly fires them off, and not always to the right person. I've had more than one message so explicit my morning coffee turned sour.

I plug my earbuds in, careful not to fall out of step with the silicon roundabout workers. Her voice kicks in: '*No, I never said that. Tomorrow night? Baby, come on. I didn't know she was going to be the flippin' instructor, did I?*' There's a pause as a woman's shrill voice filters through, obscured by fabric rustling and soft, soothing words that are clearly failing to de-escalate the nameless woman's anger. '*It was my form! I've never been good at the downward dog. Well, not in certain situations ... Babe! It was a joke! Babe!*' A pause. '*Hi! Sorry, about that. Jazz just flipped her shit. She's stormed off somewhere, but she'll be back. Pffff, women, eh? What was I gonna say? The auction! Next week! You're coming, right? You can bring Annie if you want, but if you fancy a night off, that's cool. The bar's open from 6, so I'll meet you there. It's got a fancy dress-code, so a tie, or dress, or some shit like that. Pain in the arse, but dem's the rules. See you then!*'

Suki might be able to seamlessly switch between pop-up

227

bars in Hoxton and drinks receptions on the Google campus, but I'm not like that. She can turn up, find three or four people she pretends to know, and five minutes later they're swapping numbers and taking selfies in the toilets.

As fun as it is, something about the event sits a bit awkwardly with me. The idea of watching the eye-wateringly wealthy residents of West London fling more money at artwork than I'll ever earn in my life will do that to you. I'm trying not to be cynical. Apparently, the gallery donates the commission fees to charity, but I'm sceptical as to whether that's the real reason behind the event, or whether it's because the publicity they get from one night of overblown extravagance means they don't have to be nice to poor people for another year.

Chapter Twenty-Two

'Why don't you bring this new bloke to the auction?' says Annie. I peel the lid off a strawberry yoghurt and slide the pot across the table on Annie's bed.

'I can't. Rhea just sort of ... springs these things on me. If I had more time, I'd try and use some of the charity contacts I've been working on, but it's early days to get on the phone and say, "Oh, I know we only spoke yesterday, but is there anyone who needs a perennial border planting in your community?", you know?'

Annie side-eyes the patient in the bed next to her before licking the yoghurt lid. 'Terrible habit, but I can't stop now.' Her eye is less bloodshot than it was right after the accident, but her brow and cheekbone have bloomed bright purple from where she hit the kerb. 'I can't wait to get home. I knew this weren't going to be the Ritz, but I'm not sure how many more of these watery puddings I can take. I miss that lovely Greek stuff with the curd on top.'

'Spoken like a true Hampstead woman,' I say with a grin.

'Only by postcode,' she replies, licking strawberry puree

from her little finger. 'So, what are you going to do, love?' I lean back in the plastic-covered chair and puff my cheeks out. I've made enough difficult decisions in the past month to cover the next decade, surely. I don't know why, but choices have seemed so ... monumental recently. In the past I've kept my head down, because at least if something went wrong, it can't have been my fault.

'Look, I'm not going to pretend that I know how your job works,' Annie continues, 'but fancying someone has been around since time immemorial and so has the idea of doing good deeds for those who ain't got as much as we 'ave. Stop over-thinking it, love. You can spend too much time wondering about the whats and wherefores, then before you know it, time's moved on and you've lost your chance.' I look up, not quite sure if Annie's still talking about my upcoming date. What is she going on about? 'People are different. They want different things. See different things as being right or wrong.' Annie folds an empty muffin case into a triangle and smooths out the edges with her thumb.

Now, I could be wrong, but I've overheard enough episodes of *The Archers* round Nanny's house to know when someone is talking in double-entendres. The more I've thought about Annie's box of illicit letters, the more confident I am that her tangents about Arthur the Abominable Shit and 'life's second chances' are directly related to 'H'. The language, the writing, the passion ... it just doesn't add up. There's isn't even a photograph of her and Arthur in her house. If there was, I'm sure he'd be scrawny and milky white with a waxed moustache and mean little eyes. So, who is 'H'?

Even though I've been with Annie for nearly a month, I barely know anything about her past. Every time I mention her son or ask her about what it was like to move down to London in the Sixties, she only ever answers as 'we', never 'I'. I'll work on it, when she's back home. It would eat you up, having to bury something like that for so long. I don't know how she does it. I once stole a pair of earrings from a multipack of studs in Topshop and the guilt still plagues me today.

'You're right. Of course.' I tap my toes together and the chunky rubber soles of my boots thud rhythmically.

'I'm only right because I've seen and done all the wrongs before,' says Annie, folding her hands into her lap. 'Oh, one thing love. Can you see if Julie can come round next week to do my hair? I look like a choir boy whose dangly bits haven't dropped. No mirrors up round here, but I can see why.'

I swing my rucksack over one shoulder and tuck a *Gardener's World* magazine underneath her pillow. 'Oh, George asked after you. Margaret didn't say anything, but she sort of ... nodded when I said you'd be back in a couple of days, so that's good, right?'

'Oh, right. That's nice,' she says with a furrowed brow. 'We haven't said much to each other for – Christ – must be years now. George has always been kind. He's done a good few favours for me in t' past. Thought it rude to stop with paper swapping now, since Arthur died, though I don't think too much of the paper he buys. I still collect them off George at the gate in t' garden. Another old habit. Arthur didn't like him coming in the house when he were out.'

'What was wrong with George coming over when Arthur wasn't about?' Annie blankly smiles and looks ahead, her focus on the middle distance.

'I don't suppose I remember.'

***

I'm sure I've had more messages in the past two hours than I have in the past two years. I'm going to have to move onto a different price plan at this rate. Earlier, when I drained the saucepan of boiled noodles, peas, and sweet chilli sauce, a little emoji of a hand waving appeared as a Lovr notification on my phone along with

Hey, it's Freddie

I checked all the doors were locked and window latches shut before I risked looking at my phone again. It's only the second time I've slept home alone in the past decade, so naturally I'm on high alert for robberies and abductions. Or creepy Craig popping up at the kitchen window – the more likely scenario. Seconds later, my phone pings again:

Sorry, should have made it clear! Rhea (your colleague?) has told me about the app and it sounds great. Looking forward to meeting the brains behind it all.

Oh, and he's finished it off with a winking emoji. That's suggestive, isn't it?

It's pushing ten o'clock and I've moved from the kitchen to the living room, where I've slipped so far down the sofa that my boobs have formed a shelf of sorts, against which I've propped my phone. David Attenborough's breathy narration on an old episode of *Blue Planet* has a hypnotic effect on my already overtired eyes, and, after nodding off for a third time, I look at my phone to see if Freddie has messaged again. Somehow, I manage to swipe the camera on and the sight is like an injection of caffeine at the back of my eyeballs. Bloody hell. My own quadrupled chin appears on the screen below my incredibly oily nose and a helmet of spiral curls pushed low over my forehead from the tracksuit hood I've pulled tight around my head. I need to get to bed.

I swing myself off the sofa and manage to drop my phone as a painful twinge runs up my spine from the awkward position I've been in for the past hour. Fuck, is this what being in your late twenties is like? Or maybe it's living in a house with winged armchairs and rails around the bath; you start assimilating half a century too soon. I bend over slowly, half expecting my back to spasm again, and my phone buzzes, making my stomach lurch.

Freddie seems ... normal? The dozen or so messages that we'd sent back and forth hadn't flooded me with fear or made me want to flush my phone down the loo, which is a novelty for me. He works for a company that organises corporate away days, he looks after his grandparents' dog now they're both in an old folks' home, and he isn't vegan. Too good to be true? I switch the lights and sockets off downstairs and put my phone on a shelf in the medicine cabinet whilst I scoop my hair up into a bun. A message appears on the screen.

Ha! Good one!

What does that mean? What was a good one? I miss my toothbrush and a globule of toothpaste drops into the sink. Oh. No. No, no, no, no, FUUUUCCCKKK! I fumble at the screen and let out a deep, low moan, like a heifer giving birth. Somehow, I've sent Freddie a picture of my own face – or that's what it might be – if it didn't look like a close up of someone's wrinkled thumbprint. I drop my phone in the sink. How could it betray me like this?! I pace the bathroom tiles. I think I might be sick. Another buzz reverberates around the sink and my phone vibrates closer to the plughole. This has got to be a joke. After the golfing abandonment of last week, the idea of writing up a date that's cancelled before it's taken place because my slumping, fatigued face has offended Freddie isn't something I can contemplate right now. I jab at the screen through squinting eyes and when I catch what's there, I lean in closer. Surely not. He's sent a picture back: an upward shot of a cross-eyed, sandy-haired man with dark eyebrows, a broad, prickly chin, and a mouth pulled wide in an incredibly unflattering gurn. Underneath, a message:

Would be rude not to join in.

I get into bed still staring at the screen. Am I in some alternate universe? Of all the possible reactions, this hadn't crossed my mind. In a way, it's worse. Now I have to come up with some sort of response. God, this is stressful. The more time I let elapse, the more awkwardness settles in. *Come on, Elissa, think!* I need something witty, casual, and possibly a little self-deprecating. Before I can think on it any longer, I type out:

It's like reverse catfishing. A face-to-face meeting can only be an upgrade!

I send it, and switch my phone off for the night. Annie's going to crease when I tell her about this tomorrow.

Chapter Twenty-Three

I had a call from the hospital to say that Annie would be home this evening, so I've given the house a once around with the hoover and tidied away the letter explosion from her bedroom floor. I was incredibly self-restrained and I only glanced over two or three more chosen at random from thirty years' worth of dated envelopes. The more I read, the more certain I am that the love she had from 'H' is what she'd hoped to get from her marriage to Arthur. It makes me feel so incredibly sad for Annie and a tiny, weeny bit sad for myself. H's letters (okay, I may have had a *very* quick look at the rest) are beautiful and raw and poetic and make my last Valentine's card from Tom seem utterly vanilla in comparison. There was no 'I want to carve your name in trees' from him, that's for sure.

In the past week, the days have grown deliciously long and balmy. I'd forgotten what it's like to have proper evenings, as opposed to ones where you come home late and go to bed early for want of something to do. I prop my chin on my knee and look for signs of the hospital minibus from the front step. Closing my eyes, I let the last of the sunshine bloom behind my eyelids in tones of pink and deep orange.

'Evening, Elissa!' I blink at a tall, broad figure blocking the sunshine. When I recognise who it is, I jump up to greet him. I go for a handshake (I'm not sure why. There's something about his Fifties newsreader accent that makes me come over all formal) and lean against the garden wall.

'George! How are you?'

'Keeping well, thank you! Lovely evening to be outside.'

'Yeah, it is. I'm waiting for Annie, actually. She's due home soon.'

'Ah, wonderful, wonderful,' he says, rocking back and forth on the balls of his feet. Despite the warmth, George is wearing a long-sleeved shirt, a woollen vest, and a navy tie pulled up high beneath his chin. He holds his hands behind his back and glances over his shoulder towards his house, four doors down from Annie's.

'I did actually pop over with a bit of a favour to ask, if you didn't mind, of course.'

'Oh, sure! Fire away, sir!' I hold my smile for a little too long out of embarrassment that I've just called George 'sir', but he doesn't seem to notice, what with all the fidgeting and feverish glances.

'It's Margaret, you see. I'm afraid I'm not in her good books at the moment.'

At the moment? Every time I see her, she's frowning or snapping at him for not clipping the right bit of bush, or

237

for eating the wrong biscuit with his tea. I can't imagine her without furrows in her forehead.

'Our little dog – you remember him? Aurelius, his name is. Well, I let him out in the garden, you see, and he had rather a good time digging up Margaret's bulbs. Ate half of them too. Can't think why. He gets lean beef mince for his dinner. Anyway, they're a special variety of tulip that we brought back from Amsterdam and I'd really like to replace them.' George takes out a linen handkerchief from his trouser pocket and dabs his forehead. 'Except, I can't find a shop that sells the little buggers, so ... I was wondering if you might assist me with the *internet*,' says George, emphasising the word as if it's a mysterious place he's never been.

'Oh! Right! Of course, George. I can do that. I'll get my phone and we can look it up now if you like. There isn't much you can't get online.'

'Oh, um, not right this second. Margaret's in the bath.'

'Okay,' I say slowly, not really sure what that's got to do with it.

'The thing is, what I'd really appreciate is some help getting *on* the line. I know they say you can't teach an old dog new tricks, but Derek at Bridge Club uses the internet for a whole host of things. He even told me –' George leans in and shields his mouth '– that he watches cricket on the loo.' He chuckles and clasps his hands across his round belly.

'Well, I could come by after work tomorrow?'

'No, no ...' says George, flapping his handkerchief, 'the weekend, if you're able.'

I don't hesitate before saying yes, which feels odd, but nice. My usual habit involves scrolling through a mental list of excuses. Not today.

'Margaret will be up in Hertfordshire with Rosemary, our daughter. Two sets of twins. All boys. Need the occasional wrangling. Aurelius doesn't travel well, so I'm staying behind. Shame, really,' George says, in a way that implies he has no shame at all. 'Anyway, as always, it's been a delight.' He nods his head to me and I just about refrain from curtseying.

As I turn to leave, Nigel appears around the corner with Annie on one arm and her carpet bag hanging off the other. George gives her a wave and lingers, teetering on the balls of his feet, until Annie reaches us.

'Heard about your fall! Nasty stuff. Glad to see you up and about again. It doesn't look that bad, you know,' says George, pointing to his own face in a circular motion. He's lying. Annie looks awful. Her bruise looks dabbed on, it's so broad and dark.

'Yes, well. It looks worse than it is,' says Annie, as I take her bag from Nigel. 'Hi, love,' she says to me, blinking back up at George, as though anticipating he'll leave.

'Oh, George was just saying about his grandchildren. Four boys! Yours are boys, aren't they, Annie?' I say, step-ping to the side to form a small circle as she turns to walk past us into the house.

'Are they, now?' says George, his lip twitching with delight underneath a curtain of combed moustache hair. 'I didn't know you had any!'

'Yes, well, they live in Australia, so ... that'd be why.'

'Oh. That's a bugger,' says George. There's an awkward pause, made worse when George decides to whistle through his teeth.

'Let's get you in. I've got samosas to go with our tea,' I say, my cheeks straining from the effort of smiling away the tension.

'As you were,' he says, heading back along the path with his chin tucked into his chest.

Chapter Twenty-Four

Saturday morning starts early with a chorus of birdsong. Far too early. The single-pane sash window in my room, although beautiful (my Instagram feed will attest to this), does very little to block out noise. It's like the birds are right inside the room, singing their horny love songs down my earhole. I groan and look at my phone. 6.13 a.m. I get up, lean on the windowsill and watch the world come into focus. Annie is sitting at the little garden table, steam billowing from a china cup, her fleece jacket zipped up to the top. On the table, one of 'H"s letters lies open before her. I sit back a little, worried that she'll spot me peeping from upstairs, but going by the look on her face I doubt she'd notice if it started pissing down with rain.

This is the first time she's ventured out of the house since returning from hospital. I was worried that it was because she was scared of slipping over again, but she claims she doesn't want people staring at her bruise, which is now mustard-coloured and still looks bloody painful. 'Honestly,' she'd said, 'last week I looked like I'd been knocked about and this week it's like my liver's packed in, I'm so bloody yellow.' I told her about the unfortunate selfie incident over dinner and when I showed her the picture, she actually spluttered a mouthful of fajita back onto the plate. She agrees that Freddie seems nice, if 'a bit hairy' for her liking. Yesterday, he messaged just to say, 'Good morning.' Imagine! Tom barely messaged when he was in Vegas, and even then, I was the unintended recipient. I was hoping that showing Annie some of Freddie's messages might encourage her to talk a little more about Arthur, or 'H', but so far she hasn't mentioned anything. I might have to schedule in some tactical probing.

I'm already anticipating a disco nap before the charity auction tonight, but for now I put on a big hoodie and head downstairs. Annie is coming in from the garden as I walk into the kitchen and she quickly slides the envelope into the pocket of her fleece when she spots me.

'You're up early, love,' she says, smoothing a hand across her chest where the letter sits.

'It's the birds. Didn't have this problem in Stockwell. Actually, I did, but it was mainly football chants from outside the Irish bar.' Annie sits down at the scrubbed wooden table and starts writing a list in swooping cursive. Nanny had nearly identical handwriting. It must have been the way they were taught at school. When my generation reach pensioner status, I wonder if we'll use nostalgic emojis instead. It's like reverse progression; we're heading back to hieroglyphics.

'Fancy scones for lunch? I think I might try and pop to the shops today,' Annie says, her bottom lip pulled in.

'Are you sure? I can come with you.'

'No, no, that's all right love. I'd like to try and go by myself. I've got to do it one day, haven't I? I don't want to end up like I was before, looking for reasons not to go out.'

'Well, if you're sure. But take your phone with you, just in case, okay?'

'All right, Mum,' Annie replies with a wry smile. 'You've got to get ready for tonight, anyhoo.'

'Yeah, I suppose so.'

'You don't sound too excited.'

'I am. I think I am. It might be a laugh, but you know, Freddie ... I don't want to end up doing something stupid in front of him. And I've got to try and do something with this,' I say, pulling a frizzy corkscrew curl straight until it pings back again. I'd forgotten to wear my silk wrap last night before I went to sleep and, as much as I loved Tom Hanks in *Castaway*, I don't want to embody the stranded-on-a-desert-island vibe.

Annie puts her pen down and drums the table with her fingertips as though she's tapping the keys of a piano. 'When I was seventeen, going on eighteen, a few of us used to go round Eileen's to do our hair and the like, for dances down at the town hall. Hours, it used to take. We'd fumigate the place with hairspray,' she tells me. 'Bouffants were in, back then. It's no wonder Eileen went down with lung cancer, in the end. Well, it were that or the chain smoking. Eggs,' she continues without pause, adding it to the list.

'Is that where you met Arthur? At a dance?'

'Arthur? No, we met at the university. In the canteen. I didn't used to eat there often, but Thursday was pie day. Worth saving the bus money for.'

'And did you go on, like, proper dates?'

'I suppose they were, of sorts. We'd go to dances together and to the pub, with his friends usually. He came to ask my father if he had permission to take me out, you know. He was quite traditional in that sense. But not romantic. He didn't like coming around mine much, for Sunday dinner or owt. I thought he liked taking me out – hotels, restaurants, or little pubs in Derbyshire, but ...' Annie pauses and rolls her tongue round the inside of her cheek. 'He were just a bloody snob,' she finishes, spitting the words out. That's confirmed a few suspicions.

'Didn't he ever ... send you a Valentine's card, or anything like that?'

Annie snorts. 'No, he never. He'd have his secretary phone me up with dinner reservations, but no. He'd more likely write an Ode to Joan of Arc, or Lady Godiva— Shit, Elissa!' I jump, squeezing the bottle of honey in my hands too hard and sending it in an arc across the worktop. I've pushed her too far. I need to let it go. She's clearly distressed by me bringing up the past like this.

'I'm sorry, Annie, it's just—'

'Morning, ladies!' says Creepy Craig, inching around the

244

corner as he clips a ring of keys back into a belt loop. I stare at the ceiling, wishing I'd put a bra on before coming downstairs.

'Craig. Bit early for rounds, isn't it?' says Annie, folding her arms. I take a noisy bite of my toast and fold my arms too.

'The early bird catches the worm, as they say.' He chuckles and smooths down his greasy fringe with the palm of his hand. What's he really trying to catch, though? A peek at someone undressing? 'I put you right at the top of my list when I found out about your little fall. Someone's got to make sure you're being looked after!'

'Elissa has been very helpful, thank you.'

'Well, she helpfully saw you to hospital, didn't she?' He titters, putting his hands on his hips. 'No more trying to bump the ladies off, miss!' says Craig, waggling a finger at me. God, I hope that's not what people think. 'I'll have to keep an eye on this one, won't I?' His eyes rock down my body and I feel like my insides are going to squirm up my throat and plop onto the floor.

'I don't think so, Craig. We're fine, aren't we, love?' I nod furiously. 'So you can be off. Don't want to hold you up.'

Craig splays a toad-like smile across his face and walks back towards the door. 'One last thing. Elissa, we'll need to do another suitability assessment, because of the ... incident.'

'I 'ardly think that's necessary!' says Annie, pulling herself to her feet.

245

'Oh, it is. You're far too important to us, Mrs De Loutherberg! We have to make sure you're being catered for adequately, on every level. Can't take any risks, can we? See you next week, ladies,' he says, closing the door so gently I can't tell if he's actually left the house.

'If I were stable enough to stand on one leg, I'd kick him in the bollocks!' says Annie. 'Don't think on it, love. He's a sod who gets a power trip from empty threats.' Annie's voice strains as she walks into the hallway, where I hear her slide the chain across and double-lock the front door. I smile weakly and pick at a thread on my sleeve. When I look up, she's standing in the doorway, cheeks tinged pink, the corners of her mouth sagging as she breathes deeply, mouth agape. 'Now, there's a rack in the front bedroom that I think you'd like to see.'

***

'Are you sure?'

'Well, unless I decide to dress up for the chiropodist next time he comes round, I doubt it'll be getting much use.'

I look down at the beaded dress draped over the bed and put my only pair of black heels on the floor next to them. Yeah, that'll work. In theory, anyway. I wiggled it on earlier, paranoid that my hips would pop the seams open, but once it was up and over my waist the zip pulled up easily, even though it was a little stiff from years hung beneath a plastic cover.

'I can't believe how many you've got.'

'Nothing drier than a drinks reception with medieval historians in whatever European city they descended on twice a year. I wasn't expected to do much other than ask after people's wives and look the part. I took the perks where I could.'

Annie's collection of vintage dresses is unreal. She must have forty or fifty gowns – frills, swooping necklines, tulle, and metallic brocade. An end to dinner dances forced them under plastic and into a spare wardrobe. Some even had the labels of designers I recognise (the list isn't long).

When Annie insists I borrow one for the auction tonight, I choose a teal mini dress with a sea-green overlay on the bodice that shimmers with tiny hand-stitched beads. It's enough, without being too much. Well, it's a *tiny* bit too much, but with scuffed shoes and loose hair to cover my shoulders, it's miles better than the old white bodycon dress I'd rediscovered this morning, tinged green in parts from spilt Sourz Apple.

Annie coos and tuts as I stand by the front door and flaps her hands about like an affectionate pigeon. I pull on my black woollen coat, zip it up, and look down with knitted brows. The boldly short Sixties hemline is completely hidden by my coat and, combined with my cloppy heels, I definitely look like I forgot to put on trousers.

***

247

After a day of slate-coloured skies and air thick with the threat of a downpour, the gilded streets of Mayfair break into sunshine so bright the birds start singing with renewed gusto as though the day's reset. I flick my hood up, even though I'm sweating slightly from the stickiness of the tube (where does all that hot wind come from?) and try and use tourists donned in rain ponchos as a modesty shield for my bare legs and heavy eyeliner. My chest thuds, partly from nerves and partly from the effort of staying upright. My calf muscles are screaming.

I get to the pub far too soon and hover outside, considering whether to walk around the block once more. It's only 6.03 and I don't want to seem overly keen. My phone buzzes. Here it is, the excuse I need to abandon ship and head to the gallery to start on Jägermeister shots at the free bar.

Freddie:

I'll be there in five mins.

Right. Five minutes. I can't walk around the block because I might bump into him and then it'd be awkward because I need a table, or at least the cover of darkness, to disguise my corned-beef legs and scruffy shoes.

In an effort not to be a loitering loser, I go inside, order a glass of wine, and perch at a table with a good view of the door. I unzip my coat to the waist and try to visualise what I look like from outside the window. I hope it's the image of a nonchalant woman comfortable with her own company rather than an anxious weirdo trying not to split the seams of a fifty-year-old dress. I haven't eaten anything for dinner and the further down the wine glass I get, the more my thighs feel fuzzy.

Fifteen minutes pass, and then another fifteen. I refuse to check my phone for messages, but make sure the sound is turned all the way up. I've left a finger of wine at the bottom of my glass so it doesn't get taken away by the bar staff, but after an hour, even they're giving me sympathetic looks.

I know I'm in the right place, because there are only two Unicorn and Hare pubs in the country and the other one is in Birmingham, so unless I've got this *really* wrong, he just hasn't turned up. Perhaps he's been hit by a train. Or twisted his ankle. Or got caught up saving a kitten from a drain. Or maybe he's just a bellend. I break my own rule and double check that my internet is working by sending an email to myself. Within seconds, the 'hello' I'd pinged off boomerangs back to me. God, this is a new low. The Lovr app hasn't crashed either.

The crowd in the pub has swollen and someone's arse pushes into my arm as the gaps between tables fill with pint-wielding men in their thirties. A number of televisions boot into life and there's a small cheer as two giant rugby commentators with lumpy ears appear on the screen. Right, this has to be my cue to leave. I open up the app to tap out a pithy response, but any sign of previous interaction has disappeared completely. Bloody Rodney and his weekend server maintenance ... I tip the last of the wine to the back of my throat and elbow my way outside, straining to listen as the dialtone kicks in. The call connects, but no one speaks.

'Hello?' I say, hearing the strain in my voice.

'Who is this?'

'Elissa. From work.'

'Oh. Yes. Why are you calling?'

'Are you doing something on the app? Some technical thing that means it's not working properly?'

'No. Not working today. On holiday. Margate.'

'Right, sorry, Rodney, I didn't realise.'

'What's wrong with the app?'

'It's a chat thread. I was using it, like, an hour ago. And now it's gone.'

'That only happens when a profile is deleted. Chat is deleted too.'

'But I haven't deleted my profile! It's still there!'

'Not you. The other user will have deleted their profile.'

'Oh. Right then.'

'I'm going now,' says Rodney.

He's bloody hung up on me. I breathe out a low, ragged breath and look up at the pigeon spikes lining the window frame of the pub. I turn around to face the wall, because if anyone asks me if I'm okay, I'll turn into a shaking mess of mucus and tears and I'd really rather avoid that if I can. My phone buzzes, and I stupidly feel a little flutter in my stomach before noticing it's Suki who's sent me a voice note: '*Where the*

fuck are you? Pull your knickers up and shift your fanny over here! There's a warm glass of prosecco with your name on it!'
She trails off to a chorus of shouting, whooping, and cackling.

***

'Oh, mate. That's brutal. What a cock! My cousin, I think you've met her once before, has the funny eye? Yeah, she got cloaked a few weeks ago. Twat said he was at the end of the road and then, poof! Deleted his account, blocked her all over social media, the lot! I don't know what the point of it all is, you know? To go that far and then pull back at the last minute. It makes you think, do they get a kick out of abandoning someone? The older I get, the more I think the world is full of weirdos and perverts.' Suki drains her glass, deftly swapping it with another as a roving waiter passes close by.

'Cloaking? Is that what it's called?'

'Like, Harry Potter? Invisibility cloak? Put it on and disappear? I know you're a Hufflepuff, babe, but I thought you'd know about that.'

'I haven't been ... by myself for that long!'

'Say it.'

'No.'

'Go on. It's delicious. It might even be my favourite word.'

I roll my eyes in mock exasperation and smile at Suki, who is wearing a suit better than any of the men's here. 'Single.'

'That's it. Look, dating isn't always easy. You know that grungy girl I was into last year? Might have been before

251

you started at Lovr. Anyway, I got the clap, didn't I?' I cough some of my prosecco back into my glass. 'Ha! All's good down there now, obviously. What the fuck was I trying to say?' Suki flicks her nose and takes a swig. 'Oh, yeah, basically, in the law of averages, at least half of the people you meet are shits, and men are the shittiest of all. So, you've avoided one today. Good! You've saved yourself from being dicked about by a manchild who won't commit until he's found a younger version of his own mother. Oh, look. There's Calum. Calum!' Suki calls over to a man with a small ponytail and a velvet jacket. 'He's a riot, swear down.'

Calum walks over with the air of a man unused to moving quickly for anyone.

'Calum, Elissa. Calum's into art. Bit of a collector, aren't you?' says Suki, grinning.

'Hardly. I end up here with work a fair bit. If you loiter long enough, they throw wine at you in the hope you're pissed enough to buy a canvas.'

'Yeah, can't say anything here's taken my fancy,' I say, turning to look at a piece hung beside me that I'm fairly sure contains real human hair, 'pissed or not.'

'Ah, it's all shit, isn't it? Art is something rich people buy in the hopes it'll make them seem more interesting. Saying that, I think I've got a work of art stood right in front of me.'

Oh, Jesus. Suki is standing just out of Calum's eyeline, which is lucky because she's bent double in a silent laugh, her eyes twinkling with strain. She gives me a thumbs-up and retreats through the crowd, leaving me with Calum.

'What is it that you do?' Ah, here we go.

'I'm a social media manager. For an app.'

'Ah, a MacBook-wielding Shoreditchian?'

'Not quite, no.' I force a laugh. If it's passing judgements he's after ... 'How about you? Art critic? Hedge fund executive?'

'Private investigator.'

'Oh.' He's stumped me there. 'That wasn't what I was expecting.'

'It never is.'

'What a cool job. *Really* cool, actually.'

'Ah, it's all right. Sometimes I'll get a brief that's got some meat in it, but most of my clients are husbands or wives seeking evidence of an affair. It's my bread and butter. I was in here tailing a guy who kept buying pieces that never turned up in the family home. Wife got a decent divorce payout, I get a good commission ... that's the job really.' Calum smacks his lips together like he's chugged through this story a hundred times before. 'Social media manager then. So ... you get paid to go on Twitter all day?' I don't attempt a rebuttal, because I've learnt by now that people aren't looking for an explanation, just enough proof that you don't work as hard as them.

'Yes, exactly. Twitter all day! I'm essentially Donald Trump!' I laugh at my own joke and am met with a pitying smile. I cough and drink the rest of my prosecco. 'A PI, though! Is it tough? Do you have to do, like, training or anything?'

'Not really. It's not as hard as it sounds. There's so much on the internet that as long as you've got a few key details, you can find pretty much everything you need. It's those ancestry websites. People are obsessed with logging names, dates, birth certificates ... They do half my job for me.'

I run my tongue along my top teeth and think. 'Hypothetically, if you wanted to find someone from, say, the Sixties, how easy would it be to locate them?'

'If they're dead, very easily. Death certificates are the easiest to find.'

'Oh, well, I'm hoping he's not. Dead, I mean.'

'Is this about some sort of absentee-daddy issue? Because I can do that, just not ... at a party, like.'

'No. It's not! It's a friend of a friend. They fell out of touch years ago.'

'You're very invested for a friend of a friend.'

'Well, I am, I suppose.'

'Look.' Calum pulls his wallet out of his back pocket, flips it open, and slides out a black business card with a phone number printed on the back in white. 'If you've got a full name and a previous address – home or work – you should be able to find out something useful. Whether they want to be found is a whole other issue.' He hands me the card between his first and second finger. The bravado makes me want to laugh. 'If all else fails, give me a call. I wouldn't want to make it too easy for you.' Calum winks, hooks my hand around his velvet-clad arm, and steers us back towards the bar.

Chapter Twenty-Five

'If you're gonna be sick, love, I can't take you.'

'Course she's not, are you, babe?' Suki says as she folds me into the back of a taxi and roughly pulls down the skirt of my dress.

'Maybe.'

'Shut up!' she says with imploring eyes and a grin barely contained on her face.

'What was that?' the taxi driver says, twisting round in his cab.

'She said Hampstead! Say you're not going to be sick.'

'I'm not going to be sick, mister,' I add, trying to sound grateful and compliant, but the effect is more Victorian street urchin.

Suki taps her card on the pay sensor. 'There! All sorted. Babe –' she puts both hands on my shoulders and even though she's perfectly still, I'm unsure which copy of Suki's swirling face I should look into '– you were buzzing tonight. Absolutely on form.' I hold Suki's wrists as she

255

tries to pull away. I have no idea what half of her garble means, but I gather I'm being sent home.

'I didn't do anything embarrassing, did I?'

'No! Not at all! I think everyone got a good view of your arse when you forgot to lock the loo, but other than that? Ha! What a night. Get home safe, bud, okay? Bye!'

As the cab lurches off I try and sit as still as possible, but when we turn sharply at a junction my forehead bumps into the glass, leaving an oily smear of foundation on the window.

'There's water there, love. Just behind me, see?' says the driver, whom I seem to have endeared myself to now I've confirmed that I won't be vomiting any time soon.

'Mmm, great!' I say, reaching for a bottle. 'Five stars for you, Mr Taxi Man!'

He chuckles and catches my eye in the rear-view mirror. 'I'm a hackney cab. We don't do ratings.'

I twist the cap off and glug the water down with such inebriated joy that quite a bit spills down my chest and between my boobs.

'Nice gaff,' he says as we reach Evergreen Village. I push the door open with so much force that it bounces on its hinges and closes again. Since when did simple tasks become so mammothly difficult? Right, let's try again. I open the door and swing my legs out, except where I once had shoes, there are now bare feet which are a little swollen with welts along the toes and ankles.

I walk as quickly as possible past the porter's office,

where the door is outlined with light and the sound of tinny music videos filters through a gap in the door frame. I'm not sure if Nigel's on duty tonight, but I'd still rather sneak through unnoticed. As I pass through the archway and turn the corner, I plant my foot on a chip of bark that hurts so much I stumble sideways and land heavily on the raised border of the green.

'Ow, fuck!' I hiss under my breath, biting my bottom lip as a throbbing starts up in my temples. Around the green, silver shades of moonlight reflect off Roman blinds as twitching fingers twist the leaves open, no doubt wondering why a barefooted, moaning youth is sprawled on their pristine lawn. I use the term 'youth' pretty loosely here. The fact that my shinbones are throbbing from uncoordinated dancing is testament to my declining physical state. I might have to borrow Annie's walking frame tomorrow. The hospital sent it over, but she's refused to use it and only keeps it in the shed because they wanted to charge her for taking it back to the depot.

I roll onto my stomach and stand up like a toddler – bum first, planting my feet on the floor before attempting fully vertical movement. Before I get a chance to yank Annie's dress down over my arse, the security light screwed in under the porch throws my 'bed knickers' into full spotlight. With the amount of curtain-twitching going on, I'll be reported for public disturbance during unsociable hours. I rummage around in my handbag for keys and clutch onto the brass door knocker for stability. I scrape at the doorknob in an attempt to find the lock, but it keeps jumping away from my hand when I get the key near. *Click.* I'm in. Where's my Nobel-bloody-prize?

As I push on the handle, the door opens and my whole body slides along the varnished wood until I'm standing in Annie's darkened entrance hall.

'What are you doing back, love? Everything all right?'

'Er, yeah! Yeah! Fine! It finished. The thing. All the art got bought. Not that I bought any. Too expensive,' I say, sliding my big toe down the other foot to help slip my shoes off, before realising I'm not wearing any. 'I drank a bit too much. A lot too much. Sorry to wake you up so late. I think I woke everyone up, out there ...' Oh no, I can feel my throat tightening. I can't have gin tears tonight, not in front of Annie.

'What do you mean?' Annie asks, folding her arms across her quilted dressing gown. 'Do you know what time it is?'

'I know, I know, I didn't think I'd be back this late. I was going to get the last tube, but—' I hiccup and swallow the rest of my sentence.

'You could still get the last tube, you doughnut. It's 9.45.' *Oh no, not again.* Annie starts to giggle, her pale blue eyes sparkling. 'I'm sorry, I shouldn't laugh,' she says whilst doing exactly that. Nine forty-five? I'm sure my primary school disco finished later than this. 'Oh, love.' Annie pats my arm and pushes an entangled ringlet behind my ear. 'You've smudged your makeup.'

'Have I?' I sniff and switch on the hall light. I immediately

258

regret the decision. I've got a rim of red lipstick that reaches far past my natural lip line, my foundation has been wiped clean off my chin, and whatever mascara I was wearing has smeared down my cheeks.

'Oh. I look like a helpline advert.'

'Don't worry about that now. Bed. And water. I would say you'll feel better in the morning, but I'm not sure you will,' says Annie, pushing me gently to the bottom of the stairs. From the living room, her floral sofa is thrown into view, a nest of blankets and a stack of now-familiar letters strewn across the coffee table.

Chapter Twenty-Six

Taking Annie's advice, I glugged down a pint of water before I went to bed and as a result, I've woken up with a stomach so taut and swollen I'm visibly in the second trimester of a wee baby. Whilst I'm sitting on the loo, I flick through various apps in an attempt to figure out how a couple of hours in a Mayfair art gallery could spiral so drastically out of control. Speculation doesn't last long after I get to Suki's Instagram story. I remember the shots of tequila we drank that someone has usefully memorialised in the form of a boomeranged video clip, but if it wasn't for the teal dress sparkling in the light of a camera flash, I'd struggle to recognise the person conducting a row of women to neck a line of Jägerbombs.

It's almost masochistic to log into the Lovr app, especially with the knowledge that Rodney, Rhea, and anyone else who actually reads the data emails will be able to tell how many times I've read my messages in the past twenty-four hours. As expected, Freddie's chat thread is stubbornly absent from view. At this point, I've nearly convinced myself that he was part of an abstract dream, but I'd taken a screenshot of the mistaken selfie exchange and sent it to Maggie, so I can't have imagined it. *Eurgh*. Nothing evokes the Sunday blues like having your love, work, and life failures packaged up and rolled out to colleagues in the form of highly reflective briefing notes.

In an attempt to make myself feel less like a sausage wrapped in clingfilm, I get dressed and am met with the smell of toast halfway downstairs. After quashing the instant anxiety that I'm having some kind of stroke, a sense of nostalgia sweeps over me, of duvets on the sofa, Calpol, and breakfast for dinner. But there's an equally huge part of my brain telling me I don't deserve to feel comfort. I don't deserve toast in a nice living room, without pleather sofas and humming pizza boxes. I don't deserve Annie, standing by the kettle in a hand-knitted cardigan, the mauve bruise especially bright above the pillow-white wool she's wearing.

'I tell you, I haven't done this since Richard used to go out in Camden in, oh, must have been the Eighties, when he was eighteen or so,' she says cheerfully, dropping two tablets into a glass of water that fizz and froth on contact. Annie lifts the glass up to eye-level. 'Good job they work. The use-by date were a few years ago, but what's in 'em to go off? Here. Plain toast, too. Did you drink the water, like I said?'

'Yeah,' I say sheepishly, reluctant to take the glass from her, like doing so would be an admission of my excruciating hangover. 'I'm far from being a teenager, though.' Annie watches as I drink the water, grimacing from the flavour of stale artificial orange. I wipe my mouth on my forearm.

'Cor, what a face you've got on you! What're you being so hard on yourself for?'

I lean against the kitchen cabinet and bite into my slice of toast. Annie was right; it's on the cusp of what I can stomach. 'I promised you I wouldn't do anything silly, or make you regret having me here, you know, after last time.'

'Jesus Christ! You sound like George when he's brought home the wrong butter for Margaret. You going out and being two sheets to the wind is hardly a crime and it's got nowt to do with me. You're young, but you are a bugger for talking about yourself like you've just turned eighty-six, not twenty-six. If I wanted to have some prim and proper yuppie come live here, I wouldn't have chosen you. D'you know what?' Annie continues, holding her cup of tea with two hands. 'Yesterday I heard someone on the radio talking about Tinder and I knew what they were going on about. You help keep me in the loop and I haven't felt like that for a while, so you can stop this pity party, all right?' She pulls her chin into her chest and raises her eyebrows at me until I nod in agreement.

'I take it this Freddie bloke wasn't much to write home about?'

'Oh, no. Definitely not. He doesn't exist. Or, he does, but he doesn't. He basically dropped off the face of the earth just before we were due to meet and has become untraceable.' I stop short of telling Annie about my most recent theory: that he was covertly working for MI6 and got called away on a secret mission moments before getting to the pub. It's definitely too pathetic to say aloud.

'So, er ... when was the last time you spoke to Richard?' I say, trying to act casual by blowing on my toast to cool it down, like that's a normal thing to do.

'Not since the last grandchild was born. His wife sent me an email with some pictures in, but I didn't see it for months and months. I couldn't remember my chuffing password. I found it when I had to register for some council thing, written into the back of an old address book. I did send an email back, but I'm not sure it got there.'

'You might have typed in the email address wrong.'

'Maybe.'

'Have you tried video calling? My parents aren't great with technology, but we do chat occasionally when they're on a stopover in the Bay of Biscay.' I think back to the last time I called. Mum said I could go back to Hereford for Easter if I 'needed a break from London', but that would be giving in and I can't do that.

Annie starts wiping down the kitchen counters, her back turned towards me. 'I know what you're saying, love. But Richard has made it quite clear that he's got his life out there in Australia and he doesn't want me in it. I'm not in the business of causing any more pain than I have already.'

'But ... your grandchildren. I'm sure they'd love to get to know you.'

'They've got a grandma,' Annie says abruptly, clutching the edges of the countertop, 'and a grandpa. Just next door. They're not wanting.' I swallow the last of my toast in one stodgy lump and feel it shifting down my throat uncomfortably. 'What did you say George wanted you for, the other day?' Annie says, changing the subject.

'Oh, he wants to secretly buy some tulips for Margaret, so I said I'd help him find some online. But she might be roasting their yappy dog for dinner as punishment for him digging up the bulbs in the first place.'

Annie giggles and bites her lips, looking towards the open garden doors as though expecting Margaret to be earwigging over the fence. 'She always been mardy, that woman. They've been in Evergreen longer than I have. I've only been inside theirs once, when we first got here. You wouldn't believe it, but she makes the most exquisite cakes. The Bakewell tart we had! I've had nowt like it since. What a mean cow, eh? Keeping a skill like that to yourself.' Annie hangs the dishcloth over the tap and shuffles over to the back door, where the late May sunshine casts dancing shadows on the tiles.

'But George has always been nice, hasn't he?' I ask, pushing a knuckle into my temple.

'Oh, yeah. We get on. He done a lot for me, back when we first moved down here. And he's never asked for nowt off of me, even though he could have, a hundred times over.' Annie scratches underneath the strap of her watch and winces a little as she shuffles in her chair.

264

'You don't seem to speak much nowadays.'

'Ah, we do,' says Annie, pulling a dining chair out with a series of noisy jerks, nodding down to the newspapers haphazardly stacked on top of it. 'See? Still swap the newspapers.'

'Yeah, well, me and the guy behind the hot counter at Gregg's are on first-name terms; doesn't mean we're mates,' I say, running my tongue over my furry teeth.

Annie twists her lips into a tight pucker and narrows her eyes. 'Feeling bold this morning?' she says, the hint of a smile playing in the corner of her mouth. I stick my tongue out. Annie does the same back. 'I know what you're saying, pet. George is a good egg. It was hard coming down here, giving up my studies. I wanted to do a master's, but by then we thought a baby might be on the way, and ... well, there were eventually, but it wasn't easy.'

'What do you mean?'

'Ah, you know. I was on my own a lot. For quite a while. That does something to you, burrows itself somewhere in your chest. For me, anyway, it weren't just when I was rolling about here like a tin can in a car boot. Arthur was often ... disappointed in me. Frustrated when I didn't laugh at his colleagues' jokes about Renaissance carpenters. He'd give me the silent treatment when I didn't have his favourite cut of meat for dinner. So, I weren't just alone when I *was* alone. I did something that made it worse. He never let me forget that. He died such a long time ago

– must be over twenty years now – that I've got used to it again. Being stuck in my own head.'

Standing at the sink, Annie smacks the bottom of a Fairy bottle to release a goop of washing liquid. 'You're making it harder, though. To keep everything up here,' she says, motioning to her forehead. I smile, which turns into a grimace as I swallow another gulp of Berocca, the inside of the glass slick with an oily tide mark from where the bubbles have fizzled out.

'But there's Gloria too, isn't there? The one from yoga?'

'I'm surprised you remember her; you were barely conscious,' says Annie, pulling the tea towel through a cupboard handle.

'Ha. Well, her trousers were hard to forget.'

'Hmm, so is she, and not for a good reason. She's one of those people who asks you a question just so she can answer it herself. It's all "Oh, you going anywhere nice during summer? Oh, well, *my* daughter is taking me to Guernsey for a week. Isn't she good?" It's like, all right, Gloria, calm down.'

'Did you just say "like", Annie? You're starting to sound like me.'

'Perhaps I am. Not quite as cynical, though.'

Annie shuffles into the hallway, where I can hear her sifting through coats and jackets.

'I'm not cynical.'

'Well, might I remind you about the other week, when I asked if you wanted to invite that nice Maggie around for dinner?'

'Mmm.'

Annie comes back, one hand on her hip, the other at her brow. 'You said she was busy before you'd even asked her.'

'Yeah, well, she would have been.'

'Mmm,' replies Annie, mimicking my tone of voice. I put my glass in the sink and stand in the doorway to the pantry, scanning the shelves to look for something beige and stodgy I can take back to bed with me.

'If your laptop has been playing up, why don't I have a look at it? We won't have to keep relying on the Scrabble book when you're trying to pull a triple word on me again. It's all online.'

'Only if you can't think of anything more interesting to do today.'

'I can't, honestly.'

'Knock yourself out.'

Chapter Twenty-Seven

When you're a kid, Sunday afternoons are for lying on a blanket in the garden as your hair, damp from swimming lessons, turns crispy in the sunshine. Later, they're for sitting through family roasts, trying to keep down oily potatoes as the remnants of alcopops and cheesy chips sit high in your stomach. It's packing up leftovers for Monday's lunch, playing cards with your nan, and painting toenails whilst watching reruns of *Friends*. Up until I left university, Sunday afternoons were sacred. Nowadays, the hours I spend alone on a Sunday feel crushingly lonely, even though Annie's in the same house. With Tom, if we binge-watched Swedish detective series all day, we were doing it together. Surely, I've got fewer reasons to feel so needy now? Dinner with Annie and watching *True Crime* has become a routine of beautiful familiarity, but there are pockets of time where I feel like a passenger in someone else's life and it prickles in the centre of my chest. On Sunday afternoons it hurts the most.

They're *not* for rearranging your underwear drawer

268

whilst sinking into a spiral of despair about what the following week will bring, which is the exact task I abandon before meeting Maggie on the South Bank, just as every tourist in London decides to swarm the banks of the Thames.

'They say they don't do reservations, but every single place is full! Where's the democracy in that? We don't all have time to queue for sushi.'

'I know,' I reply unenthusiastically. I'm quite relieved we couldn't find anywhere to get a late lunch; my debit card bounced when I went to buy a Rubicon from the corner shop and the ten-pound note sitting loose in the bottom of my tote bag has got to last me until Tuesday when my expenses get paid. Instead, we go to a little supermarket where I buy the last soggy wraps on the shelf along with a huge bag of salt and vinegar crisps; much more within budget.

Maggie leaves half of her wrap, limp lettuce hanging out of the end, and licks the salt off her fingers, waggling her foot to shoo away brazen pigeons.

'I've got to tell you about Annie. But before I do, you have to promise to reserve judgement until I've told you the whole grand plan.' I wiggle my eyebrows to build anticipation, but Maggie doesn't seem hugely interested. Whilst I tell her about 'H''s letters and the mystery of why Annie's son won't speak to her, Maggie's eyes wander down to where the Thames laps at a tiny strip of exposed sand, a.k.a The Saddest Beach in the World. Just as I tentatively

269

reveal what I did before I left the house to come here, Maggie pops up like a meerkat.

'Is anyone supervising those children?' she says, craning her neck over the iron balustrade.

'Yeah, like, their parents or something,' I reply.

'There could be all sorts down there. Dirty needles, for one.' She tucks a leg underneath herself to raise her eye level higher. 'Sorry, did you just say you hacked into Annie's emails?'

'Well, yes and no. I *have* gone into Annie's emails, but only because she told me to reset her password. Beyond confirmation emails for council tax and pensions, there's nothing in there even remotely interesting. I just pinched an email address – that's all!'

'Elissa! You can't do that!'

'Well, hear me out. I've got a plan.'

'Oh, I'm not sure I should listen,' she says, covering her ears with her hands. I pull her arms down and laugh.

'Come on, I swear it's not that bad. You know I told you that Annie has a son in Australia who won't speak to her and she won't say why?'

'Yes ...'

'Well, I think I might know something about it. And they're both so stubborn that all it'll take is a *little* bit of coaxing and they could have some sort of relationship again. It's such a shame, Maggie. She's got two grandchildren she's never seen and no one here in London, except me, but I'm a stopgap, aren't I?'

270

Maggie purses her lips and re-crosses her legs. 'So you're going to impersonate her?'

'Oh my God, no! I've emailed him from me – my account – just letting him know how we're getting on, what happened with the fall, that she'd mentioned the grandchildren ... nothing out of the ordinary.'

'Hmm, I don't know ... Don't you think you're going behind her back? I know you want to be helpful, but you have to think about why it is she avoids the subject, and what wounds you might be reopening by doing this. I'm not saying that you're doing a bad thing, but ... just be aware of the consequences, you know?'

'I know, I know ...' I say, squeezing her leg when I notice a tinge of stroppiness enter my voice.

'Something to think about, that's all. It's really nice that you want to make Annie happy. Truly, I haven't seen you this ... *settled* in a long time. But you've had a lot on your plate recently. Everything that's happened with Tom, and then this campaign at work ... Do you think it might be good to focus on that instead? Last time we spoke you seemed really enthusiastic about the relaunch. And I thought you moving in with Annie was a great solution to the whole flat situation, but that's not the ultimate goal, is it? Maybe it'd be a good idea to redirect some of that focus. You never know, you could impress work so much they'll think, "Yes! She does deserve a permanent contract!", and that'll be one less thing to worry about.' I have a slouch and I'm sulking, but she's *sort of* right. I close my eyes and sigh.

'Oh, pickle, I don't mean to sound negative. It's just ... I know how hard you've been working at that place and I want you to get what you deserve.'

'But that's the thing, Mags. I don't deserve it. I've fucked up everything I've done at work in the last few weeks. I lose followers on Twitter more quickly than I gain them, and I can't even go on a date without making a mess of it. I'm making a difference to ... no one.'

'That's not true,' Maggie says, using the teacher voice she subconsciously switches into for consoling and counselling.

'It is. I'm not looking for sympathy, Maggie. It's just a fact. I've been playing it safe for such a long time, and not just at work. Where has it got me? Annie's eighty-three and she's put herself in second place her whole life and she might seem okay, but she's fucking lonely. *She's* the one who deserves more. I want to do this for her.' I take out the clasp holding my hair back, ruffle my fingers through the roots, and roughly twist it into a tight bun, looking out to where the sun is refracting on the Thames like it's a broken mirror.

'*Is* it for her?' says Maggie.

'Well, I'm hardly trying to reconcile Annie and her son so I can put it on my CV. "Wonderful with geriatrics, especially in conflict negotiations regarding historical misunderstandings".'

Maggie taps my knee with her knuckles. 'Oi, you know what I mean.' I don't know what she means, but I agree anyway. 'So, how many dates do you still have to go on?'

'One.' I pull a face and kick the toe of my sandals against the pavement. 'Although it was meant to be more. I was supposed to be organising some of my own, but I'm only allowed to pick from the guys who've pre-emptively agreed to have their pictures used on the site. That explains a lot, actually.'

'Sheesh, poor you.'

I pull Maggie to her feet and hook my arm through hers, figuring that Annie will be ready for dinner if I start heading back to Evergreen Village now. Before we reach the escalators inside Waterloo station, I stop Maggie next to an offensively lit advertising board featuring a model whose face ratio is 90 per cent cheekbones to 10 per cent eyebrow pencil.

'I might need your help with something in a few weeks. Unusually for me, I've come up with a plan – of sorts – for when this butchered campaign goes tits up. I'm not sure if I can pull it off, though.'

Maggie tucks us closer to the wall and glances up at the codex of train times on the departure boards behind me. 'Of course. It's so nice how much we've seen each other recently.' She pauses and hoicks her satchel up onto her shoulder. 'We've been drifting in different circles for a bit, haven't we? I suppose it's the teaching and being stuck in the London bubble – for both of us.' I can't think of what to say, so I pull her into another hug and we stand there for a moment, swaying, letting the city move around us. 'I'd love to help,' she continues. 'I haven't seen you this determined since we had that trifle-eating contest in first year of uni.' We break apart and laugh.

'Well, you know what they say: God loves a trier. And look, if nothing comes from emailing Annie's son, at least I tried. I can cope with a rejection, but she's obviously reached her limit, otherwise she'd still be trying to reconcile. If Richard still won't talk to her, she never needs to find out.'

'I hope for her sake that's not true.'

Chapter Twenty-Eight

I've managed to save money this week by cooking at home with Annie, eating leftovers, and spending the evenings playing Scrabble rather than loitering around for a pint with Suki in the sunshine. As a result, my vocabulary has seen a drastic improvement. I used the word 'disambiguation' in conversation with Adam earlier, even though it was out of context. He was satisfyingly perplexed.

Despite it being the most illogical of all office management systems, Rodney sends us our productivity reports on Thursday afternoons, but Mitchell isn't included in the email chain and so any sense of accountability is well and truly lost. Against all the odds, my productivity is up by 37 per cent, putting me at the top of Lovr's leader board. As a reward for my focus this week, I use my last hour of work to have an online browse for a spring jacket, the Goldilocks of coats, if you will. It's that time of year when you wake up with cold cheeks, but find that you have to peel off tights in the toilets by 2 p.m. In the last fortnight I've lost two jumpers to the pavements of Shoreditch as they've slipped from the handles of my rucksack, and one of them was the perfect shade of mustard. I can't go through the trauma again.

Everyone is blissfully quiet in the workspace today. Rhea and Mitchell are up in Manchester at a conference (how Mitchell is still invited to speak on panels about 'Leadership in App-Based Business' is a mystery), and everyone else has got their heads down on building, trialling, and networking for the new launch in a few weeks, despite none of us being clear on what it is we're actually relaunching.

The problem I'd anticipated in blogging about my date with Freddie had been solved with the same method my old landlord employed: use fake images and be vague about the details. Adam found me a copyright-free photograph from the internet and edited the bloke in the picture onto an innocuous brick wall background. I had to ask him to tone down his white teeth too; no Londoner would believe he maintained such high standards of dental hygiene. Underneath, I'd constructed a false timeline of events, which ranged from 'Freddie' paying for a rickshaw to the gallery (as if you'd spot one of those in Mayfair) to his admirable sense of charity when bidding for a series of pieces done by the children of China's rural mountain communities (he has a penchant for silkscreen prints, apparently). By the time I'd finished, I'd turned the fictional Freddie into a fairly pretentious caricature – a modest revenge for a man who at the very least deserves a swift knee to the bollocks.

With half an hour until I'm legitimately allowed to leave,

I head across to the lobby under the guise of checking for post in the locker room. Just as I input the door code, the handle clicks and swings open, bringing me within three inches of Rodney's impassive face, half hidden behind a stack of padded envelopes.

'You all right with all that, Rodney? Look, I'll take some off you. I came to see if anything needed bringing through anyway.'

'No, no. These are mine. I post them.'

'Right, er ... got lots of birthdays coming up?'

'No,' he says, blinking furiously.

'Cool.' I step to one side to let him through, but he moves with such a painstakingly slow tread I'm convinced moss will grow on him before he gets out the door.

'If you want to get home on time you're going to have to let me help you,' I say, attempting to sound altruistic, but really concerned about not making it to the doughnut shack down the road for when they start discounting the day's leftovers. Rodney narrows his eyes and contemplates me.

'Okay. But you can't tell anyone about this.' I roll my eyes and take half of Rodney's envelopes from the pile, balancing them on my hip.

'Going by other discoveries from the past few weeks, this hardly registers on the scale of illicit affairs of the workplace. What are these, anyway?'

'Computer parts.'

'For ...?'

'I sell them. My mother sends me parts in bulk and I have additional agents for particular items she can't source.'

'Are you running a black-market operation?' I say in a strained whisper as we cross the lobby.

'No. All legal. Side hustle.'

'But there must be ... forty parcels here, Rodney.'

'This is half of normal volume. Spring is always slow for business.'

'Is it ... profitable?'

'It covers my rent.'

'Christ, good going Rodney,' I say, silently chastising myself for not being more naturally business-minded.

It takes us a good few minutes to shove them all in the postbox. When we're done, Rodney wipes a sheen of marbled sweat from his forehead with an index finger. 'Remember my appreciation for you not to speak of this. It is disloyal of me to use the store cupboard for personal use, as stated in the code of ethics. I appreciate your discretion.' With that, he turns and quicksteps back into the building with arms pinned straight by his sides.

Back at my desk, I brush crumbs off the keyboard and wiggle the mouse to boot my screen back to life. I don't know why Rodney thinks I'd be a stickler for company policy, because I'm pretty sure I flout it several times a day. Anyway, I'm hardly the worst offender. Mitchell and Rhea have a lot to answer for.

I log into my personal email account (another misdemeanour) and amongst the adverts for mid-season sales I spot a name that sends a jolt to my stomach. It's Richard. *The* Richard. Richard-Who-Won't-Speak-To-Annie-And-Is-Probably-A-Tosser Richard. My heart is pounding. Up until this point it hasn't felt real, and right now I'm feeling more Emma Woodhouse than Nancy Drew. *Shit*. I bite my bottom lip and click through to his reply.

Elissa,

I've been sitting on this for a fair while now and must have rewritten the lot half a dozen times. To be honest, I thought this might have been some sort of scam, but I can't see how you'd know the little details about my mother and the area I grew up in otherwise.

In truth, I have been thinking about her a lot, as much as I don't care to admit it. Perhaps it's something to do with fatherhood. Seeing two boys into the world has given me a whole lot to think about and I can't help but reflect on my own Ma and Pa. I was quite happy to leave things be and move on, but like I said, becoming a father has given me a perspective I didn't have before.

Now, I don't mean to say that I was wrong to blame my mother for a lot of what happened. I gauge from the tone of your email that she hasn't been forthcoming about it all. I feel bad for saying it, but it pleases me that she still feels guilty. I know I might sound like a prize-winning arsehole, but just because she's older now it doesn't mean she automatically has her slate wiped clean.

Jackie's parents help out with Jackson and Codey (my

sons) a lot. It's great they're so close. But at the same time a creeping sense of homesickness has set in that I can't seem to shake.

I don't know whether it's hearing about Mum's fall (I am glad she's doing okay), but despite it all, I know that I couldn't live with myself knowing that our stubbornness (it's a shared trait, for sure) had stopped us from at least listening to each other, even if afterwards nothing changes.

My boys are 7 and 10. I work far too much. I'd like to take some annual leave at the end of the month and bring them over to England to see the dino fossils at the Natural History Museum, the Heath, and some of my old haunts from when I was a kid. It'd be a good opportunity to talk to Mum. I appreciate that you've taken the time to set her up with the internet and a mobile (I've been there with Jackie's parents and it's not a task I'd wish on anyone), but I think I've got to see her face-to-face. I said a lot to her before I left for Australia: a lot that I'm ashamed of and some that I'm not. That said, I'd appreciate it if you didn't tell her I was coming. We can talk about the logistics of it all closer to the time, but for now I'll just leave you with my thanks.

She won't think it, but there's barely a day that goes by where I don't think of her or Pa. Thank you for reaching out and thanks for keeping an eye on her.

Richard.

Oh my God. I'm not sure what outcome I was expecting, but this definitely wasn't it. At most I thought Richard would give her a call and maybe a birthday card from now on, but a visit? Christ. I'm in over my head here. Although there's a tiny self-indulgent voice at the back of my brain that really wants to know what went wrong between them. I scroll back and read it over again. No, this is definitely a good thing. Annie's actually going to meet her grandsons! Who wouldn't be thrilled about that? Annie makes the best lemon drizzle cake and can whack out a batch of jam tarts like no one's business; that's the only credential you need to be a good grandma.

The dull sound of ceramic on wood brings me back into the room. Bismah stands in front of me with both hands wrapped around a cup of tea.

'You look miles away,' she says, blowing on her mug. It's really sweet that she's made me a drink (it never usually happens), but it also means that I've got to stay for at least another twenty minutes because I can't drink tea until it's lukewarm, and for that I'm resentful.

'Oh, tomorrow I'm not in. If Mitchell asks, can you say I looked a bit peaky this afternoon?' *Ah, this is why I got a tea.* 'I've got an interview. I know I'm meant to have told him, but I honestly couldn't face the hassle of him throwing a strop and going off on one. I'm not expecting to get it or anything – just a precaution, yeah?'

'Yeah, yeah, of course,' I say.

Bloody hell, Bismah has a legitimate sounding Plan B,

Rodney has been working on his hardware empire since he started, and it seems highly likely that Adam is silently cracking on with his CV knowing Mitchell is out of the office. This must be what all the podcasts talk about when they go on about having 'alternate income streams' ready. It hasn't crossed my mind at all.

I rest my chin on my hands and look around the workspace. At a guess I'd say that everyone else is giving zero fucks about the future of Lovr and I can hardly blame them for that. I can't afford to sit around and hope for the best. Not any more.

***

That evening I get back to Hampstead amongst a crowd of Londoners half drunk on the false promise of an early summer. Young professionals sip prosecco from plastic cups with suit jackets slung over forearms, the sunshine deliciously warm on bare skin.

I head up the hill to Evergreen Village using slow, lolloping strides, lingering beneath a tunnel of trees, now devoid of blossom, but pricked with waxy leaves. Its ring of Gothic-style houses looks strangely austere in the face of such joyful sunshine. As I near Annie's house I'm reminded of the impending arrival of Richard-Who-Actually-Seems-Quite-Nice and my stomach twists unpleasantly. Before my fingers find the gate latch, George trundles up the path that runs alongside his house and raises a hand to slow me down.

'Glad I caught you. Golly!' He wheezes and takes out a white handkerchief to dab his forehead. 'I am terrible for getting puffed out these days. Margaret has said I must exercise restraint when it comes to Scotch eggs, but I'm far too old to turn down the simple pleasures of life.' He chuckles and twists the ends of his moustache. 'I have much to thank you for, Elissa, and a little to be cross about.'

'Oh? Why's that?'

'The tulips.'

'Haven't they turned up?'

'Oh, no, no. Boy, did they turn up! One small issue ... You were so kind as to set me up with an account and then, of course, you found a grower in Holland on the Amazon – not the river – I realise that now. But when a nice Polish chap asked me to sign for the delivery, I was a tad confused at the size of the box. Now, I don't know how it happened. I did everything you told me to. I had your instructions written down *right* in front of me, but, alas.' George turns to walk back down the alleyway and beckons for me to follow. When we step out into the garden, I blink at the riot of colour that pops up out of every tub, border, and hanging basket either side of a neat gravel path. Inside, Aurelius sits with his nose pressed up against the back door, his back legs spread out behind him like a trussed turkey.

'Crikey. You've gone to town, George!'

'Well, this is my predicament, you see. I only intended to buy ten plants, but I mustn't have been wearing my varifocals when I was ordering, because 100 arrived. You

283

see the lilac-fringed tulips over there?' He points to an old wheelbarrow likewise filled with flowers. 'They included twenty of those as thanks for my custom! I've barely sat down since they arrived. The ol' knees are shot to bits.'

'And Margaret is happy?' I ask, looking at the grid-like planting method George has employed along the borders before he clearly got a little frantic and started shoving them anywhere, including into welly boots and an old colander.

'She's thrilled. Doris over at number 11 can see them from her bathroom and brought the ladies from Bridge Club over to have a look. Astonishing, really –' George lowers his voice, glancing at the upstairs windows '– seeing as they haven't spoken since 1998. A misunderstanding over some rat poison and an elderly cat. Nasty business. But it's all forgiven now,' he says, chuckling. 'The only thing is, I've had five calls from other folks asking me to set them up on-the-line. I'm really at the edge of my capabilities, Elissa. We'll run Amsterdam out of tulips if I make this mistake again.' He gestures to the garden and steers me back down the alley. 'So, if you were open to the idea – and you really mustn't feel obliged to take it on – I was wondering if you might host a little "surgery". Bring some of the old folk up-to-date. What do you say?'

I put my hand on Annie's garden wall and tap the front of my teeth. This is perfect.

'I think I can do one better than that,' I say. 'No, I can. I can *definitely* do one better than that. Do you reckon I could have the phone numbers of all those people you mentioned?'

Chapter Twenty-Nine

'**Y**ou're in a bright mood,' says Annie, hooking her gardening fleece on the back of the pantry door.

'Do you know what? I am.' I put my bag on the floor and lean against the washing machine as it spins noisily and jiggles my bum.

'Praise the Lord, it were bound to happen soon enough,' she says with a wink. 'Something good happen at work?'

'Oh God, no. Work is still horrendous, but there's a sense of calm, like when that string quartet start up as the *Titanic* is sinking, even though people are jumping overboard and getting hit by its giant propeller.' I unzip my rucksack and slide some groceries onto the kitchen counter. Kidney beans, tomatoes, jacket potatoes, and a bag of spinach that we'll inevitably only use half of before it turns soggy and brown. 'You're looking bright today yourself. Did the doctor come round?'

'Yes. He's very happy with how "the recovery" is going,' Annie says, making bunny quotes with her fingers in faux exaggeration. 'I've got the final all-clear for concussion, so anything I forget from now on is just me going senile.' She chuckles and stretches her arms up above her head, hands shaking slightly. She really does look a lot better. Her skin isn't so sallow and her eyes are bright. 'I went to the shops today. Oh, and you'll never guess what.'

'What?' I say, smiling.

'Margaret only went and invited me round to have a look at all the chuffin' tulips George has planted. Can you imagine? Never thought I'd see the day. I feel bad now for all those times I called her "long face".'

Annie walks over to the dining table and closes the handful of clothbound engineering books she'd been working from. She marks her page in one of them with a scrap piece of graph paper and neatly stacks her notes on the bookshelf. Every day since she's been back from hospital, she's pulled down a heavy engineering book and worked through it, scribbles of sums, tables, and graphs etched out with a mechanical pencil. She still uses an ancient calculator from the Seventies that's now so tired it needs a full two hours in the sunshine to boot up its solar battery.

'Hey, I'm so glad you're feeling yourself again,' I say, trying to ignore the feeling of mounting guilt that resembles a squid headbutting my stomach from the inside.

'Thanks, love. Helped in part by the meals you've made, no doubt. And the crumpets with the good butter you brought home last week.' I smile. Thanks to the sweep of veganism across East London you can't hope to find marinated tofu on a Friday evening, but butter is a different story. I'm surprised they don't keep it behind modesty screens with the cigarettes and whiskey.

'Did you notice I've been including more than one type of vegetable in our dinners?' I ask.

'I did. You spoil me.'

I nibble at the skin around my thumb nail and watch as Annie bends to the lower shelf, one hand wedged on her knee for support. I should tell her about Richard. It's not fair to spring this on her.

Annie straightens up and rubs the small of her back. 'I swear those books get heavier each week. So, who's the next victim for this dating malarkey? You haven't got long left now, have you?'

'There won't be a "next victim", hopefully. No one at work knows their arse from their elbow at the minute. Rhea's stopped sending round the briefing notes each morning and all the feedback I've been sending Mitchell gets sucked into a black hole that I never see again. If you'd told me a few weeks ago that the company would be in such a bloody mess I'd probably be happy to see the whole thing fizzle out. Then I could do something normal, like work in a café, or earn commission wrangling hen parties into strip clubs somewhere in Soho, you know?'

'Ladies go to strip clubs nowadays, eh?'

'Oh yeah. It's the *Magic Mike* effect.'

'Who's that?'

'I'll show you one day. Maybe. Although if your heart

gives out from the oiled abs, I'm not to blame.' I unzip my bag and wiggle my laptop out, open it up, and put it on the kitchen table.

'You're not going to show me now, are you?' Annie says, putting her glasses on. I laugh and trace lines on the keypad to boot the screen to life.

'No! We'll save it for a birthday treat.' I open up a document I'd been working on in the week whilst everyone else pinged off CVs and registered for job alerts. 'I wanted to run something by you. Ignore the graphics – I don't know how to use the fancy design software, so I've used clip art.'

'Right. What am I looking at, love?' Annie says, pulling a chair up to the laptop.

'It's my "nothing-to-lose" plan, or, its catchier name, the "Lovr X Community Fair". I could spell "fair" with a "y", you know, make it oldie-worldie, but that's negotiable. Remember the idea I had originally: the informal dating combined with community work?'

'Oh, yes, yes, I do remember,' she says, nodding.

'Well, it's sort of a "spring fair" type thing, with stalls and activities to bring together people in the community, as well as users from the app. But I don't want it to be a bunch of young professionals rocking up, doing two hours of work, and buggering off again to boast about how charitable they are; it's a skills and experience swap. I'm thinking gardening advice – George with his roses and "Steve from Islington" who realises how mindful gardening can be whilst he helps shift mulch around.

We could do lessons on how to set up video calls, knitting and crochet, chats about career and industry, that sort of thing. And they all happen at the same time, with food and tea as well, so people will want to linger and chat. People my age would happily spend £50 on a permaculture course, but they have no idea that all that knowledge is living round the corner. What do you think?'

Unable to read her expression as she squints at the screen, I bite my lip and glance sideways at Annie. When it was just me planning this, I felt fine, but saying it aloud makes it sound stupid. I pull my sleeves over my hands and scrunch the material up in my palms.

'I think it's a right good idea,' she says after a pause, turning to look at me. 'You haven't got long to sort it all, but I can already picture it out there on the green. You know, I'm sure if you phoned ElderCare they'd be happy to put their name to it. They're always going on about community involvement, but beyond the companion programme I'm not sure they do owt else.'

'I've already spoken to Alina. She's sending over some banners and said she'll share the event on their social media. I just need to get everything else organised. There's the kit, equipment, a PA system, the schedule ...' I say, checking things off on my fingers, 'and I've got to convince people to come, somehow. Ideally, we'd get loads of exposure and then we can try and maintain interest from there. It's got to represent everything Lovr can offer going forward. A total re-brand, like my original idea.' I clench my teeth and look at Annie, who squeezes my elbow, her eyes crinkled like crepe paper.

'We can do this, love. Just give me a job and I'll get cracking.'

***

By the end of the following week, the area around Annie's kitchen table looks like the headquarters of a major military operation. On every surface there are stacks of receipts, brochures, posters, and cardboard boxes full of flyers that I've just picked up from the printers. I couldn't figure out how to make it look any less shit – my attempt at drawing a happy older woman on the computer looked more like an appeal for sufferers of a withering disease – so instead I used a technique honed from years of covering exercise books in school, and made a collage from pages pulled out of magazines with names like *Homes & Gardens* and *Good Old Days*.

Honestly, I think they look bloody good, all things considered. I stuff a stack in my rucksack every morning, leave an hour early, and pop into shops and businesses on the way to work to ask if they'll stick them up in the windows. I've shifted 700 in five days and my step count is off the charts.

Despite all this, my efforts at work have gone largely unnoticed, except by Rhea, who said my event sounded 'cute'. Adam openly voiced that 'old people have about as much selling power as Keith Chegwin in a mankini' and Mitchell hasn't been in since last week, meaning Bismah has been to another three or four interviews without him knowing. I've been keeping a meticulous record of receipts and expenses, particularly seeing as I'm almost at the end of my overdraft, but it'll be a few weeks yet before I can claim anything back.

Luckily, most of the ideas we've added to the whiteboard (we have one of those now) in 'Lovr X Community HQ' can go ahead with stuff I found in Evergreen's disused clubhouse, or the bits that charities and businesses have donated along the way. Margaret convinced (or threatened) the local garden centre to donate secateurs, trowels, and cuttings for George's rose workshop, but the laptops have been the biggest success so far. Rodney, who has been far more communicative since I discovered his secret business empire, salvaged a load of defunct tech from the store cupboard and spent a few hours tucked behind his divider changing batteries and circuit boards so that we've now got six computers ready for use in the 'Silver Surfers' internet workshop (I was worried the name was offensive, but Annie assures me that the geriatrics will find it funny and blamed my generation for taking everything too seriously).

With just over a week to go and Mitchell still AWOL, the fair is yet to be vetoed, so I'm powering on until I'm told otherwise. My motivation has been helped by a new evening ritual, of sorts. When I walk round the green after work, a handful of Annie's neighbours shuffle down their garden paths to ask for updates, but my responses have become so robotic that at times I convince myself that the planning really *is* going well, despite the incredibly tight time-frame. Other than the residents, who are the only guaranteed attendees, I have no idea if news of the fair will travel outside Evergreen's walls.

Along with my underlying anxiety about Richard's arrival in a few weeks, a fresh feeling of dread has pooled somewhere beneath my belly button: the fear that no one will turn up. Before I left this morning, Annie, busy tapping out a 'press release' for the local paper using just her index finger, flat-out dismissed my worries. 'What are you expecting?' she'd said, the gold chain attached to her glasses glinting in the sun. 'Those that'll come are those that'll come – no point wasting time worrying about what might not be.' She has a point, but then again, she isn't part of the generation who ignore calls from unknown numbers for fear of sustaining a conversation with a stranger.

Without a running list of attendees, I'm rigid with uncertainty. The Facebook event has a handful of people 'interested', but that's not enough of a guarantee for me. As a result, I've been pounding the pavement with my flyers, Blue Tack, and masking tape (I've found that you can't rely on the phrase 'I'll put it in the window later' – it's infuriatingly non-committal – but if you provide the equipment it's too awkward for them to refuse).

***

I head up yet another hill, my thighs sore from chafing in the sticky warmth. I'd just been to a local garage (where they agreed to put a poster next to the pumps), a record store (who also agreed to loan us some speakers – result!), and was about to turn down a lane beside The Heart and Hound, when I spotted a tiny greengrocer's that's been closed since I moved here months ago.

A bell pings as I open the door and from the back of the narrow shop, an older man raises a hand to acknowledge me, tucking in a fold of his shirt as he points to two unloaded fig crates. He instructs the younger man about where to display them in a deliberate, wavering Jamaican accent.

'Sorry, sorry, I'm coming. The boy has let the place fall apart since I've been gone, but it's okay,' he says, inching himself up onto a stool next to the counter, 'I'm back now.'

'Hi!' I start, ready to barrel through my spiel. 'I'm organising a community event up at Evergreen Village this weekend and was wondering if you'd take a few of these off me to put up in the window? It's aimed at linking members of the community across generations ... a skills swap, food hall, gathering sort of thing. It's going to be fun, I hope!' I say, laughing a little too loudly, my go-to response to cope with the awkwardness of talking up an event I'm not sure will be any good.

The shop owner interlocks his fingers and rests them across the top of his belly, his eyebrows knitting together as he exhales on an outward hum. 'Anyone can come to this fair? It's a free thing?'

'Yeah. All free and open to anyone. If you just wanted to come up and have a tea and some cake, or take part in one of the workshops, it's all good.'

'Where did you say this is taking place?'

'Up at the Village. Evergreen Village. Do you know it? It's on the corner at the top of the hill with the weird neo-Gothic arches and—'

'I know where it is,' he replies with a slow nod, scratching the whiskers on his chin. 'JJ, we still got enough left over at the end of the week for a basket?'

'Yeah, reckon so,' the younger man replies from behind a stack of green bananas.

'I'll make you a fruit basket up, for a raffle if you're doing one of those. Is it a fair if there's no raffle?' he says. I smile and nod my head in agreement. *Note to self: organise a raffle.* He takes a stack of flyers from me and taps them on the countertop to straighten the edges, scanning the words on the page. 'They've never done anything like this before. Open the place up, no? I'd remember – I've been here since I was twenty-three.'

'Wow,' I say, buckling the straps on my rucksack again, 'you must have seen a lot change round here.'

'Not half, not half ...' he replies, nodding at another customer who has come in behind me.

'Well, thanks again for the fruit basket offer. Oh –' I turn back around, my shoes squeaking on the polished concrete floor '– can I take a name to put on the list of businesses who have donated?'

'Yeah, yeah, put my son on there. He does all this now,' the older man says, motioning to the shop. 'JJ Higgins. Honeydew Fruit & Veg.'

I fall over thank-yous and goodbyes as I leave, and head up a shady side street thick with ivy-laden trees that line an old cobbled path. I tuck Honeydew's business card in my back pocket. The corners jab me through the thin material of my shorts all the way home.

Chapter Thirty

A few days pass in a cushioned haze of low-key work days (we're still missing our supreme leader) and long dinners outside with a laptop between me and Annie (we've spent a good few nights watching tutorials on the decidedly dry subject of 'finance spreadsheets', aided by Irish coffee).

Although she's been absent almost as long as Mitchell, sightings of Rhea have been reported around the office. At around 10 a.m. on Friday I went to the loo, and although I'll admit to having a cheeky scroll through my phone whilst in there, by the time I returned Rhea had already left. With so few days until the fair, I'm keen to run my plans by the team, but as I think about calling Mitchell, courage fails me at the last minute and I assume he's got bigger things to worry about. It's not dissimilar to when I need to check my bank balance. I'd rather live with the *idea* that I've got money in my account, because the *fact* that I have absolutely nothing is much harder to process.

As I cross Hoxton Square (a full thirty minutes early) I fall into step behind a woman with a hypnotically swishy ponytail and bum cheeks so peachy I'd recognise them anywhere.

'Rhea! Rhea! Hi!' I pick up my pace and catch her by the time we reach The Butcher Works. We squeeze into the revolving doors at the same time, but they're not designed for two people simultaneously, which I quickly realise when my tote bag crushes between her knees as we shuffle the bloody thing round. She slips out into the lobby quicker than I'm prepared for.

'Rhea! Can we catch up? About the fair I'm organising at the weekend? I had some ideas about a name change. What do you think about "The Festival of Love"? It's sort of—'

'Sorry, I've got to sort something out, so ...' She pulls out her phone, nips past the doors to our office with her head down, and trots up the stairs two at a time. Rachael looks up from behind the front desk. She shrugs and drags an emery board across her thumbnail.

When I head through to the office, the first thing I see is Adam's back. He and Bismah look incredibly conspiratorial, all bent heads and tight lips. Rodney is off to one side, his head angled in their direction. I drape my scarf over my yoga ball chair and join them, but they ignore me, so I demote myself and move to where Rodney stands.

Before I can interject to ask what's going on, the glass door swings open and bounces hard off the door stop. It wobbles noisily on its hinges, framing Mitchell, who stands before us sporting a new chinstrap of tufty facial hair.

'Meeting room,' he utters. He looks awkward and

297

stiff, like a grubby pigeon walking around on stumps. Rodney blinks twice and we fall into a sombre funeral march behind him.

When we get to the meeting room, Rhea is sitting with her arms neatly resting on the table. She scratches her neck and clears her throat as we sit down. Mitchell hasn't moved from his position at the window since we came in, which might have produced an air of intrigue if the room looked out onto a glittering cityscape. Instead, our view is the boarded-up pub next door and a couple of skips that art students regularly sift through for offcuts of wood. I shuffle in my chair and notice that we all have an identical document in front of us that none of us have opened. Things must be bad if paper is back on the scene.

'We're done, kids,' says Mitchell. Rhea looks down at her nails and picks at the polish. 'Finished.' Adam rubs his forehead, Bismah's lips tighten, and Rodney blinks impassively. I experience the immediate sensation that I've swallowed a live toad. 'We fought, we battled, but it wasn't enough. By the end of the week we're shutting up shop. The investors had me bent over a barrel and I've taken a right royal pounding to soften the blow for you lot.'

'You'll find details of your severance package in these documents,' chimes in Rhea, unflustered. 'We cease trading as of today, but payroll will run as normal at the end of the month. Except for you, Elissa. As you were expenses only, we're compensating you up until close of play today.'

'Hang on, is that right? Can you do that?' I say, looking

298

from Rhea to my document, which on second glance is far slimmer than the others. *Fuckity, fuck, fuck!* I was counting on Friday's payment to fund a hot-water cistern for the refreshments marquee.

'Oh, we have popped a £20 gift voucher in there. To say thank you,' she adds, as I sit unable to speak.

'If you don't mind, can you sign off on the reference I've written myself?' says Bismah, getting up from her chair. 'It's in your inbox. There's an insurance place in Tower Bridge I've got a position at, and I can head over this afternoon if you want us out, like, now.' Rhea glances up at Mitchell. He nods so slightly it could be mistaken for a twitch.

'Sure, thanks, Bismah.' She shrugs her long black cardigan up onto her shoulders and hovers by the door, raising a hand to us before she leaves. Lucky bitch.

'Bismah?' says Mitchell.

'Yeah?'

'Drop your laptop off to Rachael on reception before you leave. Same for you guys,' he says. *Shit.* I've been dependent on mine in the evenings to organise stuff for the weekend. What's going to happen to the fair?

'Just a quick one: this event I've organised, um, I tried to catch you earlier, Rhea, but ... I've put a lot into it and—'

Mitchell pinches the bridge of his nose. 'What, in the Queen's arsehole, are you talking about?'

'The Festival of Love. The big launch event for the re-brand? I've just about got everything sorted for it. What's, um, what's going to happen with all that?' Mitchell clutches the back of a chair with both hands and rocks like he's about to launch off a diving board.

'What do *you* think is going to happen, sweetheart?'

'Well, that depends, I guess.'

'Yes ...?'

'It depends on whether you want to keep your name to it. It could ... it could be good PR if we frame it as a celebration of all that we've done so far?'

Mitchell starts laughing so quietly it sounds more like bubbles gurgling through a water cooler, getting louder and louder until it becomes so awkward I don't know whether to join in or start crying.

'What *have* we done so far, eh? I won't knock your idea, darlin'. I liked the whole philanthropic, geriatric, community bollocks. I love my nan to bits, but it's just not sexy enough! No one wants to plug money into a social scheme. It's a fucking drain, I'll tell you that for free.' I pinch the skin between my thumb and finger and count to ten in my head. I will not cry, not this time. 'I can't even sell off the email addresses we've collected because of some legal bollocks. We're fucking broke, Elissa! You know what that means? The piggy bank's empty.'

'Rhea told me that I could claim back my expenses on stuff I've bought for the fair ...'

'Rhea?' Mitchell hisses. 'I can't— I ca— You take over before I do something stupid,' he says, interlocking his hands behind his head and turning back towards the window.

'Look, Elissa. We're going into liquidation. We still owe rent here –' she sits back in her chair and takes a sip of coffee '– and Mitchell's had to re-mortgage his flat in Farringdon. This is hard on all of us.'

Mitchell whips back round and shoves his hands in his pockets. He tries to smile, but it dies on his mouth. 'If you want to hold your little fair, go ahead. Sing "Que Será Será" with a bunch of decrepit bints who'll mistake you for the daughter that never visits. Do what you want, but we're not paying for it.'

***

'What are you doing back? Poorly?' says Annie, drying cutlery from the draining board. 'Are you okay?' I hover in the doorway and nod, trying to unknit my brows. 'You don't look right. Get yourself on the sofa. I'll make a jasmine tea.'

I do as I'm told. In the living room, I sit on the edge of a seat cushion and lie down sideways, my boots still on the floor. What are my chances of getting a paid job when the only thing on my CV is an expenses-only position at a failed start-up? What am I going to say to Annie about the fair? And George? There's no point to it now. Then again, was there ever a point to begin with?

'Here you go. I've given you the Princess Margaret teacup. I know you like her.' I nod. Annie puts the back of her hand to my forehead and frowns. 'You're a bit hot.'

'I'm fine.'

'You're not. Stay there.'

I look over at Annie's TV, where Lorraine Kelly sits demurely on a luridly purple couch interviewing a man about how to spot fake suede. I don't want to move. If I stay here, I can meld into the upholstery and I'll never have to think about jobs, or invoices, or consumer hooks ever again. Out of my eyeline, I hear the rubber of Annie's Velcro slippers squeak on the kitchen tiles.

'Ay, what's this about?'

Annie's face has dropped. Her chin sags and her eyes are tight. She holds my work laptop against her stomach and her hand shakes as she moves her finger over the mouse pad.

'What?' I sit up and am quickly familiarised with the crushing feeling that I've done something wrong, except this time it's not misplaced.

'I wanted to go on the NHS website, but you'd left something up and I saw ... I've seen ... What's this about, Elissa?' I walk over, take the laptop off her, and open the screen wider. Last night, I'd logged into my emails after we'd drawn a layout for the marquees and hadn't closed it down before I went to bed. The last chunk of Richard's message is on display. She's read the whole thing.

'I didn't plan for it to come out like this. It's good, isn't it? It's good. He wants to see you.' Annie turns away from me, her hand violently shaking next to her leg. She stands by the sink, her shoulders up by her ears. Outside, the birds explode in a riot of noise as a ginger cat jumps down from the fence.

'You had no right.'

'I know, but it doesn't matter, Annie. Richard wants to come and see you. With the boys. I thought ... I thought it would help.'

'I never asked you to.' Annie closes her eyes and pinches the bridge of her nose. I thought she'd be annoyed, but not like this. If only she'd found out when her grandsons were here, she wouldn't be angry. How could she be?

I feel cold, from the inside out. When Annie speaks, her voice is bold and defiant. 'You don't know.'

'What don't I know?' I ask, angry now. 'I don't know anything because you won't tell me. You shut down every time I ask. This is your son, your grandchildren.'

'Don't you think I know that?' says Annie sharply, turning around. Her eyes shine and she briskly wipes them with the back of her hand. 'Don't remind me of what I've lost. I'm reminded every bloody day. Every day,' she repeats, her voice wavering.

'I'm sorry. I thought it would be nice. I thought it might make you happy.'

'You don't know.' Annie looks to the ceiling and draws a deep, jagged breath. 'This won't help, what you've done. I accepted it long ago, and so has he.'

'But he wants to come over. He wants to see you.'

'Only because you strung him a story about a silly old woman who's locked herself away from the world.'

'Is that what you think?' I say, the words catching in my throat.

303

' 'His father took all the grievances he had about me and pushed them into Richard's head. Why did he grow up with parents who couldn't bear to be in the same room? Me. Why did he never get a hug off his dad? My fault. Why did his father take up every overseas tenure he were offered? Because I pushed him to do it. Because I was selfish and jumped into bed with someone else. Someone who was stupid enough to make me think that I was worthy of anything resembling love.'

Annie's words hang in the air.

'Annie ... I'm sorry, I—'

'Didn't think?' She picks up two cups and slides them onto the open shelf next to the window.

'I don't know what to do.' I shift from one foot to the other and a stark beam of sunlight hits me square in the eye. When I close them, flares of orange and green burst on the back of my eyelids. 'What can I do?'

'Give me some time,' says Annie. She pulls the tea towel through her hand and hangs it from a knob on the cutlery drawer. I nod and step backwards into the living room, swing my bag onto my shoulder, and leave.

Chapter Thirty-One

'Are you gonna get dressed today?'
'Maybe.'

'Okay,' says Suki, lacing up her plimsolls. 'Are you sure you don't want me to ask Leon about the job?'

'No. I'm not ready to think about doing the whole social media thing for a while.'

Suki puts a bit of dry toast in her mouth and takes a tub from the fridge to put in her satchel. 'Do what you need to do, babe.' She flicks crumbs off her chest and pulls her trousers up by the belt loops. 'Help yourself to anything from the cupboards. Be good.' With a wink, she's wheeling her bike out the door and I'm left alone.

In an effort to differentiate between day and night, I fold up the spare duvet I've been sleeping under for the past three nights and sit back in the same position, except this time I've showered, which is more than I can say for yesterday. I track time by what adverts are shown on telly. Around 11 a.m. you've got life insurance and funeral payment plans, at 1 p.m. there's bingo, and at

3 p.m. the kids' toys come on, which are a total assault on the senses.

I decide that it would be a good idea to at least *look* like I've not been a human slug all day and move from the sofa to the breakfast bar with my laptop. I refresh the seven or eight job sites I've got open every couple of hours, but each new listing that I'm (somewhat) qualified for is more underwhelming than the last. There's always a juicy hook in the job title, like 'Senior Online Community Manager', but when you start reading, it turns out that you're on a zero-hours contract, the office is in Croydon, and the only person you're managing is yourself. I've only got until tomorrow before I have to give the laptop back. After that, I'll be down the local library trying to wrangle a computer from one of the blokes who only ever seem to look at pictures of Jessica Simpson from 2002.

I look at my phone for the 7,314th time since I left Evergreen Village. Annie hasn't called, and I'm absolutely terrified of ringing her myself, which I know is super cowardly, but *she* was the one who needed time. Of all the consequences I've considered since the email incident, I've whittled it down to the three most likely. One: she won't forgive me and will want a new companion, someone who has such a vibrant life that they won't over-involve themselves in hers. Two: she's reported me to ElderCare and I'm now on a list of 'people who exploit the elderly'. Three: she's died of shock in the greenhouse and because it's my fault I'll get tried for manslaughter and go to prison.

Amongst it all, I keep replaying everything she said to me. I thought *I* carried around too much misplaced guilt, but if mine's a pebble, Annie's is a mountain. Surviving years and years of an oppressive husband and not ending up with the person you truly love is enough to skew anyone's sense of self-worth.

Each time my phone tinkles my stomach does a flip, but so far it's only been messages about the fair. I haven't cancelled anything. I can't bring myself to do it. The compost guy I spoke to earlier said he can hold off a delivery until tomorrow morning, and the marquee is getting put up today, so the fair is still going ahead, whether I'm there or not. I think of the plans we'd pinned to the board in Annie's kitchen, and the folder of receipts she'd organised with little tabs. If she still won't speak to me by the weekend, I'll have to come up with another plan.

Just as I'm on my way to the fridge to see if there's a corner of cheese I can nibble, Suki gets back from work. I hold the door open as she rocks the bike onto its back wheel. 'Jazz home?' she asks.

'Nope, not yet.'

'Great, I've got some fucking good gossip.'

'What?'

'So, I was having a beer at lunch with some of the tech guys and – you're gonna lose your shit, mate, hang on,' Suki says. She lowers herself onto the swing and pulls her ankle onto the opposite knee. 'You know all the investors bailed on Lovr, right?'

'Yeah, we got told that already.'

'But do you know *why* they bailed?'

'I assumed it was because they didn't like what we'd done so far with the re-brand.'

'Wrong.' Suki pushes back and swings, pinching the ropes between her elbows. 'You know when Mitchell and Rhea were going up to Manchester to talk bollocks on a panel about "leadership in tech"?' I nod. Suki's unashamed glee is infectious and I find myself mirroring her smile. 'Well, he was fucking lying. He's been booking a suite for weeks at a time and claimed it as a dodgy business expense. He's done it loads over the past eighteen months. Except he was never at a conference or having meetings. He was shagging Rhea and using Lovr's capital to pay for it. A thousand pounds a night! That's why you guys went bust. He only got found out because someone saw him in the hotel lobby when he was supposed to be in Dublin at a big tech expo. Oh, and he's been fiddling the books. What a fucking ringpiece!'

'Stop!'

'Babe, I'm serious. Everyone's been talking about it. Adam knew something months ago, so he's shitting it.'

I whistle and lean on the kitchen counter. 'You know that photo of Mitchell's bare arse is useless now, don't you? You've lost your leverage.'

'I know! I thought about that on the way over. Gutted, mate.'

'I can't believe it.'

'Really? I can.'

'Fair point. God, it's disappointing, isn't it? That men like that live up to every poor standard going?'

'It's why I won't go near them, babe. That and the whole ... penis thing just freaks me out, you know?'

'Mmm.'

'What's up? I thought you'd be fucking thrilled.'

'What? No, I am. It's just ... I can't believe no one's said anything before now. I'm still getting work emails and there's been nothing. I mean, it's pretty quiet but—' I scroll through the mail I've sporadically received and hover over the thread between me and Richard. All my accounts have been streamed into one folder, and for some ungodly reason, I've overlooked this one. Suki hops off the swing and reads over my shoulder.

'What is it? Please let it be another picture of them at it—' She turns to face me. 'Oh, mate. Did you know he was coming?'

'He wasn't supposed to be here until next week. *Fuck!* If Richard turns up now, Annie's going to lose it.' I scan down the email again. 'Oh God. Yep, his sons are with him too.'

'When did he send the email?'

I look at the time stamp. 'Yesterday. But that might be Australian yesterday?'

'So, he could either be flying over Asia, or he's been in London for –' Suki presses a button on her Casio watch '– seven hours.'

'Shit! I've got to get over there.'

'How come? Leave them to it. I'm sure they'll be fine,' says Suki, kicking off her shoes. She opens the fridge, unscrews the cap of a cranberry-juice carton, and swigs from it.

'I was meant to be meeting him in Hampstead, to mediate.'

Suki raises her eyebrows in quiet disbelief and shrugs. 'You poked the bear. Get over there, zookeeper.'

***

By the time I turn the corner onto Evergreen Lane, my trainers are rubbing so much I'm hopping on every other step. Suki ordered me a taxi, but there was so much traffic around Belsize Park that I jumped out and ran the rest of the way, quickly realising why these shoes have spent the last few months at the back of the wardrobe. I stop before the archway into the Village and try to swallow enough oxygen to stop my ribs from twinging. What am I going to say?

The next challenge is to get across the green without being stopped by any of the neighbours, which is near impossible without tunnelling underground. As I hobble through the archway, Nigel pops up behind the stable door that leads to the porter's office.

'Miss Elissa!'

'Oh, yes, hi,' I say, trying to look equal parts impatient and courteous.

'I have a number of delivery notes for you. And Mrs Poulter has er ... quite a long list that she's wanting to show you.' Thank God for the Margarets of this world. I'm sure I'll be explicitly reminded of everything I've forgotten to do by the time she's finished with me. 'This fair has kept us busy,' he chuckles. 'My mum has won Scrabble three times this week. Three! I've not sat down for long.'

'I'm sorry if you've been rushed off your feet because of me, but, er ... Nigel, has Annie had any visitors at all?' I say, tucking a coil of hair behind my ear. Nigel disappears into the office and comes back with a battered logbook. He traces down the page and taps his finger somewhere near the bottom.

'Yes. This morning. An Australian gentleman. And two boys. Very ... energetic.' My stomach jolts.

'Are they still there?'

'Yes, Miss.'

'Oh God.'

'Is everything okay?'

'Yep.' I hover in the archway, my hand pressed to my forehead.

'Would you like the delivery notes now?'

'No. I mean yes, but not right now. I just need to, ah ... yep.'

Leaving Nigel bemusedly holding the logbook, I break out onto the green and squint as the bright sunshine reflects off the sides of a white marquee, its unpegged tarpaulin undulating in the breeze. A little further on, three men in chunky boots and cargo shorts unroll another, smaller one, which creaks and strains as it unfurls onto the grass.

I unlatch Annie's front gate and walk up to the door, my heart racing. Beside the dull thud of a mallet hitting wooden pegs, I can't hear a thing. I rap the door with soft knuckles. Nothing. The longer I stand, the more jittery I feel. I pull the bell rope and hear it ring somewhere inside the house. Still, nothing. Tapping my thigh, I stand on tiptoes to look through the stained glass in the front door, but all I can see is a darkened hallway in a spectrum of colours. Glancing over my shoulder, I scan the green's perimeter to see Margaret straining over her garden fence. Her eyes narrow and she darts indoors. Sure enough, she emerges seconds later with a clipboard and marches up the garden path, elbows first. *No*. Not now! I panic and try the door, which is mercifully unlocked, and close it behind me, my breath shallow.

I expect to hear screaming, banging, and voices bitter with decades of bad blood. At the very least, some weeping; that's what years watching Australian soaps have taught me about domestic conflict. But amongst the familiarity of cups clunking on wood, and the scraping of chair legs on kitchen tiles, there's laughter. Children's laughter. The kind that comes straight from the belly. More disconcerted than anything else, I lean around the door frame and look past the living room into the kitchen, where Annie is sitting at the scrubbed dining table. Beside her sits a broad-shouldered man with a short beard and a very tanned bald patch. Spread across the table are the letters I'd found in Annie's bedside weeks before. I take a step into the living room and make it all the way up to the food hatch before Annie notices me. She puts down her teacup, but doesn't say anything. My bag slips off my shoulder and dangles from the crook of my arm.

'Hey! Elissa, right?' says the man. He pushes back his chair and stands, reaching out a hand to shake mine. I take it and reluctantly make eye contact, noticing Annie's brow line and pale blue eyes in a different face. If you took away the tan and gave him a bit of a real-ale gut, he wouldn't look out of place propping up a pub bar. 'Richard. Richard De Loutherberg. Mum's told me a lot about you,' he says in an English accent clipped with an Australian twang. Ordinarily, I'd follow a statement like that with 'all good things I hope?' but that seems like a highly inflammatory move, everything considered. I cough to clear my throat.

'It's really nice to meet you. Look, I'm so sorry about how this turned out.' I want to look at Annie, but I can't bring myself to do it. 'I feel like a prize-winning twat. Oh, sorry. I mean, I feel like an idiot,' I say, flushing pink as a boy of around eight appears on the back doorstep, looking at me with curiosity. 'I shouldn't have got involved.'

'You're right. You shouldn't have,' says Annie, getting to her feet to stand next to Richard. 'But I'm bloody glad you did.'

'Really?' I say, my throat tightening.

313

'I'll just be out with the boys,' says Richard, patting Annie on the shoulder. She reaches up to touch his fingers, but he slips away and heads outside, leaving her with one arm awkwardly crossed over her chest. Richard scoops the boy up with one arm and he howls in cheerful protest, followed by his brother, who roars like a dinosaur.

'Now Richard knows everything,' she says softly, watching her son in the garden, as the boys throw crab apples at his back. 'He didn't take it too well, not to begin with. He had a good relationship with his father, and I can't take that away from him, no matter how 'is dad were with me. But he knows enough. I don't want to explain it away. Just help him understand ... why I did it. Why I went with Harold. He doesn't get why I didn't just leave Arthur, but when you've got nothing of your own and in those times ... it weren't an option. And it were my fault that I let it poison the family. I'll hold my hands up to that,' Annie says, swallowing. She fiddles with her necklace and takes my hand. Hers is silken and cold to the touch. 'I didn't want a live-in companion, but I thought it might get rid of Craig, so I did it anyway. I didn't think I'd have a second chance with my son, but, well, here he is. There's no point counting yesterdays when we've got tomorrows.' I blink and take a deep breath in, pulling her into a hug.

'That's really good. You should get that put on a magnet,' I say, laughing through sniffled tears. Annie pulls away and jokingly slaps my hand like she's telling off a small child.

'Cheeky.' She smiles and dabs at her waterline with the

314

soft underside of her thumb. 'You back, then? I'd planned to have another "fall" if you hadn't turned up by tomorrow,' she says, winking. 'That got you rushing back last time.'

I groan and smile inwardly. 'Yep. If you'll have me.'

'Gi' o'er,' she says. I must look confused, because she rolls her eyes and bumps me softly with an elbow. 'Course I'll have you.' Her gaze wanders over my shoulder and when her eyes widen, I turn to follow it. Outlined through a patchwork of stained glass is a bouffant helmet of hair. 'Oh, 'eck. It's Margaret. And I think she's got her clipboard.'

Chapter Thirty-Two

'Bit to the left. Bit to the right. No, back the other way. Not that way, the other way. George, are you listening to me? Left, no LEFT!' barks Margaret from the other side of the road. George stands on an upturned bucket and I'm halfway up a stepladder with a length of gardening twine clamped between my teeth and an arm that's slowly turning blue. George pats his head with a handkerchief and readjusts the banner that we're trying to winch up the fence.

'How about now, sweetheart?' he says to Margaret, wobbling as he looks over his shoulder, which causes his hand to shift a few inches down again.

'George, I can't hold this up for much longer. I'm going for it,' I say, chucking the string over a wooden post. I shake my arm out and tie a crude knot as George finishes off a maritime twist and steps carefully off the bucket.

'It's the tiniest bit skewy, but I'm sure it'll do,' says George as he rolls his shirt sleeves up.

'It absolutely will not,' exclaims Margaret. Hitching up her skirt, she strides up the stepladder I've just vacated, her bottom lip a thin line of disapproval. She fiddles with my inexpert knot and pulls the string taut like she's the skipper on a racing yacht. George and I share a look as she nimbly hops down, dropping her pleated skirt in a way that suggests she has no time for modesty.

'Honestly, George, it's like there aren't a hundred and one things to do. Come on!' He follows her through the archway and I leave them to it, pausing to squint in the early-morning sun. As grateful as I am that Margaret rapped on my bedroom window with a broom handle at 5.30 a.m., I now regret my decision to allow her free rein over the fair. She's found a megaphone from God-knows-where and has been periodically ordering people about since the birds started singing. I'm beginning to understand why George tiptoes around like an escaped convict. I would too if I still had a television curfew at eighty-five.

With a few hours to go until people (hopefully) arrive, I force a cup of tea into Margaret's hands and peel the clipboard from her reluctant fingers. Around the green, the last of the tables are going up and I resist the urge to start draping bunting about the place. *Priorities, Elissa, priorities.* Stepping inside Annie's entrance hall, I take a minute or so by myself, and listen to the sounds of Richard's boys asking questions and scraping cars along the kitchen tiles. I peek round the archway and watch as Annie strokes the youngest's hair while pointing at something on the screen of a laptop. Next to her, Richard nods and comments in the clipped tones of a hybrid accent.

317

Just as I'm starting to understand what it was like for Peter Pan to watch Wendy through the nursery window (not as weird as it sounds ... I think), Jackson's mechanical car zooms along the skirting board and comes to an abrupt halt at my toes. He giggles and puts his hands over his mouth as I scrape the car along the floor to send it back his way. As everyone else turns in my direction and I'm outed as a true gawker, the front door opens and Maggie tiptoes over the threshold with an apologetic smile.

'Sorry to butt in, but there's a delivery man here who wants to know where to put the champagne.'

'The what?' I say, scrabbling to my feet. Outside, a man in a high-vis jacket stands with one leg crossed in front of the other, tapping a pen on the handle of a well-laden trolley stacked with proper wooden crates, packing straw visible between the slats.

'Elissa Evans?' he says.

'Yep?'

'Do you want them here?' he asks, handing me a clip-board to sign.

'Well, I'm not sure because I never ordered ...' I scan the document and my eyes come to rest on the substantial figure paid on the invoice. 'Yes, um, in the marquee next to the telephone box? Is that okay?'. He nods, slides the pen behind his ear, and carefully rocks the crates back to wheel them away again.

'You didn't tell me it was *that* kind of event,' Maggie says, joining me out on Annie's garden path.

'It's not! What am I going to do with three crates of champagne? It's hardly mini-whiskies and scented drawer liners, is it! All the other prizes are going to look crap in comparison!'

'No, no, it's great! Think of all the punters it'll bring in! You might even make your money back on all the banners and bits,' she says, hooking her arm through mine.

'Who sent it?' I ask.

Maggie looks at the delivery note stapled to the top crate. 'Calum? Calum Davis?'

Calum from the gallery auction? Christ, I didn't think I made that much of an impression. I feel my cheeks burning, as though he's presented them in person. 'Wow,' I utter. Maggie side-eyes me knowingly.

'How does he know where you live? You didn't, you know ...?'

I squirm as Maggie pokes me in the ribs. 'No! As if!'

'How does he know your address, then?'

'Well, he is a private investigator, so it's part of the day job, I imagine.' I watch as the crates are wheeled behind a flap in the marquee. 'Champagne! Real champagne! We can use it on the tombola to hide the out-of-date Bailey's. Do you think that's all right? We don't need a bodyguard for it, do we?'

'Just because it wasn't on the plan, doesn't mean it's bad,' she says, pulling a line from her mental log of inspirational quotes.

'Yep. Yep, yep, yep, I know,' I say, frowning. I'll have

to make sure one of the volunteers keeps guard in case someone tries to nick them. Maggie looks over her shoulder.

'Come back in for a sec. I think Annie wants to show you something,' she says, leading me inside.

From the garden, Codey screeches with glee as Jackson shakes the branch of a cherry tree, sending a shower of petals over his brother. 'Oh, there you are, duck,' says Annie as we come round the corner. 'I'm not sure what I've done or how I've done it, but I thought you'd best have a look.' Annie pushes her chair back from the table. From a distance I recognise the event page I set up last week.

'Oh God, don't tell me,' I say, covering my eyes. 'If no one's coming we can drink all that bloody champagne and try and forget about it.'

'Would you stop raving and just have a look?' Annie says, tapping the screen. 'Will that do it?'

I look at the numbers on the screen and blink. 512 attending. 1.2K interested. Behind me, Maggie starts giggling.

'I, um ... er, how? A couple of days ago ... What?' I press my temples and look at Annie, who sucks her teeth and sits back all self-satisfied with her chin jutting out.

'Not as senile as I look, am I? Here,' she says, scrolling down the page, 'I got my hands on George's iPad and pressed a little button that looks like a film camera and my own face sat there blinkin' back at me – gave me the fright of me life – but I thought, "Stuff it, why not?" and I recorded a message telling people about my friend Elissa and her idea about the skills swaps to make the old folks happy, and, well, I might have played up the little old lady act a smidge – I made my voice a bit wobbly – but it's done the job.' Whilst Annie talks, I have a glance over some of the comments on the page. As far as it's possible to tell, they seem genuine.

'Think we might need all that champagne, don't you?' says Richard as he pulls Jackson up onto his lap, the boy's knees streaked with muck and grass stains.

***

'Oh, bloody hell, look who's turned up,' says Annie, jerking her head towards the archway that leads to the green, where Creepy Craig stands talking to Nigel the porter, hands clasped behind his back. 'Who does he think he is? Lord of the bloody manor?' Next to him, Nigel points in our direction and Craig follows his gesture to where Annie and I are stacking plastic cups, but rather than walk over, he paces around the green in long, lolloping strides.

Maggie, who isn't only a teacher but a Girl Guide leader, has joined up with a sister group in North London. As Craig goes out of sight, Maggie, Annie and I are reassembling the cake table to fit in another donation of vegan brownies (what is wrong with teenagers nowadays?) from one of the guides, who is so heavily decorated with badges I seriously question whether she's had time to make any actual mates.

With an hour to go until the metaphorical doors open, a number of Evergreen's residents amble into the marquee, some looking a little confused (not that unusual) and others apparently grateful for a chance to sit down on collapsible chairs in the shade. George sidesteps carefully round tables to reach us. As he nears, I notice a crop circle of sunburn brightening on his bald patch. He twists his moustache and puffs heavily.

'You haven't had much let-up, have you?' I say sympathetically.

'Not sure why all these lot are having a break,' Annie says, 'I know for a fact that Brenda hasn't done so much as swept a leaf, but she's already put away two slices of cake.'

George coughs out a deep, wheezy breath. 'Pipes in the Seventies. Horrible things. My apologies,' he says, spluttering. 'It's Craig. He's been directing everyone in here. I only laid out half the sundries for the pruning workshop. Can't think what he wants.'

'Let's hope it's not a motivational speech,' I say to Maggie as she hands out aprons to the Girl Guides running the tea and cake stand. Like a bad smell, Craig drifts into the tent and stands looking at everyone with the air of a headmaster who forever regrets the ban on capital punishment for children.

'What's he about?' says Annie, eyes narrowed.

'Thank you all for coming in here as promptly as you're able. Judith, lovely blouse.' An ancient woman sitting on Craig's left jerks and tilts her body away from

322

him. 'Now, I've got a little bit of bad news, I'm afraid.' His voice is dripping with the kind of sarcasm reserved for older people termed 'difficult'. When Craig is old, I hope his carer puts him to bed with a glass of water just out of arm's reach. I hope they never wash his dentures. 'This "fair" that you've put together, hmm?' he continues, trying to catch the eyes of everyone in turn, 'is, in fact, an unsanctioned event.'

'What?' bleats Derek from the back, twiddling with his hearing aid.

'I said it's an unsanctioned event. Do we know what that means?' He pauses unnecessarily. 'It means it can't go ahead because Elissa –' at this, the Evergreen residents (well, those that can physically manage it) turn to look at me '– hasn't done her paperwork properly. Have you, poppet?'

'What do you actually mean, Craig? Can you get to the point? Because we're all very busy,' I say, feeling my heartbeat boom in my chest. But of course, he's enjoying this all too much to cut to the chase just yet.

'It's my duty as your warden to make sure you're all looked after. Isn't that right, Doris?' Doris clasps one hand in the other and opens her mouth, bottom lip quivering, before closing it again like a boggle-eyed koi carp. 'And as part of that care, it's my responsibility to exercise safe-guarding where I feel it's necessary. Elissa has not completed a risk assessment. She hasn't employed effective stewarding for an event of this size. I've already had to employ first aid on Henry due to overexertion.'

323

'I only needed a cup of water,' pipes up Henry in a wonderful, measured Welsh accent.

'Thank you, Henry, I haven't quite finished, if you don't mind,' Craig barrels on. 'As I was saying, your health is too important to me and everyone else at ElderCare to turn a blind eye, so I'm afraid we're going to have to cancel today. It's the last thing I want to do, of course,' he says, rocking back and forth on the balls of his feet, 'and a difficult decision. It's incredibly unfortunate that we invite people into our homes only to be further neglected, and even taken advantage of. Am I right in understanding that this fair isn't solely to serve the residents, Elissa?'

I'm the one who looks like a trout bobbing for air now. Annie squeezes my wrist. I can't disagree with Craig. Annie knows that the original plan was to save my job, but that isn't the case any more.

'What did he say?' barks Derek, an inch from Gwen's ear. She winces and shuffles away from him. 'I can't hear. What did he say?'

'Something about the fair being cancelled,' replies Gwen in a stage whisper, 'I'm not quite sure, though. What was it you said, Craig?'

Craig rolls his eyes and slaps his thighs like he's beckoning a dog. 'The fair. Is. Cancelled. Okay? I'd start taking down the signs if I were you,' he says, maintaining eye contact with me. 'You don't want to encourage anyone untoward to come in off the street.' All my words are stuck in my throat, like when you swallow too much hot

324

pizza and the cheese congeals in a stodgy lump that won't go down. I turn to Annie, but she's not there. Instead, she steps forward and clutches the back of each chair one by one until she reaches the front with white knuckles, her gold rings glinting like knuckle-dusters.

'Just a few things before you go, Craig.' He turns around with a sigh, hands halfway up to remove a sign that hangs beside the marquee entrance. 'I've been having a few words with the others here at the Village. Some of us have been here years and years, since before you were born. My son Richard, there he is—' Annie nods to where Richard has slipped in through a gap to stand beside me. He waves, having unknowingly stepped into a conversation he was at the centre of. 'I gave birth to my son in that front room over there. And, well, things have been up and down over the years, and people have come and gone. We've not been the kind of neighbours we remember from when we were young. But I've had more conversations with this lot in the past few weeks than I have done in years. I'm nearly done, I promise,' says Annie, turning to us all. 'When this place was turned into old folks' accommodation, the sign out the front said, "A sanctuary for the elderly", and it is, sometimes. But it's also been a prison –' she slowly turns and stares at Craig '– and you're the biggest crook here.' At this, Craig's smirk wavers and he smooths his oily hair back behind his ears. Annie is radiant. She's like a geriatric Boudicca if you swapped the flowing red hair for a purple rinse and an M&S cardigan. 'Did you know that Beryl has a cat?' Annie continues, mimicking a voice honed from years watching police procedural dramas.

'Yes,' Craig replies unconvincingly.

'Oh? So you'll know that Beryl's cat has been going missing. He's a house cat, see. Blind, I think?'

'That's right, Annie!' chirps up the crispy, plummy voice of a petite older woman who has nearly disappeared inside the folds of a camping chair.

'Well, since George has got to grips with his laptop, he's turned into a bit of an enthusiast. Set a camera up in Beryl's kitchen to see how the cat's been getting out.' Craig shifts from one foot to the other and runs his tongue along his bottom lip. 'Do you know what she saw when she watched the recording? Because I think you do.'

'Go on, give it to him, Annie!' says Beryl, punching the air with such vigour her floppy hat slips down over her eyes.

'It was you, sneaking into her house and going through her drawers with your grubby little fingers. Three hundred pounds she's had go missing. And what did you tell her when she wanted to report it?'

Craig begins to interject, 'Now, we've all had a bit too much sun today and—'

'You told me it was my tablets making me forgetful!' shrills Beryl, as others in the marquee lean across to voice complaints of their own.

'He told me I couldn't bring my little dog here!'

'I knew I'd put that money to one side for a mower ...'

326

'You ate my daughter's birthday cake!'

'He always keeps the change when I ask for teabags!'

'All right, everyone. Everyone!' Annie says in as much of a shout as she can muster. She straightens her sleeves and clears her throat. 'I'm sorry for what I'm about to say, but Craig?' He looks up, face drained of colour, piggy eyes narrow. 'Please, for the love of God, fuck off.'

Beryl gasps. A Girl Guide squeaks in shock.

'Ay, I didn't know grannies spoke like that!' another says, looking at Annie with admiration. Derek loudly asks those near him to repeat the conversation. By the time the marquee simmers down, Craig has disappeared.

327

Chapter Thirty-Three

'This is a disaster.'
'It's early days yet,' replies Maggie, stepping out into the sunshine. George is patiently sitting next to the secateurs he's lined up on the garden wall and Gwen has already plonked herself down at the 'Silver Surfers' station, along with a handful of other residents who want to get in on the amateur surveillance scene after hearing Beryl's success story. I glance back to the Girl Guides hovering around the cake.

'The buttercream is melting.'

'We can put it in Annie's fridge.'

'It does say 12 p.m. on the banner outside, doesn't it?'

'Yes.'

'Is there a train strike on?'

'Er, no I don't think so.'

This is worse than waiting for people to turn up to a birthday party. I cross one leg in front of the other and sit on the floor, looking every bit the unpopular eight-year-old.

'Look, just think about how much you've brightened

everyone's weekend. What would they all have been doing otherwise? I overheard a lovely chap earlier say he hadn't worn outdoor shoes since September. Oh, hang on. Grace? Grace! Try not to keep prodding the teacakes, okay?' says Maggie, turning back towards the marquee and the now restless Guides.

I pluck at the grass that had been sacrosanct until today and check my phone. The numbers on the event page have gone up, but still no one has arrived. As I scroll through the comments, looking for an explanation, I hover over a notification that has just appeared at the bottom of my screen. 'Tom Gosland has liked your event.' Tom. My Tom. I click through to his profile, where his picture boasts a snapshot of his new life: laptop out, beer in hand, a beach for a backdrop. In a weird way, I don't feel envious of his cushy expat life. He's doing his own thing, and I'm happy for him, but I don't need to see it. I take a moment to look at him, or this *version* of him that I hardly recognise. I click 'remove'. Another message appears. 'Are you sure?'

Through the archway, a woman in low-slung, loose jeans and a man's shirt walks in, huge turquoise headphones clamped vice-like to her ears. She scuffs the pavement as she turns a full circle, looking up at the eccentric oval of houses. Without hesitation, I press 'Yes', lock my phone, and slide it into my back pocket.

'This is some Downton Abbey level shit!' says Suki, waving at the residents who have stopped what they're doing to ogle her.

'I didn't realise you were coming down!' I say, leaning to one side so that Suki's frame blocks out the sun and I can see her properly.

'Yeah, of course, babe. I wouldn't miss it. I needed to get out and give Jazz a bit of space, anyway. She's moving some stuff out. She's pretty mad with me, so ... yeah. Hey, I've organised this thing.' Suki opens the flap of her satchel and takes out a tablet and a small, square payment device. 'I know Mitchell's pissed away all the money you guys had at Lovr, but I saw Annie's video and it gave me an idea.' She taps at the screen and an internet page pops up. 'It's a crowdfunding thing. People can tap here on their way in or out as a voluntary donation, but it also gives them a tiny share in the business.'

I hop to my feet and lean over Suki's arm, turning the contactless card machine over in my hands. 'This is amazing – honestly – it's such a good idea. But there's no one here to use it,' I say, gesturing to the green. 'The only reason I haven't called it off is because all this lot got excited about a tombola.' I look over at Derek, who is using a frame to walk across the grass, barely moving an inch on each carefully placed step. 'I don't want to let them down. And this is hardly a business, is it? It's a fair. An unusual fair, but it's still a fair. Look at all the bunting.'

Suki nods at the plastic triangle flags as they slap against the wall in the wind. 'Babe, we'll talk about that last thing in a bit, but what do you mean, "There's no one here"? Are you keeping them all outside to build suspense, or something?'

330

'Outside? Outside where?'

'On the road, you pillock! Nigel has been lining everyone up. I've already gone down the queue twice with this thing,' she says, holding up the payment device. 'We've got ... £276 already.'

'Shut up.'

Suki throws her head back in a laugh and flicks the side of her nose. 'Trust!' She pulls a miniature tablet out from her satchel. I grab her wrist to pull the screen close.

'Someone donated thirty quid? Why?' I say, marching towards the archway. Suki catches up in a half-run and flops an arm across my shoulders. 'This is not a thirty-bloody-pound event. Have you seen Gwen's floral watercolour stand? She's got Parkinson's! This is bad, Suki. This is—'

I stop at the threshold of Evergreen Village and my voice bounces back down my throat.

'See?' says Suki, giving a jaunty two-fingered salute to a group of people at the front that I recognise from the canteen at The Butcher Works.

'They can't all be here for this.'

'They are,' she calls over her shoulder as she jogs down the queue. 'I'm going to catch people at the back.'

Against a fence almost swallowed by a thick, sprawling holly bush stand clusters of people tucked into the shade as far as the spiky leaves allow. I step backwards off the path and crane my neck to look round the corner and jump out of the way as a taxi comes to a stop behind me. The engine grumbles as the driver hops around the cab and when he pulls open the passenger door, a white, shaky hand places a walking stick down on the tarmac, followed by a younger woman wearing a boldly patterned head-scarf. They hook arms and step slowly towards the back of the line.

'Miss Elissa,' says Nigel, flicking open the top button of his waistcoat and blotting his forehead with a handkerchief. 'I have been asked by one of our visitors how much longer they are to be waiting. Do you have any information for me to pass on?' I turn to look at Nigel and flick a bit of gravel out of my sandal.

'Um, wait a minute,' I say. I jog back under the archway with my arm held down over my boobs to stop them from bouncing quite so aggressively.

'You all right, love?' says Annie, putting her hand on my forearm. 'You look a bit odd.'

'Yeah, I'm fine. I'm definitely fine. Look, can you do a whizz round to see if people are ready? And can you make sure Kenneth has his trousers on?'

'Elissa. Everyone is ready. Everything is fine, and what's not fine isn't worth worrying about. Now, what's the bloody problem?'

'I'll let them in now, yes?' calls Nigel from the archway.

'Yes!' shouts Annie before I have a chance to respond. 'Send them in!' She turns to me, her eyes bright. In the full sunshine, only the faintest tinge of yellow is left around her eye socket, but it might be that I only noticed because I know it's there, hidden beneath the ultra-thick concealer

332

I lent her. 'I'll check Kenneth doesn't have his wanger out,' she says with faux exasperation.

***

Within half an hour everyone outside has made their way into the village and I've twice had to use the garden wall as a sort of observation deck so I can stand, one hand across my eyebrows, to check that there aren't any bottlenecks round the 'Silver Surfers' station. I see the top of Suki's shaved head as she leans over to point at an iPad, and from his flowerbeds George instructs a group of twenty-somethings wearing corduroy and chequered shirts in the art of dead-heading roses. Margaret stands sentinel-like nearby, ready to bark at the first person to drop a clod of mulch on the wrong side of the border. She's already taken a pair of gardening gloves away from someone who 'wasn't taking it seriously', but luckily the victim of her reprimand thought she was joking and they're now working on the cyclamens, unfazed and elbow-deep in muck. Delighted at the flurry of new people and fuelled by fistfuls of cake, Jackson and Codey periodically run between stands, smears of paint on their cheeks, and fingers sticky with icing and sap from swinging from the apple tree in Annie's front garden.

'Have you seen Mum?' asks Richard, pausing on the last word as though the taste of it is unusual. 'I'm nearly out of raffle tickets.'

'Oh, yep, sure,' I say, hopping down from the wall. I

wiggle through the crowd, shoulder first, stick my head underneath a flap of the marquee, and root through a cardboard box that we'd found in the back of the porter's shed, so old its sides were sagging. I pull out a handful of half-used raffle books and rub them on my skirt to brush off the powder of disintegrating sugar paper.

'Boys, boys! What did I say about running? No, it's not his fault. Come here! Would you give them to Mum, Elissa? I've just got to sort these two out.' Richard turns and marches towards the younger of the two boys currently howling on the grass, having run so hard into the trampoline-like stomach of a rotund elderly man that he'd bounced back down to the ground with surprising velocity. I walk round the side of the marquee and scan the purple-rinsed ladies speckling the crowd, leaning backwards to avoid being in the shot of a young man wielding an old analogue camera. Next to him, a pensioner reaches up to twist a number of dials on the lens and when he steps aside to let me pass, that's when I see her.

Annie stands just inside the archway, her hands held delicately at heart level. In front of her is a man, and on the floor between them, a fruit basket. I stop and look from one to the other in quick succession, ignoring the wind as it pulls my hair out from the bun I'd twisted and pinned in place. The man turns a straw trilby hat around in his hands and looks at Annie with a smile that dimples his cheeks, despite the deep-set wrinkles around his mouth. I'm barely ten feet away, but if I broke into a Highland jig – naked – in the narrow gap between them, I don't think they'd notice. He starts to speak, and despite the melodic hum of voices from behind me I catch a ripple of conversation. His voice has the same lilt of Jamaican that I'd heard a few days before. I flush like I've seen a celebrity. This is him. This is 'H'.

'Your accent hasn't changed,' says Annie.

'Did you think it would have?'

'It's been long enough.'

'You're not wrong.'

Annie swallows and fiddles with the ring looped through a chunky gold chain that I've only ever seen tucked into her blouse. As I take a step backwards to slip away, Codey runs past me and clips my thigh with a pointy elbow, coming to an abrupt stop as he flings his arms around his grandma's knees. Annie emits a soft 'Oh!' and pats his head. Codey looks up at the man through a fringe that's plastered to his forehead with sweat. Their bubble popped by the appearance of an overstimulated child, Annie and 'H' break their gaze and I hold my breath.

'Who are you?' says Codey, exercising a frankness that I've always found quite disturbing in young children.

Annie looks back at 'H' and her brow softens. 'Well, um—'

'Harold. You must be Harold Higgins, right?' says Richard, walking to stand beside Annie with crossed arms. He glances down at Codey, who catches sight of his brother head-butting a balloon and thus distracted, immediately runs off to join him.

'I am,' Harold replies, placing the hat back on his head, 'I'm—'

'I know who you are.' Richard doesn't move. Instead, he restlessly taps his arm with his little finger and drops his gaze to the floor. 'Yeah, I know who you are. I think,' he says, his voice softening. 'If this is the same ... Mum?' Richard looks at Annie for reassurance.

'It is,' she replies in a voice so full of hope and strain that my heart aches listening to it. No one speaks. It's like the sound of chatter, clinking plates, and the warbled PA system has been turned up, pushing in on the space around us. 'Oh, for Christ's sake, I feel like Davina McCall is gonna jump out from t' bush with a camera and start playing soppy piano music. This is all very new, Richard. I promise you that everything I said the other day were true.' I glance sideways at Harold, who looks decidedly upset.

'You kept your word,' Harold says, eyes on the ground.

'About not seeing you? After it all came out? Course I did.'

Annie turns to Richard and briefly squeezes his arm, as though still unfamiliar with the intimacy between them. 'I'm not bringing it up to make you feel bad, love, but when I got blamed for the family falling apart like I did, I needed someone else to blame. I didn't feel like I deserved to be happy – with Harold – when I'd lost everything else.'

Richard shifts and runs a hand through his thinning hair. 'Mum, I—'

'Don't, love. I'm not asking for an apology.' Harold looks

at Annie searchingly, the lines deep set around his mouth. 'I didn't offer you an explanation, Harold. But I never offered anyone an explanation.'

Harold stands taller, his hands wide, imploring. 'I tried to come back.' He hesitates. 'You should have let me.'

'I couldn't. You reminded me of what I lost. Or what I thought I'd lost.' Annie roughly dabs her eyes with the back of her hand and tuts. 'Oh, look at me.' She takes a deep, shuddering breath. 'Look at you,' says Annie, glancing from Richard to Harold, her voice strained.

Feeling like I've ruined any chance of slipping away unnoticed, I turn to my right and squint at a hawthorn tree with my hands on my hips, like the appreciation of flowers in bloom was the only reason I walked over.

'This must be the week for catching up with conversations that should have happened a long time ago,' says Richard, looping his thumbs through his belt loops. I can't wait any longer, I've got to jump in.

'Ah, hi again!' I say, taking a slow step into the periphery of the circle, immediately feeling a prickling heat climbing up my neck. 'The fruit basket, great! Thanks so much for bringing it up!'

'Oh, sure, sure,' says Harold, pulling up his trousers at the knee as he bends down to pick up the basket, which is overladen with fruit and topped with the biggest pineapple I've ever seen. He hands it over to me and I smile at Annie so broadly I can feel at least three chins pushing into my neck in a way that I'm sure looks, and most definitely feels, horribly uncomfortable. Annie narrows her eyes and looks between me and Harold.

'Ahh, I like the googly eyes!' I say, noticing a pair of lopsided eyeballs stuck haphazardly onto the pineapple, giving it the look of a neurotic fruit-based serial killer.

'My grandson did it. I tried to get them off, but the fella's grown on me, you know?' Harold says. Annie laughs and covers her mouth.

'That was mine who was just here,' says Annie, patting her thigh. 'And this is Richard, my son, although I'm sure you've gathered that.' Richard holds out a hand and Harold shakes it with both of his.

'It's a pleasure, son, a pleasure,' says Harold, and adds, 'I've left mine at the shop – my son. He's taken over as I inch towards the armchair. Says I get in the way now, but I've got to keep an eye on things. Old habits.'

I pat my pockets and glance over at the raffle stall, where the crates of champagne have drawn a small crowd of people, most of them around my age. Who can blame them, really? Between prosecco and discounted bottles of Shlöer, it's a type of fizz I've only ever seen at the posh wedding of a cousin who got married in a chateau.

'Oh, God, I've got to get the raffle tickets back to Peggy,' I say, moving the fruit basket onto my hip. 'Look, I've got everything covered, so if you want to duck out for a bit and catch up, or whatever, that's cool.'

Annie hooks her little finger round Harold's and takes a half step towards him. 'We're all right, love. We've got

338

plenty of time,' she says. 'What do you say, H? That raffle won't win itself.'

***

The burnt corners of a flapjack tray bake are all we have left by the time visitors start drifting off. From the wall, I almost have an uninterrupted view to the other side of the green, which is incidentally how I found Gwen's husband smiling stupidly at a blackbird, using an empty bottle of champagne as a prop for his foot, badly swollen with arthritis. Creepy Craig may have had a point. I definitely wouldn't have considered the inebriation of geriatrics on a risk assessment form. After I've propped him in the shade with a cup of tea and a stack of rich tea biscuits, I take a slow walk around the green and share tired smiles with Evergreen residents and the last group of volunteers in the rose garden, whom Margaret won't allow to leave until she's accounted for a missing pair of secateurs.

Maggie chats to the only remaining Girl Guide and nearby Suki reclines in a plastic garden chair with her ankles propped on the corner of a table. When she spots me, Maggie breaks into a smile and leaves the girl with a bin bag and instructions to collect the paper cups.

'There you are!' says Maggie, blowing hair out of her face. Six hours wrangling teenage girls and she still has a composure that ageing reality stars spend thousands on Botox trying to achieve. Unbelievable.

339

'Nice girl,' she says, motioning to the Girl Guide with a jerk of her head, 'but a bit ... keen. I've told her she can go home, but she's not taking the hint. Did you see Grandma earlier?' she says, resuming speech at normal volume.

'No,' I say, silently thankful. When I was first introduced to Maggie's grandma, she told me that my fringe made my eyes look bulbous, so needless to say I'm slightly terrified of her.

'You all right down there, Sook?' I say to Suki, who hasn't looked up from her iPad. The corner of her mouth twitches and she flips the screen towards her so it lands on her stomach.

'Yep. I'm good. Great.' She drums her fingers on the tablet case and rolls her tongue around the inside of her cheek.

'What?'

'Nothing,' she replies, smacking her lips. She lifts her chin and raises an eyebrow as her glance shifts over my shoulder.

'Hi.'

I turn around and when I see who it is, I become acutely conscious of the makeup I've rubbed off my chin and the baby hairs that have frizzed up like a halo around my temples. Theo, who looks as painfully cool as he did when I last saw him in The Butcher Works, stands in a blue linen shirt with the sleeves rolled up. He pushes sunglasses on top of his head and blinks in the sunshine. Before I can wipe my sweaty palms on my jeans, he reaches out to shake

340

my hand and I take it, unable to say anything because my brain is desperately trying to think of a good opening line, one that's witty and confident and alluring.

'Sorry I'm so sweaty!' *Nailed it, Elissa.* He laughs and swings his arms, tapping his fingers together behind his back.

'Me too, me too. Hot today, isn't it?' Ah, good old British weather talk. This is a conversational starting point I can work with.

'Yeah, we've been really lucky, haven't we?' I say, turning to include Maggie and Suki in the conversation. They nod and parrot agreement. Suki hops up from her chair and looks at Theo with her head to one side. She's got a certain expression that's mostly reserved for when she's shagging someone new or has taken an unsanctioned two-hour lunch break.

I try and think of something to say that isn't about sweat.

'Just dropping by, Theo?' says Suki, the picture of innocence.

'No, not exactly. I've got to head back to the City sharpish, but I just wanted to propose something.' Marriage. Please let it be marriage, you bloody beautiful specimen of a man.

'Oh? What's that?' I reply. In my head, I thought it would sound coy, but the effect is more underpaid children's television presenter.

'It's a business proposal,' he says, as though he's read my mind.

'Go on.'

'I heard about Lovr going under. I know you guys were working on something really great over there before the company collapsed. But it clearly wasn't the *idea* that was the problem, right? I mean, I've been following your social media feeds all day. This event ... it's been huge.' Social media feeds? I wasn't aware we had any, other than the event page Annie took charge of, but that was last week. I glance at Suki. She's smiling so broadly her lip piercing is stretched wide.

'Yeah, it's been amazing.' I add, 'Although it wouldn't surprise me if the people who signed up to the rose garden are regretting their decision now. Margaret's essentially used them as unpaid labour.'

'Is that right?' Theo laughs and looks from me to Maggie and Suki, clearly hoping they'll toddle off somewhere. Maggie tucks a strand of hair behind her ear and Suki taps a Doc-Martened foot on the grass. Unperturbed, Theo continues. 'Elissa, we're keen to join you. These crowd-sourced community events have got serious potential for expansion across the city, further than that, even. We've been working with a Danish grassroots project for a about a year now, and with their experience and our capital, there's talk of a partnership. With you.'

'What does that ... mean exactly?'

'Well, you've had the idea, you've engaged with the community, and for a first event, well, you've done better than a lot of stuff we've launched, so we'd be looking to acquire. You'd be kept on board, in a consulting role.' At this

342

point, my limited understanding of business is no longer helpful, which is unsurprising considering all my knowledge has come from reruns of *The Apprentice* featuring Alan Sugar's tired puns about profit and loss.

'I'm afraid that doesn't quite cut the biscuit, Theo,' I say with feigned confidence, despite being 99 per cent sure that I've mashed together nonsensical idioms.

'Yeah, Elissa isn't going to just let you buy her out,' adds Suki. Ah, so *that's* what it means! She flips open her iPad case and starts jabbing at the screen.

'A consultant position could be really good for you,' says Theo, widening his stance.

A sharp elbow jabs me in the ribs. 'Ouch!' Suki darts her eyes backwards.

'Can you give me a minute, Theo?' He puts his hands up in submission. Suki wheels me round and takes three long strides to the back of the marquee, where Jackson is licking icing from the catering table.

'You don't need him,' says Suki.

I sigh impatiently and cross my arms. 'I'm all for the strong single girls' club, but have you seen him?'

'Babe, go to town on his todge, that's not what I'm saying. I mean you don't need his money, or his contacts. Your email has been firing off all day with messages from the charity, and councils, and possible sponsors, all that shit. And, look—' Suki taps through the app she's used to collect donations. *Holy shit.*

'It's not mad money, but look at the pledges. You've got

enough to do this again three times over, and if you get a good backer, which it looks like you will, you can do this on your own. Maggie agrees.' I look up at Maggie, my oldest and most trustworthy friend. She nods vigorously.

I think of Annie. I look at her and Harold on the garden wall, oblivious to the fair packing itself up around them. I think of George and his purple cheeks, beaming at his scowling wife as she fills a jug with cut tulips. I think of the unfamiliar faces who were strangers until today. I think of all the times I've felt like my chest was made of eggshell. I think of the time I got two questions right on *University Challenge* and Annie poured me a brandy shot to celebrate. I think of my nanny. I think of the mornings I've sat on the tube, seen by everyone and no one.

I turn around and feel the slight touch of Maggie's fingers on my shoulders, pushing me back towards Theo. I breathe in deeply. He looks up and his almond eyes are so mouth-wateringly gorgeous that my thighs feel weak.

'Thanks for the offer. But it's a firm no.' Theo wrinkles his nose and bites his bottom lip. I see the beginnings of a defeated smile on his face.

'I get it. Honestly? If I were you I'd be saying the same thing. I had to try, though.' He holds out a hand for me to shake and I take it. 'I'll be looking out for you, y'know?' he says. As his fingers slip away from mine, I tighten my grip and pull him closer to me.

'Hey, Theo?'

'Yeah?'

'If you were wondering, I will go out for a drink with you.'

***

The sun tips the last of its amber light into the near corner of Annie's kitchen by the time Evergreen falls quiet. I set my tea down and hoist myself up onto the kitchen counter. Beside me, strips of chicken, pepper, and onion sizzle in a skillet, the smell of paprika filling the kitchen. Having thrown a quilt over the two boys top-and-tailing on the sofa, Annie sits at the scrubbed dining table with Harold's letters unfolded before her. When I tell her about Theo, she beams with eyes bloodshot from a day of jittering heartbeats and the half bottle of champagne we've drunk between us.

'Think you can put up with me for a bit longer?'

'If I have to,' Annie says, her eyes crinkled. 'You're banned from baking owt, mind you.' I slide off the counter and lift the skillet off the stove, ready to sit down to fajitas for two.

'Deal.'

Acknowledgements

Writing a book is an inherently surreal process. You spend so long stuck in your own head that the path can seem incredibly muddy, which is why I'm hugely grateful to Team Fajita, who lifted me up and pointed me in the right direction. To Hayley Steed, my brilliant agent, and the whole team at Madeleine Milburn, who understood what I wanted to do with Elissa and Annie's story with exceptional clarity. To Tilda McDonald, for your keen editing eye and consistently brilliant suggestions. Here's to more gossiping over white chocolate mash.

To Joe – Thank you for bolstering my confidence when it waned and for the pitching practice, cups of tea, and reminders to leave the house. You make my heart sing.

To Linford – For coming up with the wonderfully silly title for this book and all the pep talks along the way. Who knew that dancing in the kitchen and eating too many onion rings would produce so much creativity.

To Rachael – Sorry for eating all the snacks when I wrote at your kitchen table.

346

To Big Nan – There's so much of you in this book, although even Annie can't claim to have whacked a mugger off his bike with a two-pint carton of milk.

To Mum and Dad – For an unwavering belief that I would make a success of writing, especially when I struggled to believe it myself. Sorry for the times I spewed fire in response to you asking: 'How's the book going?' and for keeping prosecco in the fridge for when things went well. Truly, I couldn't ask for more enthusiastic, patient, and supportive parents. You're bloody wonderful.

Libraries have been a consistent feature of my life and I want to extend another thanks to my mum for taking me there so often as a child, sometimes every day after school. Those early years nestled amongst the bookshelves heavily influenced the path that led to this point. Public libraries are sanctuaries for so many people and The Millennium Library in Norwich is where much of this book was written. Long may they live!

To my beloved Norfolk girls – Who knows what we'd have turned out like if we didn't have each other? (Less weird, that's for sure.) Thanks for the plot solving on WhatsApp, a lifetime of in-jokes, and the relentless joy you bring me every day. I love you all immensely.

To Sheffield – Thanks to the indomitable Team English at NDHS, for your enthusiasm at a very early stage when I was worried about the unknown. Also, to the students I taught, who are amongst the most creative and inspiring people I have met.

To the teachers who taught me, especially Miss Cooper, Miss Miras, and Mr Bishop – You're partly to blame for all this.

To the Comedy Women in Print Team – Thank you for allowing me to see myself as part of the comedy scene at times when I was reluctant to do so. The community of funny women surrounding the prize is the best club I could have hoped to be a part of.

On to London, the grubby, wild, and gorgeous city I have come to love. My Fridays spent in the union of the IOE threw brilliant pals my way, especially Emily and Alice. If you see your influence in this book, it's no surprise. Thanks for making me laugh until my sides hurt and for being unapologetically fierce, hilarious, and subversive women.